Honor Redeemed

Fasten your seat belts, kiddies, you're in for a wild ride in *Honor Redeemed*. Loree Lough has that innate ability as an author to suck her readers into the story from line one. You don't read a Loree Lough novel, you *experience* it. Keep it coming, girl.
—KEN FARMER, co-author of *Black Eagle Force: Eye of the Storm* and *Black Eagle Force: Sacred Mountain*

Loree Lough weaves wonderful tales that inspire hope in her readers' hearts. It's hard to find an author who can match Loree's descriptive detail and rich characterization. *Honor Redeemed* will snag readers from page one and carry them through to its satisfying conclusion. Don't miss this well-told story of love and redemption!
—SHARLENE MACLAREN, award-winning author of *Livvie's Song*, book 1 of the River of Hope series

From its "you are there" beginning at the site of a plane crash, Loree Lough will hook you and keep you turning the pages to the very end. *Honor Redeemed* is an honest, heartrending story about two people who must face and overcome personal challenges if they have any hope of a relationship. Lough's great gift as a storyteller is not only in creating characters you care deeply about, but in testing their limits. *Honor Redeemed* is a powerful story of the human condition that resonates long after the last page is turned.
—DEBBI MACK, author of *New York Times* ebook bestseller *Identity Crisis* and Kindle bestseller *Least Wanted* ·

Author Loree Lough is a pro at bringing stories and characters to life. She delivers readers right smack-dab into the middle of the action and gives them no choice but to care about the outcome. If you enjoy suspense, romance, and just plain good writing—not to mention a story that honors the courage of America's first responders—you'll love *Honor Redeemed*.

—KATHI MACIAS, award-winning author of *Deliver Me from Evil*, book 1 of the Freedom series

Loree Lough is unsurpassed when it comes to crafting warm, honest characters whose voices remain in memory long after the tale has been told. Her deft use of dialog and intense, personal plotting draws you right inside the story and makes you feel as though every character is a friend, every emotional twist part of a personal journey. Her stories just get better and better, each more un-put-downable than the one before. The name Loree Lough on the cover means beauty and grace on the page. *Honor Redeemed* is a powerful, exciting story . . . another in an ever-lengthening list of must-reads by this talented author.

—L. G. VERNON, author of *Wilderness Road*

When you pick up a novel from Loree Lough, it's like picking up a map, because she takes you on journeys that transport you to other times and places, and with each trip, you're sure to find yourself in each story. *Honor Redeemed* is one of those stories. It's so perfectly written that when you close that last page, you'll find yourself craving more from this talented author.

—ROBIN PRATER, reviewer for *Robin's Nest*

Loree Lough writes characters who are so real, they become your friends as you immerse yourself in her powerful, uplifting stories. Charming humor, snappy realistic dialog, and vivid settings that make you feel you're living in the pages will send readers on a wonderful journey. *Honor Redeemed* will make you laugh, cry, and turn that final page with a satisfied sigh, because Loree has woven a rich tapestry of love and redemption that will warm your heart.

—DIANA DUNCAN, author of *Taken by the Highlander*

HONOR REDEEMED

Book 2 of the First Responders Series

Loree Lough

Abingdon Press fiction
a novel approach to faith

Nashville, Tennessee

Honor Redeemed

Copyright © 2012 by Loree Lough

ISBN-13: 978-1-4267-1316-3

Published by Abingdon Press, P.O. Box 801, Nashville, TN 37202

www.abingdonpress.com

The persons and events portrayed in this work of fiction
are the creations of the author, and any resemblance
to persons living or dead is purely coincidental.

Library of Congress Cataloging-in-Publication Data

Lough, Loree.
  Honor redeemed / Loree Lough.
    p. cm. — (First responders series ; bk. 2)
  ISBN 978-1-4267-1316-3 (trade pbk. : alk. paper)
  1. Aircraft accidents—Maryland—Baltimoe—Fiction. 2. First responders—Fiction.
3. Search and rescue operations—Fiction.
  I. Title.
  PS3562.O8147H66 2012
  813'.54—dc23

                                        2011037244

Scripture is from the King James or Authorized Version of Bible.

Printed in the United States of America

1 2 3 4 5 6 7 8 9 10 /17 16 15 14 13 12

To Larry, my real-life hero and the love of my life

Acknowledgments

I'm so grateful to everyone at T-Bonz Steakhouse and Grill in Ellicott City, Maryland, for sharing the restaurant space with me, just as they regularly share it with real first responders.

Much appreciation to Susannah Charleson, whose writing talents proved so amazing that I had to remind myself, time and again, that I was reading *Scent of the Missing as research!*

Finally, my warm and heartfelt thanks to real-live first responders—cops, firefighters, EMTs, and of course, search and rescue teams and their remarkable, hardworking canine partners—whose dedication and courage make America a better, safer place.

Other recent books by Loree Lough

Author's Note

It doesn't take much, does it, to remind us of the nightmare that unfolded on 9/11. Blink once, and picture the World Trade Center and the Pentagon, disappearing into blistering clouds of smoke. Blink again, and envision hundreds of first responders, digging through smoldering rubble in New York, DC, and Shanksville with one shared goal: find the missing.

And find them, they did. In the process, some responders lost limbs, eyesight, or hearing, and still others lost their lives. One of the best definitions of "hero" I've ever read can be found in the Bible. "Greater love hath no man than this," Jesus said, "that a man lay down his life for his friends" (John 15:13 KJV). Remarkably, these courageous souls routinely lay down their lives . . . for total strangers!

Police officers, firefighters, EMTs, search and rescue personnel, and U.S. soldiers all begin every operation to serve and protect. I pray the First Responders series will honor the valiant men and women—and their fearless canine partners—who willingly face unknown dangers each time they report for duty.

When an emergency vehicle, or a guy or gal in uniform crosses your path, it isn't always possible to step up and say thanks for what they do, but it is possible to salute them—

if only in our minds—and echo the First Responders Prayer (written by Reverend Robert A. Crutchfield):

Father in Heaven,
Please make me strong when others are weak, brave when others are afraid, and vigilant when others are distracted by chaos. Provide comfort and companionship to my family when I must be away. Serve beside me and protect me, as I seek to protect others.
Amen

The Lord is my rock, and my fortress, and my deliverer;
my God, my strength, in whom I will trust.
—Psalm 18:2

1

*H*onor Mackenzie shivered, and not just because the temperature had dipped to near-freezing. The far-off wail of a coyote harmonized with the moaning wind, and the creak of leafless trees only intensified the ghostly atmosphere.

Crisscrossing beams of high-powered flashlights sliced through the sleety black haze and shimmered from the river's surface. The Patapsco River seemed alive tonight, pulsing and undulating like a monstrous turbid snake. From deep in the woods, Honor felt the cagey stares of a thousand unblinking eyes and shivered again as she panned a wide arc, walking backward every few steps; the crash had probably sent every critter scurrying . . . but that's what she'd told herself those scary hours with Uncle Mike, and the night a feral dog bulleted from the underbrush, teeth bared and snarling and—

"Is it just me," Elton huffed, jogging up beside her, "or do I smell gas?"

She jumped, then jumped again to make the first one look like an attempt to maneuver around a tree root. "Maybe it's that swill you claim takes off the chill." Elton was a good guy but got way too much pleasure from scaring her out of her shoes.

A puckish grin warned her to brace herself, but before he could deliver a biting comeback, a frantic baritone blasted through the fog: "Over here!"

"Sending up a flare," hollered another.

Most of the Boeing 747 that plummeted from the mid-November sky during rush hour had landed square in the middle of I-95. The cops shut down all lanes in both directions to enable the two available medevac copters to airlift passengers of the airliner—and those in the vehicles it had crushed—to Baltimore's shock trauma. And because eyewitnesses reported seeing fiery bits of the plane falling due north of the explosion, Honor's search and rescue squad was sent into Patapsco State Park. Her unit included a couple of young guys just returning from Texas, where they'd earned wilderness certifications. Like thoroughbreds at the gate, both chomped at the bit to prove they could keep up with more experienced personnel. With any luck, they hadn't yet heard the rumors about her past and wouldn't pummel her with the usual acerbic questions when the mission ended.

The scent of jet fuel grew stronger with every step, and she thanked God for the sleet. Yes, it added to their physical discomforts, but it would douse any embers hiding in the wreckage. Helped her focus on the task, instead of potential taunts, too. Elton stopped walking so fast that his boots sent up a spray of damp leaves. His voice was barely a whisper when he grated, "Oh, my God!"

Honor followed his line of vision. "Oh, my God" was right.

There, in the clearing a few yards to their left, was the tail section of the airliner. Like a beached whale, it teetered belly up on the bank, one mangled wing pointing skyward, the top half of the airline's logo submerged in riverbed muck. Twin witch-finger pillars of smoke spiraled upward, as if reaching for the treetops in a last-ditch attempt to pull itself free of the sludge.

A nanosecond later, they were on the move again, hopping over rivulets carved into the earth by rushing rainwater, ducking under low-lying pine boughs as they picked their way closer. Two pink palms slapped against a window, and between them, the bloodied and terrified face of a boy no more than ten. The sight startled Elton so badly that he lost his footing in the slimy mud. Arms windmilling, he staggered backward a step or two before regaining his balance. "Donaldson!" he bellowed.

"Kent? That you?"

"No," Elton snarled, "it's your old maid auntie." He muttered something under his breath, then added, "Fire up the radio. Let 'em know we need more boots on the ground. And equipment, on the double. We've got survivors!"

Well, at least one survivor, Honor thought, closing in on the craft. She hopped onto the rain-slicked wing and inched nearer the window, then lay her palm against the glass and matched the kid's handprint, finger for finger. "You're okay," she said, trying to look like she believed it. Not an easy feat, now that she'd aimed her flashlight's beam over his shoulder. Only God knew what he'd seen, or which of his family members lay motionless at his feet. She'd seen that frantic expression before, and it reminded her of the day when the Susquehanna overflowed its banks and slammed through a Boy Scout camp. After hours of searching for one still-missing kid, something made her look up, and she found him, clinging to a tree. Though the water had receded, he'd been too frantic to climb down. She'd probably said "Don't be scared" a dozen times before he found his voice. "Why do grown-ups always say dumb things like that?" he'd demanded.

And she'd never uttered the words again.

"You're okay," she repeated now. "Help is on the way."

"Mackenzie, get down from there."

The poor kid's pleading, teary eyes locked with hers, seeking reassurance and hope, and she couldn't look away. Wouldn't walk away, either.

In the window's reflection, she saw Elton behind her, pointing toward the biggest column of smoke. "I'm dead serious, Mack. *Get down* from there," he repeated, this time through clenched teeth.

A second later, the heat of yellow and orange flames flared on her right. The boy saw it, too, as evidenced by a pitiful wail that, because of the thick, double-paned window, no one outside the airplane could hear. "Help is coming," she said again.

And please God, she prayed, *let it get here fast.*

2

Matt parked as far from the crash site as possible, not only to avoid getting mired in the mud but also to ensure he could sneak up on the scene. The tactic helped him get lead stories before, and with any luck, it would work this time, too.

He'd been on high alert since the call came in from Liam Wills, the editor who, according to his wife, showered and slept with his police scanner. "Phillips," he'd barked into the phone, "drop what you're doing and drag your sorry butt over to I-95." Liam's voice had that edgy "this is a headline story" quality to it, so Matt wasted no time dialing Mrs. Ruford. House phone pressed to one ear, cell phone attached to the other, he'd arranged for Harriet to stay with the twins while assuring Liam that he was on his way.

He'd spent nearly two hours on the interstate, observing, listening, grabbing a quote here and a radio transmission there, then headed over to the Patapsco. Now, wearing a thick brown Carhartt jacket and yellow reflective vest—the closest match to fire department gear he could find in the Cabela's catalog—he wished he'd kissed his sleeping sons' foreheads before leaving home. More than likely, he'd make it back before they woke up, but even if he didn't, it wouldn't surprise them to find their favorite sitter, cooking an old-fashioned country break-fast when they came downstairs. He'd packed their lunches and book bags after supper, same as always, and it wasn't like they'd know he hadn't said that final, quiet goodbye, but *he'd* know, and it ate at him. If he'd planned better . . .

Friends and family claimed he had a rabid case of OCD and followed the accusation with "you should see a shrink about that." Matt took it with good-natured ease because his Marine training taught him that a man can never be too prepared or too organized. He chucked his well-supplied rucksack behind a tree and scanned every face at the crash site. For his purposes, Matt needed a rookie, and they were easy to spot, thanks to overconfident "been here, done this *a lot*" expressions. He'd spent enough time, volunteering on SAR missions, to know that a true pro, having *really* done this a lot, looked a whole lot more tense and a little bit suspicious, especially of reporters. And who could blame them, considering how often they got the facts wrong?

He spotted a newbie on the fringes of the tree line, arms crossed and wearing his best "I'm calm and in control" frown. Matt sidled up and mimicked the younger man's stance. "Man. What a mess, huh?"

"Yeah, and weird." He shook his head. "I read *Chicken Little* to my kid, just this afternoon."

Matt picked up on the newbie's "things are falling out of the sky" parallel. "What in blue blazes happened?"

"I'm guessing mechanical failure, but—"

"Okay, Phillips," a gravelly voice interrupted, "assume the position." Sergeant Sam Norley stomped up, his size-fourteen police-issue shoes splattering muddy rainwater on both men's pants cuffs.

Matt grinned. "What's the charge this time?"

"How's 'impersonating a professional' sit with you?"

"You need some new material," he said, accepting the cop's hearty handshake. "So how goes it, Sam?"

"It goes." He gave the rookie a quick once-over. "I see you've met Matt Phillips, big-shot reporter."

"Don't know about the big-shot part," said the newbie, "but I knew he worked for the *Sun*. Saw him talking to Finley couple weeks back, when that truck got hung up on the Key Bridge." He said to Matt, "Austin says you two go way back, to before 9/11."

If this wasn't a "gotcha" moment, Matt didn't know what was. Caught, trying to pass himself off as a firefighter, then reminded of his days as a down-on-his-luck beat reporter in New York. The image of the smoking mountain of rubble that had been the World Trade Center flashed in his mind's eye, and he quickly blinked it away. Better to focus on the good times that happened before that awful day because God knew there weren't many afterward, for him *or* Austin. "Don't know who was dumber back then, him or me."

"From what I know," Sam said, smirking, "that'd be you."

Chuckling, the newbie laughed and stuck out his hand. "Name's Gibson," he said as Matt shook it. "Abe Gibson."

Instinct made all three men duck and press their hats to their heads as a helicopter hovered overhead, spotlighting the still-smoldering jetliner. "So what's the count?" Matt shouted over the roar of rotors.

"How long have you been here?" Sam asked.

" 'Bout ten minutes."

"Then you must've seen the ambos . . ."

Matt shook his head. "No, I came the back way, to save time."

Sam harrumphed. "Not enough time, then." He told Matt that so far, no one knew what had brought the plane down, but, by his estimate, a couple dozen people, pulled from vehicles that skidded into the crash site, were on their way to area hospitals. "Half dozen more were medevac'd to shock trauma, and that's just here at the river. Before the sun's up, I expect that number will triple on 95."

Triple, at least, Matt thought, remembering what he'd seen over there. He was wondering if his contact at the University of Maryland's R Adams Cowley Center was on duty when Abe said, "You really okay talking about all this in front of a reporter?"

Sam responded to a signal from a cop across the way. "Be there in two," he bellowed, holding up two fingers before facing Abe. "Matt, here, is good people. Most trustworthy reporter I know."

"*Trustworthy* and *reporter* don't even belong in the same sentence."

All three men turned toward the sultry female voice. Matt recognized her as Honor Mackenzie, who'd been featured on TV and in the papers for her work with search and rescue dogs. Twice, he'd seen her in person, too. The first time had been about a year after losing Faith, when he'd covered the collapse of a parking garage, and then about six months ago, after a construction trench gave way and buried two guys laying cable for Verizon. Both times, Liam had sent him to cover the *cause* of the cave-ins, not the rescues. And both times, Matt had to suppress guilt inspired by the feelings Honor had stirred. What kind of guy had thoughts like that so soon after losing his wife? Not a loving husband, for sure.

Yet here he stood, thinking them again.

Judging by the looks on Sam and Abe's faces, they felt the same way. Not that Matt could blame them. Honor was sure easy on the eyes. "Where's Rowdy?" he asked, mostly to change the subject.

"Back in the SUV," she said, but her *attitude* added, "Not that it's any of your business."

"Well," Abe said, backpedaling toward the river, "let's hope you won't need the dog."

Honor never took her wary eyes off Matt. "You've got some nerve, cowboy," she all but growled, "impersonating a first responder."

He'd run into plenty of people who aligned with the "reporters are scum" mind-set, but she had them all beat. By a long shot.

She took a step closer. "I read all about how you won an award for that piece about that slimeball who conned a bunch of old folks out of their life savings. I guess you got *that* story masquerading as a banker, huh?"

Matt was half tempted to defend himself by admitting he'd never written a word that couldn't be substantiated, even when his gut told him the *un*substantiated stuff was 100 percent true. But why waste his breath?

She crossed her arms. "So, does it work?"

He bristled a bit under her scrutinizing glare and hoped his stiff-backed posture would hide it. "Does *what* work?"

"You know, skulking around like a sewer rat in search of really good gore for your front page."

Maybe she'd been dumped by some slimy reporter. Or a slimy reporter had written something damaging about *her*. Later, he'd find out what had turned her into an unbridled reporter-hater. For now, he said, "I'm not fussy. Run-of-the-mill gore will do."

She rolled her eyes. The biggest, greenest, longest-lashed eyes he'd ever seen.

"Get this big goof out of here," she told Sam, "before he gets hurt. Or gets somebody else hurt." Halfway between where they stood and the river, she stopped. "Hey, Sam," she yelled, "I think you oughta arrest him. For impersonating a firefighter. Think writing about that'll earn him a Pulitzer?"

"Mmm-mmm-mmm," Sam said, shaking his head as she jogged back into the woods, "if I wasn't married, and old enough to be her father, and thirty pounds overweight . . ."

He laughed, cleared his throat, and didn't stop talking about the crash until Matt had scrawled pages of notes. "Can I buy you a cup of coffee and a donut, to show my appreciation?" He nodded toward the parade of TV news trucks and reporters, trying to penetrate the line of cops that kept them far from their story. "Ain't every day the paper beats 'em to something this big."

"Just keep my name out of it. Anybody wants to know what we were talking about, I'm gonna tell 'em you were pumping me for information about Mack," he said, heading back toward the jetliner, "and I said you're not good enough for her, no matter what anybody says."

No matter what anybody said? "Good way to pique a reporter's interest!" But he didn't have time to follow Sam for details. Not if he hoped to file his story in time for the morning edition and get home before the boys woke up.

Once he'd thanked Harriet and sent her home with a fist-ful of fives—and a mug so full of milk and sugar it seemed dishonest to call it coffee—he'd put the twins on the bus and head back to Calvert Street. Traffic downtown was bound to be easier to maneuver by then, and if he was lucky, Liam would have another juicy assignment waiting in the queue.

Staying busy was about the only thing that would keep his mind off the feelings Honor Mackenzie had awakened inside him . . . and the pounding guilt that went with them.

3

$\mathcal{H}$onor hated quoting tired old clichés, but seriously, the *nerve* of some people!

Bad enough Phillips tried to pass himself off as a firefighter. If the guy was Sam's idea of trustworthy, she hated to think what the cop's version of *dishonest* looked like. No doubt, the reporter was shooting for another Pulitzer-winning story, but not even furthering his career excused the conscienceless way he'd tried to pry facts from rescue personnel, even those in the thick of administering aid.

Correction. Phillips hadn't *tried*. He'd succeeded, and the proof was splattered across the front page of this morning's *Baltimore Sun*. The memory of him scurrying back and forth, pad and pen in hand as he questioned the dazed flight crew was bad enough. But then he'd started in on ambulatory victims. The full-color photo of the copilot, head wrapped in white gauze and nose hidden by a metal splint, infuriated her. "Some people will do anything for a minute in the spotlight," she griped, tossing the paper onto the kitchen table. She wouldn't be the least bit surprised to find out he had a few *other* traits in common with her Uncle Mike.

Rowdy rested his head on her knee and whimpered, as if to say, "Easy, Mack. What's done is done."

"How'd Phillips *get* those pictures?" she wondered aloud, absently patting Rowdy's head. "I never saw him with a camera."

Rerun stepped up for a little attention and echoed his brother's whine. Honor ruffled his fur, too, then shoved back from the table. "Person can't nurse a grudge, even for a minute," she said, grinning, "with the two of you around."

The pair danced in spirited circles beside her chair, and then Rowdy tugged his leash from the hook beside the back door. "Sorry, handsome," she said, putting it back, "no time for a walk this morning." Stooping, she hugged them both. "I promise. Tonight. Before supper. You. Me. Around the block." She drew an invisible circle in the air. "Twice. K?"

They yipped happily as she grabbed her bag—more a combination first-aid kit and briefcase than purse—and headed into the garage. She grabbed the newspaper on the way, thinking to read the rest of it during her lunch hour. "That's a joke," she muttered, firing up her boxy SUV. She could count on one hand the number of times she'd taken a real lunch break in the past year and have fingers left over. According to her coworkers, Howard County General had been a beehive of activity, even before the merger with Johns Hopkins. If management had planned smarter, the crew insisted, they would have hired another clerk or two. But if they had, Honor couldn't count on overtime hours to help bypass destructive, self-pitying thoughts . . . and redirect gossip about her past.

The downward spiral began when her fiancé joined half a dozen firefighter pals in New York to help carry survivors— and those who didn't make it—from the rubble. If she'd known he'd become a victim of 9/11, too, Honor wouldn't have been so supportive of his decision to volunteer all those years ago.

Wouldn't have joined the department after his funeral in personal tribute to his sacrifice. Wouldn't have made the biggest blunder of her young life. To be fair, she'd had help with that last one. But even now it was still hard to believe that one unscrupulous TV correspondent had the power to destroy her career and her reputation with one broadcast and nearly take her lieutenant down at the same time.

Nearly two years had passed since Brady Shaw's reputation-destroying story hit the airwaves. She'd dealt with the whole Uncle Mike fiasco; shouldn't she have a better handle on the bitter, depressing emotions aroused by the article by now?

"Evidently not," Honor grumbled as she drove past the hospital entrance. Annoyed at her lack of concentration, she went into a U-turn but didn't cut the wheel sharply enough. The scrape of her hubcap, grinding against the curb made her wince and hit the brake. Which made the guy behind her lean on his horn.

"Yeah, well," she said when he sped by, mouthing God knew what and shaking his fist, "same to you, buddy."

Tempting as it was to sit in the parking lot, pounding the steering wheel and cussing her bad luck, Honor didn't dare. SAR missions had made her late for work three times this month, most recently, just three days ago. How long before her so-called pals in the billing department called her boss to task for allowing her to get away with repeated tardiness? The appearance of favoritism had been at the root of her other troubles, and Honor had no desire to help that history repeat itself.

Head down, she tucked her keys and gloves into her bag and looked up in time to see the blue-uniformed EMT at the elevator . . . but not soon enough to keep from colliding with him.

"Holy mackerel, girl," Austin said, steadying her, "where's the fire?"

"Sorry. I'm this close to being late." She groaned. "Again."

He returned her smile. "You're not hurt, are you?"

"Only my pride."

He thumbed the elevator's Up button. "That was some mess last night, eh?"

"I'll say. What time did you get out of there?"

"Not till about half hour ago. What about you?"

"Same here. Didn't even have time to shower. Just fed and watered the dogs and let 'em out for a potty break." And caused some poor guy to lose his cool. "So what's the latest?"

A furrow formed between his eyebrows. "Two went from critical to stable, one died."

"Awful," she said. Hopefully, neither of the little blond kid's parents. He'd have plenty to cope with, just being a survivor, without losing his mom or dad. Or worse, both. "Has anybody come up with a total yet?"

"Not that I know of. Just the info from that last report—twenty-seven dead."

And let's pray the number doesn't rise in the next few days.

So far, the only really positive news to filter down from higher-ups was the report stating that every passenger—those on the plane and the ones in the vehicles it had crushed—had been accounted for. That left nothing to do but wait—and pray—that every patient hospitalized by the crash would improve enough to move from the critical to the stable list and that those deemed "stable" could go home.

"Will you be at T-Bonz tonight?"

One way or another, she usually got wind of get-togethers at the steak house, where first responders observed birthdays and holidays or gathered to blow off steam. But she hadn't heard about this one. "What're you guys celebrating tonight?"

"My engagement."

Honor smiled, and for the first time today, her heart was in it. "No kidding? Austin, that's great news!" She gave him a congratulatory hug. "So who's the lucky lady . . . the one I saw you with a couple weeks ago?"

Austin nodded. "Yeah. Her name's Mercy." One shoulder lifted in a half-hearted shrug. "We go way back. Had some issues, but . . . long story." The shoulder rose again as the elevator doors opened. "That's history now, thank God." He stepped into the car. "You'd love her, Mack. And she'd love you, too. See you at seven? The wings are on me."

Honor was about to say thanks but no thanks when the doors hissed shut. And then she remembered the advice Elton gave her a couple of weeks ago: "How are people supposed to know you're innocent of what that sorry excuse for a reporter accused you of if you don't socialize a little, let the guys get to know the real you?"

She reminded him that "the real her" didn't care much for socializing. "If I didn't have to work full time to keep the wolf from the door, I'd be content, living a hermit's life." Then she wondered aloud if she had the backbone to take it on the chin when they put her to the test with hard questions and judgmental comments.

"You're already taking it on the chin," he'd pointed out, "so what have you got to lose?"

True enough, she decided, seated at her desk with two minutes to spare before starting time. A sign that her life was about to take a turn for the better?

Only one way to find out.

4

*E*lbows leaning on a bar-height table, Austin waved Matt over. "Hey, dude, you remember the love of my life," he said, sliding an arm around the dark-haired beauty beside him.

Matt kissed her cheek. "It's good to see you again. You look gorgeous, as always." Shaking Austin's hand, he added, "Congratulations, bud. Never thought I'd live to see the day."

Elton hollered from the next table. "Neither did any of the rest of us."

"Took you long enough," came another voice from across the room.

Someone else put in his two cents. "Let's not go countin' chickens till after the I do's."

Masculine laughter bounced from every wall as WJZ's evening anchor Vic Carter passed the baton to Bob Turk, who launched into the weather report.

"How come you ain't doin' TV news?" Elton wanted to know.

"Yeah, Phillips," Sam agreed. "How come?"

Julia delivered beer and sodas as her boss slid two plates of wings—one spicy, one regular—onto the table. "Good question," the owner said, " 'cause you're sure purty enough."

The wisecrack invited another round of good-natured laughter. "Better watch it, Derek," someone said. "There's a rumor going around that your wife's the jealous type."

"Like the fire chief's wife, y'mean?"

Matt didn't recognize those last two voices, but he *could* identify the new mood that had spread through the restaurant: subdued. He sat back, listening as the guys volleyed hearsay about the affair back and forth. *And they say* women *are gossipy,* he thought as each tacked on a personal observation.

In the years since her engagement had ended, they said, Honor had failed at two additional relationships. He was still bristling from the brusque inquisition she'd given him at the crash site and wondered if what he'd just overheard—about her relationship with her loo—explained her attitude *and* solitary status. Maybe the swirl of controversy stirred up by the TV news story, and the half a dozen equally damaging articles that followed, had been too much for the guys to handle.

Her heart-stopping green eyes sparked in his memory. Unconsciously, Matt shook his head, unable to believe she could have used her good looks to climb the fire department ranks. Hours spent face to face, interviewing rapists and robbers, hookers and killers had honed his people-reading skills to a keen edge. It seemed to him that despite all the effort she'd put into matching their tough, untouchable expressions, Honor had a long way to go if she hoped to hide flashes of—he couldn't put his finger on what, exactly—vulnerability? Loneliness? If she was guilty of anything, his gut told him, it was bad acting. Besides, if memory served, hadn't it been a stationhouse lieutenant, and not the fire chief, who'd shared the controversial spotlight with her? If the guys could distort something that important, they'd no doubt messed up other pertinent details, too. Matt made up his mind, then and there, to reserve judgment until he'd had a chance to roust out the facts.

As if cued by a Hollywood director, the door opened. Bright sunlight spilled into the restaurant's semi-darkened interior, silhouetting a shapely figure and haloing gleaming auburn curls.

Honor.

She moved with the grace of a gazelle . . . until the place fell silent. It was clear by the look on her face that Honor knew why everyone had so abruptly stopped talking. Matt racked his brain for something—*anything*—that might put her at ease.

Elton beat him to it. "Well now," he said, winking as he drew her into a fatherly embrace. "It's about time you got here."

Austin joined the hug. "I was beginning to think you'd be a no-show."

"How could I miss something as important as your engagement party?" she asked as Mercy walked up. "Congratulations," she said, squeezing the bride-to-be's hand.

"It was a long time coming," Mercy said, smiling up at her future husband, "but well worth the wait."

Matt remembered that it had been touch and go for Austin when Mercy turned him down flat. Remembered, too, how those closest to him worried that he might just lose his years-long battle with the bottle. Thankfully, he proved them all wrong. Six months into Mercy's highfalutin job with the Chicago Board of Ed, Austin hopped a plane to O'Hare and gave her two choices: come back to Baltimore with him, or help him find an apartment in the Windy City. *If that wasn't an example of absence making the heart grow fonder*, he thought, *I don't know what is.*

It made him miss Faith, or, more accurately, made him miss the comfort that came with knowing someone loved him, warts and all. In the years since her death, he hadn't given a serious thought to finding it again.

Until now.

"Good to see you again," he said to Honor.

One corner of her mouth lifted in a wry smile. For a minute there, it looked like she'd say "Good to see you, too." Matt hoped his acting skills were better than hers because the last thing he wanted was for her to know how it disappointed him to hear "Yeah, right" instead.

"I see you've met the Defender," Austin said, giving Matt a good-natured shove.

Her eyebrows disappeared under thick bangs. "The Defender?" she echoed.

"You mean you don't know?" Austin feigned shock. "This guy is like every superhero, all rolled into one." He started counting on his fingers. "Saved an old lady from a purse snatcher and put an end to playground bullying even before he was ten." He followed up another playful shove to Matt's shoulder with "And how old were you when you got Mrs. Abernathy's cat out of that tree? Eleven? Twelve?"

Matt felt the beginnings of a blush coloring his face. "Knock it off, Finley. Nobody wants to hear any of that nonsense, least of all, me."

Austin looked to Honor for permission to continue. Her indifferent expression was a letdown, which surprised Matt, considering how much he hated it when anyone spoke of his past good deeds. Maybe the tough-girl routine wasn't an act, after all. "Hey, isn't that Ribaldi over there?" He pointed to the far end of the bar, where a cluster of firefighters were lambasting the Ravens' coaching staff. Without waiting for confirmation, Matt left Austin and Mercy with Honor and joined the group. He barely heard their genial greetings, almost didn't notice the affable backslapping and hand shaking, because his brain had focused on getting the cold shoulder from Honor . . . and why he gave a hoot *what* she thought of him.

Ribaldi pulled him aside. "Saw you over there with Jezebel," he said with a nod toward Honor. "A word to the wise: take what you can and move on, and keep your back to the wall."

Matt glanced over, too, just in time to see that she'd caught the two of them, gawking. She frowned a bit and shook her head, then faced the other direction. Gorgeous, even when she's ticked off, he thought. "She looks pretty harmless to me."

"Yeah, well, looks can be deceiving." He looked left and right, then leaned closer and said into his palm, "You're a hot-shot reporter now. I'm sure you've got connections."

In other words, use those connections to find out more about Honor. Every investigative cell in him was twitching to do just that. But from the looks of things, the guys were about to toast the happy couple.

"Phillips," Austin hollered, "get over here and say a few words."

"Why should I?" he hollered back.

"Because as best man, it's your job, that's why."

He and Austin had been as close as brothers since long before 9/11, but lately, work had taken them in different directions. Matt chuckled to hide his surprise. "Guess that means I'm stuck throwing you a bachelor party, eh?"

Austin laughed, too. "If it's all the same to you, I'd rather have—"

A cacophony of cell phones and fire and police department radios squawked and crackled with the droning hum of voices that dispatched cops, firefighters, and paramedics to a multi-car pileup on the Beltway. Within seconds, the final slurps from coffee mugs and soda glasses was drowned out by the scrape of chairs across the floor. Regular patrons of T-Bonz understood the hasty departure and did their best to clear a path to the door.

Seconds later, only non-emergency personnel remained in the subdued silence, among them, Honor and Matt. It made him regret letting his certifications lapse. But being the only parent his boys had, he couldn't take the chance he might not return from a rescue. He'd been standing at the next table when the calls came in. Their eyes met, and he saw in hers the same spark of desire to lend a hand that rumbled in his own heart. Raising his frosty mug, he said, "That's about the best example of organized chaos I've ever seen."

She grinned, but not enough to hide a trace of sadness. Then she turned to the bride-to-be. "Some engagement party, huh?"

"Goes with the territory," Mercy said, shrugging into her coat. And grabbing her purse, she gave Honor a sideways hug. "See you soon, I'm sure."

"Count on it."

She walked up to Matt and, hands resting on his shoulders, gave a slight shake. "Don't be such a stranger, you hear? He misses you."

"Feeling's mutual." As she hugged him, Matt admitted to himself how lucky Austin was. That trip to Chicago could have destroyed him . . . if Mercy had held her ground on the issues that had separated them.

"We haven't seen the twins in ages. I'm gonna call you *this* week to set something up."

"Sounds good. They ask about Austin all the time."

Mercy laughed. "What am I, chopped liver?"

"Hardly," he said as she shoved through the door. Before it swung shut, it dawned on him that luck had nothing to do with getting Mercy and Austin back together. Faith set things in motion. Trust held them fast. Matt didn't know if he could summon either to that degree, unless it involved his boys' well-being.

"You have twins?"

Matt took that as an invitation to step up to her table. "Yeah. Boys. They're ten." He watched her process the information and wondered which question she'd ask first—if he and his wife shared custody since the divorce, or if he was an every-other-weekend dad.

She pulled a twenty from her pocket and pressed it to the table. "That oughta cover some of the tab. Catch y'later."

Then she shouldered that oversized tote that passed for a purse and walked away without a backward glance. Matt lifted his mug again and toasted the space she'd vacated. "Yeah. Later. Have a good one. Nice seeing you again. Drive safely."

The elderly couple at the booth across the aisle exchanged a knowing glance. "I don't see a ring on your left hand," the woman said. And nodding toward the door, she added, "Hers, either."

Her husband shook his head and shrugged helplessly.

Even if he had the time, Matt wouldn't have told them why he couldn't go after her. How could he explain something that he didn't understand himself?

5

Honor leaned her forehead on the steering wheel and, jaws clenched, groaned. After giving the dash a sound thumping, she got out of the car and slammed the driver's door. "Of all the days for you to poop out on me," she muttered, pacing beside the car, "why today?"

She kicked the left front tire, then kicked it again. "I've never been able to count on you, you stupid, stupid, *stupid*—"

"Remind me to thank God *I'm* not your passenger."

Honor hung her head. Of all the people who could have witnessed her mini meltdown, why him? Well, at least he'd given her a little slack, pretending he believed there was someone in the car, instead of taunting her for talking to herself.

"Dead battery," she said. "Again."

"I worked for Sears Automotive in high school. Doesn't make me an expert, by a long shot, but I can have a look under the hood if you want. Maybe it's just a loose wire or something."

Honor lifted both arms, let them fall against her sides with a feeble slap. "Oh, why not."

She got back into the car and popped the hood. "What could it hurt?"

"Careful," he said, putting the support arm into place.

"Careful?"

"All that gushing confidence is liable to give me a big head." He laughed quietly and stuck his head into the space between the engine and the hood. "And if that happened, how could I poke this," he said, tapping the distributor cap, then wiggling a hose, "and tug that?"

She crossed her arms to fend off the biting wind, remembering her decision not to wear a coat today: it's just a short trip from the garage to the car, she'd told herself, and from the car to the office. Bearing in mind the undependable nature of her car, it had been a foolhardy choice, at best. Foolhardy, but not surprising, considering the hundred rash decisions that had come before it.

He slid a bright white handkerchief from his back pocket. "Sorry," he said, wiping his hands, "but it looks like you're right."

"Dead battery."

"Sorry."

"And me without a AAA card."

Matt chuckled. "Let me give you a jump." He pointed. "My truck's right over there."

She hesitated, torn between wanting help and *not* wanting it from Matt. But she was cold and tired, and by now, her dogs' bladders would be at the bursting point. "Thanks," she said, hoping she didn't look or sound anywhere near as desperate as she felt.

Matt jogged over to where he'd parked, giving her a moment to wonder why she'd lumped him in with every other creep who earned his living as a reporter. *Because he earns his living as a reporter*, she thought, summoning her resolve as he pulled up in front of her car. It took no time for him to attach the jumper cables, then he held out one hand and wiggled his fingers.

Honor gave him her keys and watched as he slid in behind the wheel. If this is how fairy-tale damsels felt as their heroes rode up on big white steeds to rescue them, she didn't know how all those happily-ever-after endings could have been written, because—although it didn't make a bit of sense—half of her wanted to thank him, and the other half wanted to slug him.

After four failed attempts to fire the ignition, he returned her keys. "Sorry," he said again. "I was hoping I could pump enough juice into it to at least get you to a repair shop, but it looks like your battery's shot."

"So's my patience with this hunk of junk," she blurted.

"I'm happy to give you a lift home."

Now wouldn't *that* just be the perfect end to the perfect day—twenty minutes trapped in a vehicle with a *Baltimore Sun* staff reporter. "Thanks," she said, digging in her bag, "but I'd better just call a tow truck." Just last week, she'd come *this close* to buying the zippered pouch she'd seen advertised on TV. The announcer guaranteed its pockets and compartments could organize even the biggest, sloppiest purse. If she hadn't blown it off as yet another rip-off, she would have found her cell phone by now and wouldn't look like a loony prospector, determined to find gold in a depleted mine.

"Here," he said, handing her his phone.

He'd already scrolled to a highlighted number, and as she read it, he added, "The guy's honest, and affordable, and has his own tow truck."

Here she stood, shivering in the late-November wind, trying to figure out which was the dumber judgment—trust a reporter's word about anything, let alone a car mechanic, or trust the mechanic himself.

And then he smiled, warming the space between them, prompting Honor to gentle her tone. "Might as well get this beast into a shop, aye-sap." She pressed the tiny green handset icon on the face of his cell phone. "I oughta tell him to roll it into the landfill, save him the bother of hoisting it onto a lift, save me the cost of yet another repair."

"Free estimates." He pointed at the phone. "Another reason I trust Buddy."

She was about to counter with "We'll see about that" when a woman said, "Praise the Lord!"

"I should've warned you," Matt said, grinning at her reaction. "Manny and Bea are hard-core Christians. Never miss an opportunity to witness their faith."

Yeah, that definitely would have been good to know, though at the moment, Honor couldn't come up with a reasonable *why*. She stammered out her location and handed Matt his cell phone.

"Thanks. The tow truck's already on the way."

"Good." He opened his passenger door. "Anything you need from your car before Manny gets here?"

She felt the inviting heat emanating from the interior of his truck. Honor weighed her options: wait inside and take the chance that Manny would arrive sooner than Bea's promised half hour, or sit in her own car and freeze. Or, she could accept his invitation and pretend it didn't come with an implied agreement to his earlier invitation to drive her home. A fierce blast of frigid air made the decision for her. Honor tossed her bag onto the backseat and slid onto the front, staring straight ahead as he slammed the door.

"This is awfully nice of you," she said when he joined her.

"Happy to help."

"I'll give Manny a few minutes, and then I'll call a cab."

He backed into the space across from her car, then put the truck in park. "Why? I don't mind driving you home."

"It's 'Put a Taxi Driver to Work' week?" Honor braced herself for the "Save your money" or "Why not donate the cash to your favorite charity?" lecture. It surprised her when, instead, he shook his head and sighed.

"So what's with all these food places choosing T names?"

"T names?"

He started counting on his fingers. "T-Bonz, Double-T Diner, Terseguel's, Timbuktu . . ."

Small talk. Idle chitchat. It's what people did when they were uncomfortable. Honor ought to know because she'd done more than her share of it, especially since—

"So how many dogs do you have?"

"Two."

"Goldens?"

"Yeah." But how'd he know that?

Matt plucked a hair from her shoulder. "I have a German Shorthaired Pointer. His papers say Jaek von something-or-other, but we call him Cash."

She turned slightly on the seat, waiting for the explanation.

"Cost us a small fortune at the vet's, 'cause when we rescued him, he had Lyme disease, heartworm, broken bones that healed on their own, cracked teeth that had to be surgically remov—"

"Good grief. Was he run over by a truck?"

"Nope. Hunters will pay two to three thousand dollars for a good bird dog, but Cash is gun-shy."

"A breeder did all that? He must be even stupider than he is crazy, because even I know that 'gun-shy' is a genetic trait, handed down by the mother dog."

"It *can* be averted," Matt said, "but it takes time. Lots of it. And incredible patience."

She pictured Rowdy and Rerun and shuddered involuntarily.

"Still cold?" He reached for the heat controls.

"No . . . no, I'm fine. I'm just trying to wrap my mind around everything your poor dog endured at the hands of that monster. They prosecuted him, I hope."

"Nope. Gave him a choice: hand over every pup from every litter, or pay a stiff fine."

"Meaning . . . he's still breeding dogs?"

"Not legally." His jaw muscles bulged, and he said through clenched teeth, "Many's the time I was tempted to go over there and tie the jerk to a chair and do to him everything he did to Cash. After describing each thing and giving him time to think about what was coming."

Honor harrumphed. "If you ever change your mind, call me."

She spent the next five minutes telling him about the feral dog that had attacked her during a rescue a few years ago.

He winced when she showed him the scars the wild shepherd had left on her right forearm and left hand. "I'd wager he was abused, too, before some idiot dumped him by the side of the road to fend for himself."

"Weird."

"What is?"

"I've often thought the very same thing."

"And that's weird because . . ."

It didn't feel right, telling him the truth. Besides, which truth would she tell? The stuff about her uncle? The Brady Shaw story and its aftermath? What had happened to her fiancé? Just because they'd spent the past half hour, talking like old pals in the warmth of his truck didn't mean they were pals.

"Does it bug you?"

"Does what bug me?" she asked.

"That you have something in common with . . ." He looked left and right, as if about to divulge a state secret, "with a *reporter*."

"No." It surprised her a little to admit that she meant it.

He flung an arm across the seatback, which put his fingers mere fractions of an inch from her shoulder. Honor resisted the urge to scoot closer to the door.

"So how'd you get involved with search and rescue?"

She told him about how her fiancé had gone to New York in the days after 9/11 to help find people buried in the rubble. Told him how an I-beam dislodged, crushing and killing him instantly, leading to her decision to walk in his footsteps, to honor his sacrifice. No doubt, Matt had heard the stories circulating about her. Thankfully, there was no way he could know about the Uncle Mike mess. So if Matt asked a straight question about the Brady debacle, she'd give him a straight answer. If he didn't? Why put herself through the ugliness?

"I read a book by a guy who trained SAR dogs," she continued, "and that was all it took to hook me. Not just on the work, but on the dogs. I've been training them—and their handlers—for years now."

She didn't know what to make of his perceptive nod and decided against asking if it meant he'd heard about her work . . . or her past. "So, Mr. Pulitzer winner, why does Austin call you The Defender?"

She'd already heard the stories, and expected him to puff out his chest and crow about the heroic deeds that began at age ten, when he thwarted a purse snatching, and continued through to his college years, when he beat a would-be rapist to a pulp. He'd rescued a gaggle of Afghani kids from certain death by loading them onto a Humvee, minutes before an IED detonated. Much to her surprise, he blushed and blinked and fidgeted so badly that Honor felt genuine regret for asking. Having been on the receiving end of "none of your business" inquiries too many times to count, she said what she wished *her* interrogators had said upon seeing her discomfort: "Look, it's really none of my business."

"It's no big deal, really. I'm just—"

The tow truck came to a halt in front of his pickup. "Saved by the squeal," he said, laughing. Ten minutes later, once Manny and her car were on the way to the garage, Matt shifted the pickup into drive. "I told the boys I'd bring 'em pizza for supper. Tony's—see, another T place!—is right on the way. Mind if I stop at the house and keep my promise before I drop you off?"

"How do you know it's on the way to my place?"

"You told me."

I did? Next time her car broke down, she'd check her blabbermouth at the door. "Can't let two growing boys starve, now can we?"

He snapped open his cell phone and scrolled to Tony's number.

"It's illegal to drive and talk," she said.

"Good point." He handed her the phone. "Two large thin crust pizzas. Pepperoni and mushrooms on one, plain cheese on the other. For pickup. You're more than welcome to join us."

"Can't. Dogs. Full bladders. Remember?"

"Yeah. Now that you mention it, I do." He maneuvered into traffic as she repeated his order, and when she returned the phone, her stomach growled.

"Oh, boy. Now you *have* to join us. It'll be half an hour before the pizzas are ready. Plenty of time to stop by your place and tend to your boys."

Pizza sounded great. Meeting his boys, even greater. But spending more time alone with Matt? Not so great. "I really can't. They've been cooped up inside all day."

"Good point," he said again.

Moments later, he pulled into her driveway, slid the gear-shift into Park, and as she opened her door, he said, "Maybe we can do the pizza thing another time."

"Yeah. Maybe." *Not*, she thought.

She hopped down from the cab, then turned to grab her bag, only to find Matt trying to hand it to her. For an instant, his fingertips brushed hers, sending her heart into overdrive. *He's a reporter*, she reminded herself, and well-deserved or not, his nickname alone didn't make him trustworthy. Once she found her voice, Honor said, "Thanks, Matt. I owe you one."

"No, you don't." When he leaned across the seat to pull the door shut, their fingers touched again. This time, his boyish, lopsided smile made the breath catch in her throat. "Enjoy your pizza," she said, stepping back.

Hours later, with both dogs slumbering at her slippered feet, Honor was still trying to figure out how to interpret his last comment . . . and whether or not she should believe him.

6

"Where are the hot peppers, Dad?"

"You ate 'em all, dummy."

"Did not, stupid-head."

"Boys, if I have to warn you again about bickering, you're going to bed. I'm not kidding."

The twins exchanged wide-eyed shock. "But it's only eight o'clock," Steve said.

Warner chimed in with "Yeah, and it's *Friday*."

"So if you want to stay up and watch that movie, you'd better knock it off."

Cheeks bulging like a couple of chipmunks, they put their heads together and whispered. "Mrs. Ruford is way nicer than him," Warner grumbled around a mouth of pizza. "Yeah," Steve whispered. "Lots."

Grinning, Matt hid behind his newspaper, more than happy to serve as their common enemy. At times like these, he wondered how their mom would have handled the bickering and stinginess so typical of sibling rivalry. No doubt she'd refer to a favorite how-to book and bow to the so-called experts' advice. Throughout Faith's pregnancy, she'd brought home dozens of pregnancy and parenting books, and he'd found a hundred excuses not to read them until *placenta previa* confined her to bed during those last two months. Though his skepticism grew with every page, he'd kept his opinions to himself, and not a day went by that he didn't second-guess the decision. If he'd played devil's advocate instead of caving to his over-protective tendencies, maybe he could have talked her out of going the natural childbirth route.

Steve helped himself to another slice of pizza. "I wish he'd get a girlfriend."

"And marry her," Warner agreed.

"Yeah. Tommy's stepmom lets him get away with everything."

"Same with Billy's stepfather."

Obviously, they'd given some serious thought to his remarrying, he thought as the boys set up the DVR, turned out all but the lamp beside Matt's chair, and lay flat on their backs to watch *Batman*. Again. And he'd watch it with them—again—just as his dad had watched *Star Wars* a dozen times without a word of complaint. Matt's dad was one of the few who hadn't recited the tired old cliché about what a good job he was doing—filling the mother and father roles. He'd also been the only one who never flinched when, as the groundskeepers had lowered Faith's coffin into the ground, Matt vowed never to mollycoddle his sons; if doing right by them meant they'd dislike him—or worse—so be it.

"Hey, Dad," they said in unison.

Planned? he wondered for the thousandth time, or yet another "twins thing?"

"Grab a pillow," Steve said, "and c'mon down."

"You can see better," Warner agreed, patting the carpet, "from here."

The movie's intro music was loud enough to make Cash whimper, so Matt flicked off the table lamp and grabbed the

remote. If the boys noticed him turning down the volume, nei-
ther said anything. Not Warner, whose twin called him "Dad's
Mini Me," and not Steve, the smaller, blond, and blue-eyed
Faith look-alike.

Though Matt sat up straight and leaned into the couch cushions, his big white socks lined up with their shorter-legged,
sneakered feet. The dog draped his black-and-white speckled
body across all three pairs of legs, and, giggling, the boys gently pushed and shoved, pretending they wanted him to leave.
They weren't fooling anybody, least of all, Cash, who tired of
the roughhousing long before the boys and trotted to the other
side of the room for a peaceful, quiet, hands-off place to flop.

The boys settled down, too, leaving Matt free to replay their
earlier get-a-girlfriend–get-married exchange. The boys were
in kindergarten before he started dating. Once or twice, he
thought maybe he'd found a woman he could spend more than
a couple of hours with. But he'd never mustered enough affection for any of them to inspire an introduction to his sons. Not
only had he planned to initiate a meeting between the boys
and Honor, he'd invited her right into his home. It would take
time, trying to puzzle that one out, and the minute the kids
were tucked in for the night, Matt intended to start a serious
Google search, see which of the rumors about her could hold
water, and which were little more than hot air.

"Hey, Dad," Warner said, pointing at the TV, "lookit that!"

Matt stared at the screen, where cops and firefighters, EMTs,
and SAR team members were milling around an accident site
as a smooth-voiced female narrator asked viewers if they'd like
to attend a college that would help them prepare to be one of
those first responders.

"I think *that's* what we should do for our next Scout badge!"

"What, go to college?" Matt teased, giving him a playful
shove.

He groaned good-naturedly and smacked a hand to his forehead. "No-o-o, not that. At least, not yet. But remember how Mr. Wilson said at our last meeting that he wanted us to think big? 'Don't just do the easy thing,' he said. 'Push yourself.'"

"Yeah, I remember." But Matt wasn't making the connection between the commercial and the troop leader's challenge, and he said so.

"We could do that."

"I admire your spunk, kiddo," he said, ruffling his dark hair, "but you're barely ten. Not nearly old enough to—"

"No-o-o," he said again, "not the life-saving stuff, like sticking people with needles and jamming tubes up their noses and—"

"—and driving fast," Steve tucked in.

"Right. And driving fast. What I *mean* is, like, well, do you remember that kid who got lost on a camping trip someplace out west, and the Eagle Scouts helped look for him?"

Yeah, Matt did remember that story. And thanks to a sharp-eyed Scout who found the autistic boy's baseball cap in hip-deep field grasses, SAR dogs tracked the child and found him, huddled and nearly catatonic, in a hollow tree. He made a mental note to see if there had been any follow-up stories, detailing the boy's progress. "But those kids were fifteen, sixteen years old, son. Some were even older, working on earning Eagle status."

Now Steve got involved. On his knees, he faced Matt, too. "You're not getting it, Dad. What he means is, we could scout out the perimeter. Y'know, make one of those shoulder-to-shoulder lines, and walk along, looking for small clues."

"Yeah!" Warner agreed, fist-bumping his brother. "*Those* are the guys who find rings and watches and things that get trampled on, and hidden by weeds and stuff."

"Right. And a lot of the time, *that's* what leads grown-up searchers to the missing person."

"Or the dead body," Warner said, looking much older than his ten years.

"What do *you* think, Dad? Will Mr. Wilson think it's a great idea, too?"

Thankfully, the Scout leader would be the heavy if this idea didn't fly. "I can talk to him, if you want me to." He wondered what Honor—who taught SAR classes and trained rescuers and dog handlers—would have to say on the subject of kids getting involved in searches.

But no matter what the boys' Scout leader said, Matt would never sign off on their participation, no matter how "perimeter" the search might be. Nightmarish memories of things he'd seen during his own rescue missions still had the power to rouse him from sleep, and one of the grisliest had started out as a routine search for a lost child. No way he'd put his stamp of approval on anything that might expose his innocent kids to anything of the kind.

Hoots and hollers, high-fives, and stomach-bumps roused Cash from his nap, and he ambled over to see what all the fuss was about. "What's the matter, boy," Matt said, laughing as he ruffled the dog's floppy black ears, "afraid you're missing something good?"

The commercial bled into a second, and a third, and by the time the network returned to the movie, the boys and the dog had settled down. Bless their little hearts, he thought, grinning, for presenting him with a perfect excuse to call Honor. Tomorrow, maybe even the day after, lest she get the wrong impression from one-on-one contact so soon after he'd pretty much forced her to use his mechanic and gave a ride home. He'd better tread carefully if he wanted to get to know her better, and Matt definitely wanted that. What better way to accomplish that than by learning everything he could about her?

"G'night, Dad," Warner said, hugging him.

Steve followed suit. "You comin' upstairs?"

One more element in their nightly ritual, Matt said, "You bet. Who's telling the story tonight?"

Side by side, the boys stretched and yawned, then started up the stairs. Steve said over his shoulder, "Can we skip it tonight? It's ten o'clock."

"Yeah," Warner said, "and we told Mrs. Ruford we'd help clean out her basement."

The woman had a good heart, no doubt about it, and loved his boys almost as much as if they were her own flesh and blood grandkids. Matt honestly didn't know how he would have made it all these years without her help. But he'd braved the cluttered staircase of hers a time or two and knew firshand that what lay at the bottom of the last step more than qualified her to appear on that hoarders show. "Whoa. Big job. You sure you're up to it?"

They wouldn't finish in one day, the boys admitted; mostly, Harriet wanted companionship as she plowed through the mess. He had a notion to tell them they couldn't go unless they promised to wear masks and goggles, rubber gloves to protect their hands, and waders in case they stepped on something moist. Or alive. Then he remembered he'd been about their age when he helped clear out his grandpa's barn. Every mucky inch exposed a new treasure, invited a new adventure. He'd gone home exhausted and filthy, with spider webs in his hair and dirt under his craggy fingernails, but Matt would never forget that day. With no barns to dig out, this might be the closest his sons would ever come to experiencing that kind of full-out, all-boy joy.

"Be right up," he called after them. He'd let the dog out one last time, turn out the lights and lock up, and turn in. Tomorrow was soon enough to get online; maybe what he dug up there would take his mind off Steve and Warner, hip deep in fifty years of dusty, grimy junk that sweet old lady hadn't been able to part with.

He listened to the boys' bedtime prayers, then took a shower and said his own. He stared up at the black ceiling for a long time, grappling with issues of conscience: what if his Internet search turned up sordid information that backed up, rather than refuted, the rumors about Honor's past? Smart and gorgeous, she'd survived some tough stuff. If even 1 percent of what he'd heard about her had happened to him—or any other man he could name—it would have flattened them like a wrecking ball. She put on a good show with her hard-as-nails façade, but no one *chose* search and rescue unless inside them beat a heart that wanted to help others, that cared what happened to those she cared about.

A weird thought slipped into his head as he dropped off to sleep, and it made him grin:

If he played his cards right, could he be one of those people?

7

Aw, dude . . . that's low," Austin said, leaning over Matt's shoulder to read the computer screen. "And creepy. Never would-a figured you, of all people, for a stalker."

Matt kept staring at the monitor, mostly because it was the best way he knew to hide his caught-red-handed embarrassment. "Hand me the phone, will ya?"

Austin delivered the device. "Calling Harriet to send the twins home so they can see their Uncle Austin?"

"Calling the cops. To report a break-in."

Laughing, Austin gave Matt a friendly shove. "Funny. Real funny. If you ever get tired of writing for the *Sun*, maybe you can try your hand at stand-up."

The heat in Matt's cheeks had faded, making it safe to face his pal. "How'd you get in here, anyway?"

"Through the living room window. From all the heel scrapes on the sill, I figured that's how everybody gets in." Chuckling, he added, "Guess you didn't hear me ringing the bell and pounding on the door, bellowing like a bull moose, engrossed as you were with your, ah, work." Crossing his arms over his chest, he regarded Matt from the corner of his eye. "Now I've got a question for you, pal o' mine: what're you searching for, exactly?"

He could fib, but he and Austin went back way too far for that. "I kinda like her," he admitted, "but I've got the boys to consider, y'know?"

"Ah-ha. The old 'poop runs downhill' theory, eh?" He gave an approving nod. "Can't have her, um, tainting the twins." Another nod, this time at the computer. "Admirable . . . in a sick and twisted, protective parent sort of way."

"Bite me," Matt said. Then he pointed at the screen. "Says here she was all wrapped up in a big scandal some years back."

"Yeah," Austin said, pulling up a chair. He leaned both elbows on the corner of Matt's desk. "Some broad at the fire department started the ball rolling. Got it in her head that the only way Honor could've climbed the ranks as fast as she did was by trading favors—and you know the kind I mean—for promotions. Very unsavory stuff. She ended up quitting, to put an end to the speculating, but it only stirred things up more." Frowning, he shook his head. "Frankly, I'm surprised a hot-shot investigative reporter like yourself missed it."

"I was in New York when this was written."

"Flimsy excuse if ever I heard one." He chuckled again. "Personally, I never believed a word of it."

"Seems you're in the minority, then."

"You can say that again. Once the initial story hit the air-waves, it spread like wildfire."

One that was helped along with a couple gallons of acceler-ant . . . "A cryin' shame, ruining Honor's reputation that way."

"Very nearly ruined Hoffman's, too, and his marriage, to boot."

Wyatt Hoffman, Matt wondered. "County's fire chief?"

"Yep. But you'll read all about it if you keep this up." Then, "You ask me, Honor was the only one involved in the whole mess who has any scruples." The monitor flicked to Matt's screensaver photo of the twins, inducing a faint smile on Austin's face. "Stevie is one good-lookin' kid."

"Hard not to be good lookin' when you're the spitting image of your beautiful mama."

Now Austin's gaze settled on the framed picture of Faith, hanging on the wall between Matt's degrees and diplomas, then slid to the dark-haired, dark-eyed twin. "And that could be a picture of you at Warner's age."

"Steve calls him Mini-Matt."

"Warner and Steven. What's up with that, dude? Don't think I've ever heard more un-twin-like names." He chuckled. "Don't think I've ever heard the name Warner."

"Stevens was my father-in-law's name, and Faith's name was Warner before she changed it to Phillips."

"Seems a little unbalanced. I mean, what's *your* family involvement?"

Matt remembered the big blowup he'd caused, asking that very question while Faith was pregnant. He'd fallen back on the "Choose your battles well" adage his dad had drummed into his head, and, near as he could figure, his rational demeanor made her feel unreasonable by comparison, inspiring a compromise. "The boys' middle names are Carter and David, after my grandfathers."

"Carter. Nice. Might just have to borrow that if Mercy and I have kids."

If, Matt noted, not when. A subject for another day. Maybe. "So how are the wedding plans coming?"

"Actually, that's why I'm here. The only family Mercy has is a half-brother who lives in England, and you know my sad story."

Matt remembered only too well that Austin's dad had been shot during a convenience store robbery, and not long after, he lost his twin brother in the North Tower on 9/11, Austin's mom died of cancer . . . pancreatic, same kind that killed his own mother.

"So she wants a small wedding on the boat. The minister, the reception, the whole shebang."

"That's surprising."

"The small wedding? Nah. She isn't the 'drag a poufy dress down the aisle' type. If you knew her better, you'd know—"

"Finley, you named that old bucket of bolts you call home 'One Regret.'" Matt laughed. "I can believe she's anti-poufy dress, but starting married life on a note like that?" He laughed again.

"Oh, you definitely have to look into a career in comedy, pal. You're a real cutup." His smile dimmed when he said "So, anyway, no tuxedo required."

"Not even for you?" Just thinking of the stiff monkey suit Faith had insisted he wear at their wedding was enough to make Matt run a finger under his sweatshirt collar. "Man, I hope you know how lucky you are."

"Would I be doing this if I didn't?"

"Guess not. You are pushin' forty . . .'"

"Bite me," Austin said, smirking.

"When's the big day?"

"I'm trying to talk her out of it, but Mercy's got her heart set on New Year's Eve."

"You mean, 'I do' as the ball drops in Times Square?"

Austin nodded. "'Fraid so."

"Well, look at the bright side."

"Bright side? You are one cold dude, dude." Then, "Okay. I'll take the bait. What is the bright side?"

"You'll never get the cold shoulder for forgetting your anniversary."

"Good point. You bringing Honor?"

"Hadn't thought that far ahead. Not in 'who I'll escort to your wedding' terms, anyway."

Austin's raised brows and narrowed eyes implied "What kind of 'way', then?" But "Have the boys met her yet?" is what he said.

"Nope."

"What's the plan, there?"

"Don't have one." It wasn't the truth, but then, it wasn't exactly a lie, either. Matt pictured Honor, all green-eyed, stand-offish, hundred-something pounds of her. Would that mass of shiny red curls feel as soft as it looked?

"She could do worse."

He might have agreed, if Austin hadn't nodded at the computer screen. "Poor kid already did. Couple of times."

Matt must have bumped the mouse with his elbow, waking the hibernating machine. His gaze went straight to the headline on the article he'd been reading when Austin came in: "Female Firefighter Quits Amid Promotions Controversy." He thought back to what Austin had said earlier. "What really happened, between Honor and the lieutenant, I mean?"

"You know Wyatt, always rooting for the underdog. Well, he saw that she was struggling, mostly with concentration, so he took her under his wing. I'll bet he clocked a couple weeks' worth of off-duty time, making sure she could pass the written and endurance tests. I remember once, while we were all loading up after a fire, he pointed at her. Said he'd never seen anybody more dedicated and determined, man or woman." Austin shrugged. "I took it to mean he thought she was good for the department."

"Too bad everybody else didn't take it that way."

"You got that right." Austin stood, put the chair back where he'd found it. "So what are you and the boys doing for Thanksgiving?"

"Same as always. I'll throw a turkey in the oven, overcook it, and we'll all pretend to love it."

"Mercy's got a big dinner planned at her place. Her brother Leo can't make it, so she asked the Sullivans and—hey, why don't you guys join us?"

"Okay if I bring Harriet?"

"The more, the merrier, I always say."

The men walked side by side into the foyer, and as he opened the door, Matt said, "You know it's bad luck to leave a building by a different door than the one you came in."

Austin stepped onto the porch. "Then I'm safe as a babe in his mama's arms. I didn't come in through a door, remember?" Halfway into his pickup, he said, "I'll call you in a day or two, once Mercy's got the time nailed down."

"Find out what I can bring while you're at it."

"Why don't you bring Honor? Two birds with one stone," he said, and slammed the driver's door.

Meaning, introduce her to the twins, and rack up a few "getting to know you" hours at the same time.

He powered down the computer and walked into the kitchen to slap together some lunch for Harriet and the boys. On the way out the front door, he stopped in the living room. Sure enough, black streaks provided all the evidence he needed that Austin hadn't been the only one who'd slipped into the house by way of the window. He slid the lock into place, then remembered how, last year, the boys had forgotten their keys. They'd gone next door to borrow Harriet's, and when she couldn't find it in her mess of a kitchen, they'd called him. In the middle of a story, at the height of rush hour. The open window, he surmised, guaranteed they'd never have to sit through another "be more careful" lecture that lasted all through supper.

Grinning, Matt unlocked the window and grabbed the cooler. Steve and Warner weren't little boys any more. All too soon, they'd be grown and gone, and he'd be staring at heel marks on a windowsill and Matchbox car scrapes on the hardwood, wondering why he felt so alone.

Tonight, once the last of Harriet's basement dust had gurgled down the bathtub drain, he'd call Honor. They had more in common than she was willing to admit. She understood the pain of loss, for starters, and hopefully, in time, she'd see that, too. For now, he had two solid excuses to call . . . to ask her advice about getting the boys and their Scout troop involved with perimeter searches, then to extend Austin's invitation to join them for Thanksgiving dinner.

But first, he'd do something he hadn't done in a long, long time: pray.

Because something told him if she said no to either appeal, he'd need all the strength he could get.

8

Guess you're wondering how I got your number."

It was good to hear his voice, which confused her almost as much as the fact that he'd called at all. "Not really. I'm in the book."

"How's the car?"

"Got it back a few days ago, and it's running fine."

"See? Told you Manny would take good care of you."

"Yes, you did. And I appreciate it."

"No thanks necessary. The car isn't really why I called."

And here it comes, she thought. He must have heard the stories about her and decided to put her purity—or lack of it—to the test. The only question, really, was how he'd approach it.

"The twins were watching some sort of rescue on TV, and got the bright idea that they could maybe earn a Scout badge if they learned how to help with a search."

Well, this was a new one. Not even the sleaziest guys had used their kids to get to her.

"I thought your boys were only ten."

"They are."

"A lot of the *adults* I teach think that SAR is basically a walk in the park. They don't realize what an investment of time and

money is required, just to get started. It's physically demanding because the search terrain is almost never flat, and the
weather can be downright miserable. There are snakes and
bugs and poisonous plants, stagnant water and brush so thick
and thorny that not even a rabbit would go through it. And
that's all before they even *find* a victim."

"Uh, wow."

"Wow? You were at the crash site and saw for yourself how
many different conditions we find people in—from bloody
and unconscious, to dismembered or worse—and if they've
been dead a while?" Honor harrumphed. "You'd better have
a strong stomach. It's enough to give grown men nightmares,
so it's probably not the best idea for your boys to—what about
you?"

"Me? In a search and rescue course?" Then, "Well, maybe I
could train the dog."

"Cash? How old is he?"

"Five. Six, since June."

"It takes a year, sometimes more, to teach a rescue dog
the basics. Then another two, maybe three additional years
of steady field training before they're ready for the real stuff.
Rigorous, test-their-limits stuff that's a whole lot harder than
what we go through because we ask them to go places we can't
go, do things we can't do. And their bodies weren't built for
most of it. And poor Cash has been abused enough."

"You're right."

"But you could start from scratch. The boys *could* get
involved by helping train a rescue dog. I know a couple who
own two goldens, and the female is pregnant. She's a rescue
dog, and so's the father, so those pups will be—"

"I dunno, Honor. With my wacky schedule and two rowdy
boys? Wouldn't be fair to anyone, least of all, the puppy."

His rejection had come so quickly, it almost seemed rehearsed. Evidence that Matt was commitment-phobic? Not that it mattered, because even if she'd been in a position to commit, what made her think he'd want a relationship with her? She'd been tough on him, right from the get-go, for no reason other than he shared a gender with other men who'd hurt her. "At least you have the good sense to admit your failings before anybody gets hurt."

Matt whistled as she winced. *Lighten up, girl*, she told herself.

"Ouch," he said, chuckling. "Truth is, I think I was just looking to hear an expert put into words what I already knew. It'll be tough, explaining it all, especially now that they've spent their allowance on how-to books." He muttered something, then added, "Guess this is another of those 'put it in God's hands' things."

Translation: Not only had she underscored the reasons Matt needed to shoot down his boys' idea, she'd given him the ammunition to do it, too. Guilt nagged at her. Just because she had her guard up all the time didn't mean everybody else did, and Honor felt bad about playing a part in disappointing his kids. If only she could make it easier, for him *and* his boys. "You could always take a page from my mom's parenting manual."

"Parenting manual?" Matt laughed, and she so enjoyed the rich, robust sound of it that she wished she hadn't lost her sense of humor, along with her reputation, so she could crack jokes and spew puns to inspire more of it. A whole lot more. "When you asked why she wouldn't let you do something, you mean?"

"Or have something, or go somewhere, or hang around with this kid or that one." Honor felt the stirrings of fond memories, and it made her miss her mom a little. "I used to think she *looked* for excuses to say 'Because I said so, that's why.'"

"Here I was, fixin' to ask you out, sorta. Can't do it now, though."

Honor didn't know how to react to that. Shortly before the fiasco, she'd gone out with an accountant, ten, maybe eleven times. Ray had one flaw: He wasn't *John*. Once she acknowledged that, Honor knew it wouldn't be fair to keep seeing him. Then came a man—to use the term loosely—who resorted to name-calling when she said "I don't believe in kissing on a first date." And the one who'd behaved like a perfect gentleman when she delivered the same line . . . and made so many prank calls in the next weeks that she'd been forced to change her phone number. Worst of all were the firefighters, guys who were supposed to be brothers at arms, who let their buddies believe she was everything they'd heard, and then some. "Okay, I'll bite: Why *can't* you ask me out . . . now?"

"Isn't it obvious?"

Not even slightly!

"By some weird twist of science, we must have had the same mother. And she must have liked you best because when she used that line on me, she always added 'and that's final!' So, see? I can't very well go out on a date *with my sister*, now can I?"

Half a dozen clichés zipped through her mind because never in a million years, not if her life depended on it, even if they held a gun to her head, would she have guessed he'd say *that!*

"The other reason I'm calling is to find out what you're doing on Thanksgiving."

She'd feel pathetic, just saying "nothing," so Honor explained how she spent every holiday with her sister's family and that this year, because the entire Gray clan had enjoyed their Disney cruise so much last Christmas, they'd booked the shorter Thanksgiving weekend trip.

"Why aren't *you* going?"

She could handle a few hours in the warmth of family love. Longer than that only emphasized how alone she'd been since the debacle. Times like these, it was hard not to be mad at God, for making her a do-the-right-thing person, even when it hurt. "Because I can only take so much whining and complaining and bickering." She paused to ask God's forgiveness for the lie. "And then there's the stuff the *kids* do. I'd probably jump overboard on day two!"

"Does that mean you'll join the boys and me at Austin and Mercy's?"

"Maybe. Why not? Whatever . . ."

"Can you take a little constructive criticism?"

"I guess. Depends. About what?"

"You might consider ratcheting your enthusiasm down a notch or two. Y'know, just so's I don't get a swelled head or anything."

Laughing, Honor said, "Okay."

"Okay, you'll curb the over-eager 'I can't wait to spend time with Matt Phillips' gusto? Or okay, you'll come with us?"

"Both." She couldn't remember the last time she'd felt playful. Or flirty. It felt so good that Honor was almost tempted not to rein it in.

Almost.

"Did Mercy happen to mention if she needs me to bring anything?" Honor loved to cook, but with no one to do it *for*, the whole process seemed pointless.

"Aw, now, don't get me all involved in your women-in-the-kitchen stuff. I'll give you her phone number—hold on a sec, it's on the back of an envelope, right here in this stack of mail, at least I think it is, yeah, got it—and the two of you can talk

yourselves blue about side dishes and desserts and appetizers."
He rattled off the number, then said, "Hey, I've got an idea . . ."

"Uh-oh."

Chuckling, Matt said, "Just to clarify . . . I said *ratchet* the
gusto down a tad, not take a *hatchet* to it."

"Sorry." She heard herself giggle, something else she hadn't
done in a long time. "My mistake."

"Don't give it another thought." He paused. "Until the next
time you're tempted to come at me with a pin."

To pop his swelled head? she wondered, laughing. "Sorry,"
she repeated. "You were saying?"

"How 'bout if we pick you up? Your place is right on the
way to Mercy's house. That way, you and the boys and Harriet
can get acquainted during the drove over. Why, I'll just bet
that by the time we get there, you'll all be best buds and I won't
be able to get a word in edgewise."

"Harriet?"

"The woman next door. Sweet ol' gal jumps at any opportunity to spend time with the twins."

"I'm sure that's because they're great kids."

"Yeah, they are, if I do say so myself."

Which was scary. Because if they were anything like their
dad, she was sure to go nuts over them, too.

Too? Where had *that* come from! "So what time's dinner?"

"Never thought to ask. Here's an idea: you finesse the info
outta Mercy when you're asking if she prefers cheesecake or
fudge, and let me know."

"Subtle, Phillips. Real subtle."

"Hey, a guy whose dessert-making talents fall into two cat-
egories—unwrap and thaw or thaw and unwrap—can't afford
to be subtle."

"Which is your favorite?"

"Is there such a thing as fudge cheesecake?" He smacked his lips.

"I'll check it out."

He did a fair-to-middlin' Irish accent. "Ah, Honor, m'love, where've you been all m'life?"

Hiding in the shadows of lies. The admission made her wonder what was wrong with him. The longer she knew him, the more apparent it became that he liked her. If he truly was the sane and rational man he appeared to be, why would he pursue a more-than-friends relationship with a woman who had more baggage than a luggage carousel at BWI?

"So you'll call me tomorrow, then?"

"Sure. If I can get hold of Mercy."

"Well, a guy can hope."

No one since John had made her heart pound like a parade drum. She'd blame the reaction on that third cup of coffee . . . if it hadn't been decaf.

"Sweet dreams, Honor."

"You, too." Matt might have heard her, if she'd said it a tick sooner. Just as well, because he probably would have sensed that she didn't believe in sweet dreams. Not after Brady Shaw's news story hit the airwaves, anyway, when the nightmares began, sometimes two or three a night that shook her awake, gasping for breath and sweating. It took more than a year to figure out that if she ever hoped to sleep again, she needed to push herself, so long and so hard that she'd fall into bed, too exhausted to do anything *but* sleep.

Which was perfect, really, since she'd never been a sweet-dreams kind of girl.

Honor wasn't a bubble bath-and-candles kind, either, but that didn't stop her from popping her favorite Eagles CD into the stereo and lighting everything and anything with a wick while she waited for the tub to fill. By the time she'd hung her robe on the doorknob, the sparkly white foam was nearly thick enough to float a bar of soap. Eyes closed, she sunk into it, replaying every warm and friendly word exchanged with Matt. If that didn't relax her enough to conjure a sweet dream or two, what would?

Enjoy it while you can, she warned, *because old habits die hard.* How long before she slipped back into her cautious, suspicious ways? *Never would be nice.*

Smiling, she sank deeper into the suds. "Well, a girl can hope."

9

Aren't we an oddball bunch? Matt thought, grinning. The weirdness started with Austin, who'd insisted that Matt sit at the head of the table, "Because if you think I'm gonna jog from this end to that every time I get a yen to kiss my best girl, you've got another think comin'." The twins sat to Matt's right and left. Harriet, Bud, and Flora lined up on Warner's side of the table, Mercy and Austin on Steve's. Across from Matt at the far end of the table sat Honor, wearing a fuzzy, elbow-length sweater that not only matched the blue flecks in her enormous green eyes, but accented her curvy figure, too.

He could barely see the satiny white flowers etched into the fabric of the tablecloth, thanks to bowls and baskets and platters, all filled to overflowing. The blend of scents hung like an invisible cloud above them, and the steam from pots and pans hazed the windows, taking him back to those rib-sticking Grandma cooked-and-baked dinners of his childhood. Steve had drawn a plate-sized heart in the fog, and Warner fingered M.S. + A.F. inside it, and Matt wondered if the happy couple would take their eyes off one another long enough to notice.

Everyone in this sunny dining room had a lot to be thankful for, from Flora, whose cancer had been in remission for more than two years, to Mercy and Austin, who'd found each other again after misunderstandings and stubbornness kept them apart for months. Harriet had cleared eight boxes of God-knows-what from her basement, and the twins earned twenty bucks apiece for helping her accomplish the feat. Matt had their good health, a mortgage-free house, and a dependable car to be grateful for, and God willing, a shot at winning a coveted award for his article on the Chesapeake Bay. And then there was Honor, all pink-cheeked and glowing despite the rumor shadow that followed her everywhere. Matt had no idea if she could find something to give thanks for today, but she looked happy. And after everything Brady Shaw's report had subjected her to, that was something, right?

"The table looks wonderful," Flora said. "All these beautiful dishes!"

"Pass the beautiful breadbasket, please. And while you're at it, the beautiful butter dish, too."

"Bud," his wife said, "you're incorrigible." And then she kissed his cheek.

"You know, I thought Austin, there, was crazy, not taking his proper place at the head of the table, but if this is why he's breaking tradition?" He returned the kiss. "I'm more and more inclined to agree with him."

Austin kissed Mercy, just because he could, and Warner whimpered. "It's a good thing my stomach is empty."

"Why's that?" Harriet wanted to know.

"Because all this *mush* might just make me throw up."

"Not suitable table talk, son," Matt said, forefinger wagging like a metronome.

Warner responded with a quiet sigh, and Matt groaned inwardly, but not for the same reason as his son. Honor might as well have been a mile away. Not that he was in any position, literally or figuratively, to kiss her, but he sure as heck *wanted* to.

He might have given the admission a moment's thought, if Steve hadn't piped up with, "If somebody doesn't say the blessing, the potatoes will taste like cardboard and the gravy will congeal."

"Congeal," his twin echoed, snickering. "Are you fer real? Mrs. Wiley didn't really mean that you have to use *every* spelling word in a sentence."

"Your *breath* is getting ready to congeal," he shot back.

"Your face has *already* congealed."

Steve crossed both arms over his chest, and for a moment there, all gathered thought he'd been bested. Until he smirked. "Yeah, well, your *brain* must have congealed because everybody knows that's just plain dumb."

The adults laughed, enjoying the banter, but it made Matt nervous. Not so much because he'd refereed hundreds of similar verbal sparring matches over the years as something Honor had said on the phone, about not having much patience for squabbling kids.

"Li'l Stevie is right," Harriet said. "Who'll do the honors?"

For the first time since they'd gathered around the table, the room fell silent. Every head turned, every eye was on Matt. He blinked. And swallowed. "Why are you all lookin' at *me*?"

"'Cause the guy in that chair says the blessing," Austin pointed out.

"And slices the turkey," said Mercy.

The resolute expressions aimed his way told Matt that despite what he did for a living, he would never come up with the words that would help him weasel out of the prayer. "Well, don't just sit there like a bunch of zoo monkeys," he said, grinning, "fold your eyes and close your hands."

"Dad!" the boys blurted, and when the laughter died down, Matt cleared his throat. "Dear Lord," he began, and like dominoes toppling, the sound of heads bowing and hands clasping rippled down the table like a gentle wave, "we thank you for the generosity of our hostess, who opened her home to this motley crew."

"Motley," Warner whispered, giggling.

"Sh-h," Steve hissed past his own snicker.

Matt raised his voice, just enough to silence them, and grinning, continued. "We ask Your blessing, Father, on the veritable feast Mercy has prepared, and on Mercy, who for reasons known only to You has consented to marry a man who's more brother than friend. Thank you for Flora's healing, and for the good health You've bestowed on everyone at this table. Watch over the brave men and women who fight for our freedom, and their families, who wait and worry here at home. Go with every first responder, Father, as they walk into unknown dangers to keep us safe. Comfort and provide for those rendered homeless by any one of a hundred calamities. We ask these things in Your most holy name, Amen."

He barely heard the enthusiastic Amens that echoed his own, because when Matt looked up, it rocked him to see a trembly smile playing at the corners of Honor's mouth. Still more surprising were the tears shimmering in her eyes.

"That was beautiful," she whispered, and the words floated to him like a welcomed summer breeze. People liked to say that God works in mysterious ways, and Matt had never agreed more. If Austin had sat him beside Honor, she'd be all tangled up in a hug right about now, trying to decide whether to participate in the kiss . . . or punch him on the jaw.

It took a few seconds to realize that all eyes were on him again, this time waiting for him to carve the turkey. Standing, Matt picked up the big-handled blade and executed a few moves learned while on the fencing team in college. It tickled the men and boys and terrified the women.

"Just slice the bird, y'big show-off," Harriet said with a cluck of her tongue.

"Yeah, Dad," Warner agreed, "before we all faint from starvation."

Steve hid behind one hand. "He's right, Dad."

"I read someplace that it takes weeks to starve," Flora put in.

"Speaking of reading," Bud said, and launched into his annual "what really happened at the first Thanksgiving" spiel.

When someone suggested they take turns going around the table, naming one thing they were thankful for, Matt thanked God that Honor's sweet potato casserole distracted them because he couldn't think of one thing to add to his prayer . . . except to admit how grateful he was that God had put Honor into his life.

Halfway through dessert, Austin's cell phone buzzed, and he stepped into the foyer to take the call. His former jovial expression gave way to one of high alert as he said, "There was a multi-car pileup on the Bay Bridge." He grabbed his pre-packed duffle and, shouldering it, kissed Mercy good-bye. "I'll call as soon as I can."

A chorus of "Praying!" and "Be carefuls" followed him to the door, and when he closed it behind him, Mercy went into the kitchen.

He'd been in Austin's shoes, plenty of times. Matt started to follow her, hoping to smooth things over and spare his pal the "your job is too dangerous you have to quit before I go insane" nonsense he'd faced so many times with Faith. But Honor stopped him with nothing more than a brow quirk. "I'll go," she said as the chatter rose up again.

It was a simple thing, really: she'd sent a silent message, and he'd received it. Happened to couples all the time, right? Not so simple after all, when he considered that in the eight years he and Faith had been together—and they'd been about as close as two people could get—nothing even remotely like it had ever happened between them.

10

Mercy was facing the window when Honor entered the kitchen. "You okay?"

She hung her head. "I don't know if I'll ever get used to it."

"Takes a special person to do what he does," she said, laying a hand on Mercy's forearm, "and it takes an equally special person to wait at home."

A ragged sigh rumbled from the smaller woman's throat. "He changed me in just about every imaginable way—all of it good—except for this white-hot fear that takes over my mind when he's out on a call."

Honor put an arm around her, led her to the big island counter in the center of the room, and poured them both a cup of coffee. "I know what you're going through."

That inspired a tiny grin. "What! You're one of *them*. How can you know what I'm going through?"

Honor saw no spite or anger written on Mercy's worried face, but it was there, in her anxious voice. "I wasn't always one of them."

Raised brows and wide eyes told her she had the woman's attention. "What do you mean?"

"About ten years ago, I was engaged to a firefighter. Every time he was called away from a date, or a family dinner, or one of our phone conversations was interrupted by one emergency or another, I went into a funk. Pacing a path in the rug, gnawing my cuticles bloody, praying for that phone call that would tell me he was home, safe and sound . . ." Even the memory of it was enough to inspire tremors, and when she reached for her mug, Honor nearly overturned it. "If I had a dollar for every time I thought about asking him to leave the department to—I don't know, sell widgets at Wal-Mart—I could have paid for our wedding a couple times over."

"But you never asked him to leave, did you?"

"No."

"Because it would have been like asking him to cut off his leg."

Honor nodded. "Prayer. Faith. Trust in his skills. Belief that he loved what we had enough to *want* to come home . . . that's what kept me going between emergencies."

"When Austin showed up in Chicago, I was never so happy to see someone. Or so horrified."

"Because the nightmares you thought you'd escaped were standing right in front of you."

She grabbed a napkin from the basket on the countertop and blotted her teary eyes. "And because I knew as sure as he was standing there outside my door," she said, knuckles rapping the granite, "that he'd ask me, one more time, to give his whole God thing a try . . . and that even though I didn't *get* it, I'd say yes."

"And pack up your things and follow him back here."

"And follow him back here. But kids?" Mercy shook her head. "Austin talks about it all the time. How he'd love to have a houseful, and at least one boy, to carry on the Finley name. I get that, really I do. But if something happened to him out there, it'd just be me, alone with all those kids, even the one who'd carry on the Finley name."

"I hear ya, girl. But you can't let fear rule your life. Give God some credit because I'm sure *He* isn't ready for an Austin Finley up there," she said, thumb pointed at the ceiling, "riling up all the angels!"

Mercy laughed. "I never thought of it that way." Then, "So how'd you end things with your fiancé, if I'm not being too nosy?"

"I didn't end it. He did."

"Whoa. Never saw that coming," Mercy said, refilling their mugs.

"September 11 happened, and some of the guys decided to put in for vacation time and drive up to New York, to see what they could do."

Mercy grabbed Honor's hands and squeezed them tight. "No . . ."

"An I-beam gave way and pinned him down. There were so many others trapped in the rubble, and not nearly enough personnel to dig them out."

And he bled to death, all alone in a tunnel of fire and ash.

"I'm sorry, Honor, so sorry."

"Don't be," she said, wrapping both hands around her mug. "John's death gave real purpose to my life. I can't prevent tragedies and I can't save every victim, but I can do everything in my power to help put more boots on the ground."

"And if your work saves just one life . . ."

"If," she said, "the biggest little word in the English language."

"You think if I volunteered, I'd have a better understanding of what Austin does, what he goes through out there?"

"Somebody has to keep the home fires burning, give them incentive to be careful, to come *home* . . ."

"Can I ask you a really personal question?"

Honor grinned. "Sure." At least Mercy would temper her prying with a little decorum.

"How do you feel about Matt?"

She'd set her jaw, expecting the inquiry would involve Brady Shaw's story. "Matt? I—I, ah, how do I feel about him . . ."

"Down, girl," Mercy said, patting her hand. "You don't have to answer." She winked. "I pretty much know, anyway."

"Then I wish you'd tell me because I honestly have no idea how I feel about him." The words poured out like rain from a downspout . . . how they'd met, things she'd said to him, ways she'd included him in the list of shady reporters, stories they'd shared.

"I don't know him very well, myself, but Austin thinks the world of him."

"So you're suggesting I abide by the birds of a feather rule, eh?"

"Something like that."

But what if Austin and Mercy were wrong? What if Matt was like the Brady Shaws of the reporting world? Her opinion of human nature wasn't all that great to begin with. If he—

"I know it sounds goofy, coming from someone who barely knows him, but you can trust him, Honor."

"Why are you so sure?"

"I was born and raised and earned my degree in psychology in New York. After 9/11, my patients were mostly cops who'd worked at Ground Zero. They were different in just about every way you can name, except for an innate talent for reading people. If I hoped to reach them, I had to learn to play the game by their rules. Not to sound like some cocky know-it-all, but I got pretty good at it. I can't define it and don't understand it, but I respect what it tells me."

"And it's telling you I can trust Matt."

"With your very life."

"Not an easy concept to wrap my mind around," she confessed. "Considering . . ."

"Nobody with two functioning brain cells believes that clown, Shaw. An old college pal is a major player at the network. It's no secret that they keep him around because his buffoonery is good for ratings. But just between you and me? They're prepared for the day the bottom falls out of his cage. So don't give another thought to what Matt thinks of Brady's so-called work. Borrowing your birds of a feather premise, he's too smart to align himself with that scuzzball, even by way of opinion."

"Y'know," Honor said, smiling, "I came in here to console you. How'd things get so turned around?"

"Believe me, you've been a huge comfort." She raised a hand and pressed her thumb to her forefinger. "I was *this* close to calling off the wedding when you walked in here."

"And now?"

"And now I'm wondering what you're doing on New Year's Eve, because I need a maid of honor for my wedding."

11

*T*he computer monitor radiated a ghostly white light, shrouding Matt's home office with an eerie, otherworldly glow. The story on the screen was equally strange. Beside the keyboard, lay the top page of a fat spiral tablet filled with quickly scrawled notes. Later, he'd dig deeper into each detail. For now, he plowed forward in search of corroborative facts to back up gut instinct.

With one click of Matt's mouse, Brady Shaw's network-generated head shot filled the screen. Asked to identify the head of the IRS, nine out of ten Americans would walk away, scratching their heads. But hold up a picture of Brady Shaw, and every last one of them could cite his name, home-town, and a list of other PR-crafted biographical details. Were viewers really so naïve, Matt wondered, that they could be dis-tracted from the facts by boy-next-door looks and a smooth DJ baritone? If the havoc Shaw had wreaked in Honor's life was any indicator, the answer was a booming yes.

"Easy to pull the wool over people's eyes," he grated, "when you're the antithesis of a wolf in sheep's clothing."

But no matter. When the time was right, Matt's story would tell the truth, once and for all, about *Shaw*. "Smile on, Brady ol' boy," he said, clicking the X that erased the picture, "while you can."

⁓⁂⁂

Honor had a love-hate relationship with Christmas.

Between work and classes and joining in on SAR operations, she barely had time to buy gifts for her sister's family, let alone ornaments and garland and lights that no one would be around to enjoy. Most years, she leaned toward the "love" side and got her decorating fix by helping out at Hope's house. This year, the "hate" side would win because they'd changed the dates of their annual ski trip from February to Christmas week.

Once a month, she made a point of visiting Johns Hopkins, playing games with the kids in Children's Oncology, leaving Christmas to the Orioles and Ravens players whose schedules didn't allow for regular visits. This year, she'd deliver board games, CDs, and DVDs she'd bought for them. If they were too tired for that, she'd read one of the books she'd been collecting. Hospitals were awful places for kids any time of the year. But Christmas, she thought as her cell phone rang, no child should be alone on Christmas!

"You okay over there?"

She lay a hand over her heart and willed it to stop beating like a tom-tom. "I'm fine. How're you?"

"Haven't heard from you since Thanksgiving. I thought you were coming over to share some popcorn on movie night."

"I promised to try."

"Do or do not," he said, "there is no 'try.'"

"Good quote. Who said it?"

"I was afraid you'd ask that. C'mon over. Steve and Warner will know."

"I have lesson plans and handouts to prepare."

"Oh yeah. Class is in session, isn't it?"

She grinned. "Seems to me *you* said you'd try to audit the session."

"Touché, mademoiselle, touché."

"How many imitations can you *do*?"

"Imitations? I vill haff you know dat I'm the genuine article!"

"English, Irish, French . . . now German . . ."

"I'm sure you won't be surprised to hear that I'm so crazy that I have no idea when I'm slipping into a foreign accent. But-t-t . . . choo kahn't evade der kvest-shun so *eeez*-ily, dollink."

"What was *that* . . . Zsa Zsa Gabor?"

"Of course not. It was *Mister* Gabor. But you still haven't answered the question."

"I hate to admit it, but I've lost track. What question?"

"C'mon over and join us for pizza-and-a-movie Friday."

"I'm no Pulitzer-winning writer, but even I know that isn't a question."

"Touché, mademoiselle, touché." Then, "Stop me. Please. Not even I have the patience to go through all that again."

Matt laughed, then said, "So . . . ?"

She wanted to see him and the twins again, but—

"Make it easy on yourself."

"How do I do that?"

"Just say yes."

She took a deep breath, exhaled slowly. "All right. But I have to be home by ten."

"Eleven. It's a two-hour movie, and the kids like to take a break in the middle. Bathroom and junk food intermission, they call it."

"All right, eleven. What can I bring? Brownies? Ice cream? Both?"

"Just your gorgeous self." He rattled off directions. "You have a GPS, right?"

"Yeah."

"As a Pulitzer-winning writer, I have some finely-honed skills, but being able to see through the phone isn't one of them."

She laughed. Again. "Sorry."

"That's where you're wrong. There isn't a single—"

"What?"

"Never mind. How soon can you be here? So I'll know when to nuke the popcorn."

She glanced at the clock. There wasn't time to shower and change. Not without disappointing the twins. "Half an hour?"

"Perfect. Like everything else about—"

"Sorry?"

"Wear gloves. And boots. And a hat. Does that baby SUV of yours have 4-wheel drive?"

"Yeah . . ."

"Good, 'cause they're predicting snow."

"Oh. Maybe I shouldn't—"

"Yes. You should."

"But—"

"Honor?"

"Matt . . ."

"The sooner you say good-bye, the sooner you can leave."

"Good-bye."

"Remember, gloves, hat, boots."

"Yes, *dad*."

"See you in a few, then."

"Right."

"Bye."

"Matt?"

"Honor . . ."

"If you don't hang up, I can't leave."

"Good point," he said, laughing as he hung up.

She stood staring at the now-silent receiver. Something told her tonight would be a lot of things . . . but boring wouldn't be one of them.

12

Honor had visited John's apartment enough times to know that a house without a woman's touch might not be less than clean, and she made up her mind to roll up her sleeves and dig in if it appeared that Matt and his boys were living in unsanitary squalor. So it surprised her to find he'd adopted an everything-in-its-place home that felt as relaxed and cozy as any she'd seen. She'd have to get to know him better to know whether his Marine background could be credited with his gift for order and organization, or if it was part of his DNA.

"The twins have been running around like headless chickens," he said, leading her to the family room, "to get things ready for you."

They'd arranged paper plates, napkins, and cans of decaffeinated soda on the big oak coffee table. In its center, the biggest potholder she'd ever seen, and around the edges, one soapstone coaster per person. "They did a great job," she said, perching on the nearest sofa arm. "Where are they?"

"Upstairs, brushing their teeth and combing their hair."

"For me?"

"Isn't every day a gorgeous redhead joins us for movie night."

A rumble sounded overhead. Matt looked at the ceiling and sighed. "I'll bet I tell them not to run in the house a couple dozen times a day."

"Boys will be boys, eh?"

"If you say so. So you found the place okay?"

"Your directions were great."

"Good. How was traffic?"

"Not bad." Small talk again. It made her yearn for the easy banter they'd shared on the phone earlier.

"So what's playing tonight?"

"*Open Range.*"

"Really. I expected action-adventure or sci-fi, or a comedy, even."

"Steve remembered you saying on Thanksgiving that you're a Robert Duvall fan."

"That's just . . . that's so sweet. Fresh breath, combed hair, *and* a western? I'm flattered. And touched."

She'd been right. Tonight would be a lot of things, but boring wasn't one of them. "Is there anything I can do?"

"Nope. Everything's all set. Soon as the boys get down here, we'll put toppings on the pizza. Ten minutes after that, you can yell 'Action!'"

The thunder of sneakered feet spilled down the stairs. Side by side they stood, freckled faces beaming as they shook her hand. "Good to see you again, Miz Mackenzie," they said in perfect unison.

"It's good to see you, too." She winked. "I wonder . . . will you tell me a secret?"

Their voices harmonized on the word "Depends . . ."

"How do you say the exact same things at the exact same time?"

Steve gave a nonchalant wave. "Oh, it's—"

"—a twins thing," Warner finished.

"They've been doing it since they were babies," Matt said.

The quiet reminder that he'd raised them, single-handedly, made Honor want to reach out and squeeze his hand, tell him what a great job he'd done. She didn't imagine it would have been an easy undertaking for a mother and father to share. But a man alone? Just one more reason to admire him.

"Let's get those pizzas decorated," Matt said, starting for the kitchen.

The boys walked down the hall, one on either side of her. "Do you like mushrooms, Miz Mackenzie?"

"Yes, Steve, I do. And please, call me Honor. Or Mack."

"Mack," Warner said. "But that's a *guy's* name."

"Usually," she agreed. "But in my case, it's a nickname. You know, short for Mackenzie."

"I like it," he said, nodding. "But . . . which name do *you* like best?"

For the kids' sake, she pretended to give it a moment's thought. "Honor," she said, "because it's unusual."

The boys knelt on two of the four tall stools surrounding the center island. "We haven't touched anything since brushing our teeth," Steve said. "Do we need to wash our hands *again*?"

"Nah. You're fine." To Honor, he said, "Make yourself at home."

"Yeah," Steve said, "your pizza ain't gonna decorate itself."

"Isn't," Warner corrected.

Laughing, Honor slid the nearest plate-sized pizza closer.

"Don't be shy," Warner instructed. "Just dig in."

"If your hands are clean, that is," his brother said.

When she stepped up to the sink, Steve said, "So I hear you have two dogs."

"That's right," she said, grabbing a paper towel. "Golden retrievers named Rowdy and Rerun." After pitching the towel into the trash can, she looked around her. "Where's Cash?"

"Oh, he's around. He's always skittish when people first get here."

"That's 'cause we don't hardly ever *have* people over."

"'Specially not *women*."

She looked up in time to see Matt scrubbing a hand over his face. "Sheesh," he said, shaking his head.

"You must be some kinda kisser . . ."

Steve hollered, "Warner, no *way* you just said that!"

"Well why else would Dad have brung her here? He never—"

"*Brought*, not *brung,* and you don't go around talkin' about how good a girl kisses. 'Specially not with her standin'. Right. There."

"Don't you mean how *well* she kisses?"

Warner's smug grin made Honor laugh. "Since you shared a secret with me, I think it only fair to share one with you."

The boys exchanged a puzzled glance . . . and their dad hid behind one hand.

"There haven't been any kisses."

Steve's brow crinkled. "None?"

"None."

The twins stopped layering their pizzas with toppings and stared at Matt, who looked like a taller version of his boys as he blinked and blushed and stammered.

"Well, why not?" Warner blurted.

"I, ah, well, um . . ."

"We haven't known each other very long," she said, rescuing him, "so there really hasn't been time." *Shut up, Honor. Just stop talking before you dig this hole even deeper!*

"Me 'n' Steve could go to bed early."

"Warner," Matt said, "you know better."

What she'd told the boys was true. But she'd known Matt exactly long enough to realize that right now, he couldn't decide whether to smile or frown. The halfway-between result was almost as funny as Warner's original question.

Somehow, they finished topping their pizzas, and as he slid them into the oven, Matt told the boys to take Cash out. "Run him around a little and make sure he does his business. That way, he won't interrupt us during the movie." Then he set the timer and waited for the back door to bang shut.

"Look," he said, leaning his backside against the counter, "I'm sorry as I can be about all that . . . that . . . you know."

"Don't give it another thought." She shrugged. "I'd love to see the rest of your place."

He grabbed the timer and dropped it into his shirt pocket and took her from room to room, pointing out the boys' art projects and deals he'd found at flea markets and garage sales. He was particularly proud of the old spinet he'd found in a consignment shop and refinished to match the mahogany living room tables.

Honor plinked a few keys. "Does anyone play?"

"Faith did."

She picked up the silver-framed photograph on the piano's back. "She was beautiful, Matt." Returning it to its proper place, Honor wondered how hard it had been for Matt, looking into the little face that was a daily reminder of his late wife. "Steve looks so much like her."

"Everybody says that." He used his thumb to nudge the picture a hair to the right. "Frankly, I don't see it."

But he was blond and blue-eyed, slender and tiny, just like Faith.

Matt pointed at a picture that hung on the wall across the room. "My folks," he said. "If you ask me, he more closely resembles *my* mom than his."

Honor crossed the room to get a closer look. She didn't expect to agree, but because he seemed to need validation of his opinion, she prepared to do just that. Only . . . the boy *was* the spitting image of his grandmother.

"Isn't that amazing," she said, facing him.

"What is?"

"Science. Genetics. Heredity. Whatever you want to call it." She was happy for him, and for Steve, too, because it meant he wasn't forced to think of Faith every time he looked at his son.

She tapped a tree ornament and started it bobbing. "The place looks so . . . so homey. I'll admit, I'm a little—"

His timer beeped, and he headed for the kitchen. "Would you mind calling the boys while I slice the pizzas?"

"Not at all." Smiling, she stepped onto the back deck and rubbed her upper arms. "Holy cow, it's freezing out here," she said, trying to hide her surprise at finding them seated at the patio table instead of racing around in the yard. She stooped to pet Cash. "Aren't you a pretty boy," she said, kissing the top of his head.

Their mischievous grins reminded her of the Cheshire cat. *And that can't be good*, she thought, grinning herself. Crossing both arms over her chest, Honor tapped the toe of one booted foot. "Okay. Spit it out. What's going on?"

Warner stood. "We just thought you two could use a little, ah, privacy."

"Yeah, for, you know . . ."

She slid an arm around each boy's shoulders and drew them into a sideways hug. "I'll make a deal with you. You stop talking about . . . you know . . . and if it happens, you'll be the first people I tell."

Warner jerked open the screen door. "Well, okay. But it's *when* it happens, not *if*."

She would have given anything to ask them how they could be so sure. And then Steve said, "He never brought a lady home before. Ever. So yeah, *when*." He hung his coat in the cubby across from the washing machine. "You wanna know what I think?"

"Not really," Warner teased, tucking his in beside it. "But I know you. Only way we're gonna keep you from tellin' us is with duck tape."

"Duct tape," Steve droned, "with a *T* not a *K*. And what I *think* is, if Honor isn't doing something else for Christmas, she should come over here and fix dinner for Dad and us. If she can cook, she's a shoo-in."

Nodding, Warner sauntered into the kitchen. "Y'know, I like the way you think, bro . . . sometimes."

They were in the doorway, smiling, when Matt turned to face them. One brow rose, and he narrowed both eyes. "All right, out with it. What're you three stooges up to?"

The twins sing-songed "Nothing" as Honor shrugged.

Shoulders slumped, he hung his head and chuckled quietly. "Oh man, oh man, oh man," he chanted, "something tells me I'm in bi-i-ig trouble."

Warner whispered into a cupped hand, "If he thinks he's in trouble now, just wait until *when* happens."

Matt's head jerked up, and before he had a chance to ask what it meant, Honor said, "So when does the movie start?"

13

*H*e'd never seen Cash take to a person the way he took to Honor. Never knew the boys to attach so quickly to someone new, either. Sitting close and flinging an arm over her shoulders would have required moving the contented ten-year-olds who'd settled on either side of Honor, supposedly because she was holding the popcorn bowl. Matt could have said, "What about me?"

Instead, he propped his feet on the coffee table, more than content to watch her. Honor was a whole lot more interesting than the movie, anyway, flinching with every gunshot, frowning when the bad guys beat up the sidekick . . . misting up when the big guy died. Yeah, he'd made a good call, inviting her here. The only real mistake he'd made since meeting her was that he hadn't kissed her.

But he would.

Tonight, if she'd let him.

It was pitch dark outside when the kids decided it was time for a bathroom break. "Let Cash out, boys," he told them, "and this time, make sure he *goes*, will ya?"

A moment later, the back door slammed twice, telling him they'd both gone outside with the dog. Something about skulking around in the dark had appealed to him as a boy, too, but never more than when the safety of home was within easy reach. When the door slammed again, they'd run into the room, pink-cheeked and breathless, to report that Cash really had *gone* this time, putting their unwritten "no hugging in front of company" to the test. "So what do you think?"

She'd just stuffed a handful of popcorn into her mouth, and her jaw froze at his question. "About . . . ?"

"Those monsters of mine. Are they driving you crazy yet?"

"Hardly! I think they're wonderful."

"Not too bratty?"

"Not bratty at all."

"Or too loud and rambunctious?"

"No, not even . . ."

She stopped talking so fast that he thought a kernel had gotten stuck in her throat. He leaped up, reciting the Heimlich steps in his head, but only made it as far as the curve of the sectional before she said, "I get it. You're referring to that stupid crack I made about my sister's kids and *her* nieces and nephews."

Relief that she wasn't choking collided with disappointment. *Well, there goes a perfect chance to put the boys' suggestion to the test.* The ridiculous thought inspired a smirk as he realized mouth-to-mouth wasn't one of the steps. Then he realized she'd figured out what he meant, despite the vagueness of his question, and remembered that extraordinary moment on Thanksgiving, when she'd known what he'd been thinking, just by locking those gorgeous eyes on him.

"I only said that so you wouldn't feel sorry for me, spending a major family holiday, all alone. The truth is, I love kids, and every yelling, screaming, running, jumping thing about them. And your boys . . ." She hugged the popcorn bowl a little tighter, as if *it* was a kid. "Your boys just couldn't be sweeter. You've done an incredible job with them."

"Thanks." Relief of a different kind swirled in his head, because if she didn't like them, well, it was over before it started. "And speaking of not spending holidays alone, what's this stuff the boys were babbling about? Something about you coming over here to cook Christmas dinner?"

"It was just a silly suggestion."

"Silly? You're kidding, right?"

She put the bowl on the table and tucked her legs under her. "I told them we'd have to run it by you first, so—"

"We could invite Mercy and Austin, and Flora and Bud, and Harriet. Our whole Thanksgiving gang."

Had her little gasp been inspired by his reference to "we" and "our"? Matt followed up with, "And if there's somebody you'd like to add to the list, do it."

He watched her process it all, frowning, raising her eyebrows. She widened those sometimes-blue-sometimes-green eyes, then tucked in one corner of her mouth. That beautiful, kissable mouth. If Brady Shaw was here right now, he'd punch *him* in the mouth, for stealing even one second of Honor's joy. Well, if Matt had anything to say about it, Shaw would get what he had coming to him. Then Honor licked her lips and his mind went blank, and when she smiled at him, his heart pounded so hard that he worried she could hear it from her spot near the arm of the couch.

He glanced at the clock. An hour, yet, before the boys went to bed. He should never have sent them outside with her earlier, because it messed up the schedule. It'd be eleven before the boys settled down, midnight before he could trust that they'd fallen asleep. Now disappointment of a different kind thumped in his head because how was he supposed to put their suggestion to the test if—

They thundered into the room bellowing, "Dad, Dad!"

Warner whipped off his hat. "It's snowing like crazy out there!"

Steve did the same. "I bet there's six inches on the ground already!"

Matt cut another glance at the clock, then stood and started walking toward the back door. "In an hour? No way."

"Yes, way," Steve said, running alongside him. "You'll see."

Honor followed, too. If the boys were right, she'd leave. So he hoped with everything in him that they were wrong.

"Oh my," she said over his shoulder, "it's just beautiful."

Nowhere near as beautiful as what I'm *lookin' at.*

"Let's start the movie up again," Warner said.

Steve hung his jacket beside his twin's. "Wanna swap a slice of pizza?"

"No way. You put mushrooms on yours."

"Only half."

Honor took a step forward, laying a hand on each boy's shoulder. They turned to face her as she said, "At the rate it's coming down, there'll be a foot on the ground before the movie ends." She chucked their chins. "So I can't watch the end of it with you."

"Aw-w, bummer."

Cash chose that moment to trot up and beg for a pat, and she stooped to oblige him. "Believe me, I'm more disappointed than you are. But Rerun and Rowdy are home alone."

"Yeah. We know." They walked with her to the foyer. "So will you come over for Christmas?"

Honor cut a fleeting look at Matt, and he tensed, wondering what she'd say. She hadn't declined the invitation, but she hadn't accepted it, either. He lifted his shoulders and smiled, hoping she'd read his mind again. *Say yes. Just say* yes.

She grabbed her coat, and Matt took it from her. "Y'know," she said as he helped her into her coat, "I think a repeat of Thanksgiving will be fun. Let's just pray everybody else hasn't already made plans."

He let his hands rest on her shoulders a second longer than necessary. "I was hoping you'd say that," he said, giving them a little squeeze.

She reached up and patted his fingertips. "Maybe next Friday, we can finish watching that movie. Nothing better than seein' a bad guy get his just desserts."

The image of Brady Shaw, getting his, flashed in Matt's mind, and it made him grin.

"Drive safely," he said as she stepped into the snow.

"I will."

"G'night, Honor," the boys chorused.

"Sweet dreams," she said.

And Matt's heart raced because she was looking at him, not at his boys, when she said it.

An hour later, the snow had filled in her bootprints on the walk, and drifts hid her tire tracks in the driveway. He'd already checked on the boys and let the dog out and cleaned the last of the movie night mess from the family room. Too late to call, make sure she'd gotten home all right? "Only one way to find out," he muttered, biting the corner off a slice of cold pizza.

After just half a ring, she said, "What, you think I don't know how to drive in snow?"

Man it was good to hear her voice. "What," he echoed, "you don't say hello when you answer the phone?"

She laughed. "I'm fine, as you can see—hear, but thanks for checking."

"Somebody's gotta make sure your dogs are properly cared for."

"Touché, monsieur."

The reminder of their earlier call inspired a quiet chuckle. "Wanna borrow my pin?"

"I was thinking more along the lines of a chainsaw."

"A *chainsaw!*"

"Thanks to your boys' compliments, the only way I'll get my big swelled head through the doorways is if you carve key-hole shapes into them."

"And you think *I* should try stand-up."

"Please. One joke does not a comedian make."

The mantle clock struck midnight. Perfect timing, he thought, because if he wasn't bewitched, he didn't know who was. "Well, I'd better let you go. I promised the boys breakfast at the Double T."

"Ah, the home of the 24-hour breakfast . . ."

"Yeah, they love the place, so I expect they'll be up at dawn." He paused. "Hey, why don't you meet us over there?"

"I'd love to, but I'm working tomorrow. If the snow doesn't cancel class, that is."

He remembered how she'd put lesson plans and handouts on hold to join them tonight. "What time does your class start, if it isn't canceled, that is?"

"Nine."

"Where is it?"

"The fire hall on Route 99."

"One hour? Two?"

"You'll be out of there by noon. If it isn't canceled."

Did he sense a "gotcha" in that last comment? If so, he had it coming. Matt grinned. "What should I bring, teach? Safety harness? Rope? Compass?"

"Oh, I think even a reporter can find the fire hall without a compass. Paper and pencil will do."

"Well, don't save a seat for me. You know. Just in case the kids throw me a curveball after breakfast."

"Got it."

He could almost see her, giving that little nod of her head when she said it. "Well, g'night then.

"G'night."

He waited for the telltale click as she hung up. When he didn't hear it, he said "Honor?"

"Matt . . ."

"You didn't hang up."

"Oh. I was waiting for you to do it."

"Why?"

"I don't know. The person who calls has to hang up first?"

"What's that, Rule Six in the Phone Call Etiquette book?

"More like Two, I think."

He chuckled. "The sooner you say good-bye, the sooner you can get to bed."

"Bye."

"Sleep tight and all that."

"Matt?"

"Honor . . ."

"This could go on all night."

"Hang the Phone Call Etiquette book. You hang up first."

"Why?"

"I dunno. Ladies first?"

"All right," she said.

And with that, she hung up! Matt sat staring at the buzzing receiver for a moment, knowing before it made contact with the cradle that he'd sit front and center in that class of hers tomorrow, even if it meant rushing the boys through breakfast. It wasn't likely he'd nod off with her at the front of the class, even though he'd sat through the sessions before. He'd have to watch it, though, because his own SAR training qualified him as an instructor, and the last thing he wanted to do was undermine her authority up there. Especially with that craziness hanging over her head.

"It's for their own good," he muttered, climbing the stairs.

A dad with CPR and SAR training had to be a good thing, he thought, tiptoeing into the boys' room. Warner had kicked off his quilt, as usual. And, as usual, Matt pulled it up, then pressed a kiss to his forehead. On the other side of the room, his twin snored softly, one foot poking out from under his blanket, a hand tucked under his head. He sighed and stirred slightly as Matt kissed his cheek. And as Matt was pulling the door to, Steve whispered "Love you, Dad."

"Love you, too," he whispered back, knowing the boy was too sound asleep to hear it.

As a young Marine, he'd silently scoffed when a married pal got a little pie-eyed on the first night of a three-day pass. "There's a lotta different kinds o' love in the world," he'd slurred, tapping the wallet-sized photo of his infant daughter, "nothin' tops the love of a dad for his little girl."

Matt took a last look at his sleeping sons and said a silent apology to that Marine. Yeah, having a dad with CPR and SAR training was a good thing, but having a mother was better. He couldn't think of a more fitting candidate than the woman they'd entrusted with their little-boy secret, mere hours after meeting her.

14

I can't believe you made this," Mercy said, holding up the wooden cutting board.

"I gotta say, it's the perfect two-in-one gift. Kitchen appliance for the little woman, here, reminder of my bachelor days aboard One Regret." Austin ran a fingertip along Honor's rendering of his tugboat. "Must've taken hours to woodburn all these details into the water and sky."

"And look, sweetie, she even put the name across the back end."

"Across the stern, *sweetie*." Groaning, Austin shook his head. "I'll never make a sailor outta her."

Steve sat on the sofa arm nearest Austin. "Is that why you're selling it?"

Smirking, he looked at Mercy. "Nah. Between our jobs and her condo, there won't be time to take proper care of her."

"Why don't *we* buy it, Dad?"

"Because," Matt said, "between my job and your school, and Little League, and Scouts, *we* don't have time to take proper care of her, either."

"We can't quit school," Warner said, "but you can."

Matt looked at Honor and smiled. "What? Give up before I earn my . . ." He pretended to search his memory for the proper term.

"Wilderness training."

"Right. That. You want me to quit before I earn my Wilderness badge?"

"Certification," she corrected gently. "You'll have to join the Scouts to earn a badge."

"He's already got a whole drawer full of 'em," Steve said.

Warner nodded. "Yeah, Dad was an Eagle Scout, y'know."

"No, I didn't know that. But I'm not the least bit surprised."

Matt felt his face redden. He'd never known a woman with the power to turn him into a weak-kneed, bumbling idiot, just by smiling at him. He didn't want to think about the mess he'd be if he ever got around to kissing her.

"Your turn," Honor said, handing him a rectangular box.

"Seems a shame to unwrap it," he said, fiddling with the perfectly-tied red bow. "Maybe I'll just put it on the mantle, next to the carriage clock and the—"

"Here," Warner said, hands extended, "let me do it."

"You already had your turn," Steve said, clutching his DVD.

She'd put a lot of thought and time into every gift. For the bookworm, a silver marker inscribed with Harriet's initials. A cutting board for the couple who loved to cook, and the latest releases of *Shrek* and *Transformers* for the twins. She'd *had* to secure Austin's help in getting a photo of Flora and Bud to slide into the carved driftwood frame she'd given the Sullivans. And Cash got a canister of hand-baked dog biscuits. Matt couldn't imagine what might be inside the box on his lap.

"I'm with the kid," Bud said, wiggling his fingertips. "Open that baby, or give it here."

"You guys sure know how to stifle a mood." Matt said, chuckling as he slowly peeled away the silvery wrapper. The boys were hanging over the back of the sofa, and every few seconds he felt the breeze of a frustrated sigh. When he lifted the box top, Warner said, "Finally!" and Steve applauded.

Matt pulled back the tissue paper.

"Well," Bud said, "what is it!"

"Something knitted," Flora whispered.

Austin leaned forward. "A scarf?"

"No," Matt said, holding it up, "it's a sweater."

"Not just a sweater," Harriet said, "a cable knit. And just look at the precision of those twists!"

He met Honor's eyes. "You made this."

"I did." Her lips slanted with a shy smile. "I hope it fits."

"Only one way to find out." Standing, he slid it over his head, then tugged the sleeves and hem into place. "Perfect," he said. "But how'd you know what size to make?"

"I'm just a good guesser." She grinned. "I guess."

Not that he was looking, but Matt couldn't find a single flaw. It must have taken weeks to produce a hand-knit sweater so perfect that it looked machine-stitched. Honor worked a full-time job and clocked hours of overtime, in addition to teaching SAR classes and volunteering for missions. It had only been a week since they'd discussed spending Christmas together. Either she'd knitted so fast that her needles sparked, or she'd made it for someone else.

The very thought made every muscle tighten. "When did you have the time to make it?"

Shoulders raised, she braided her forearms and tucked both hands between her knees. "I don't require a whole lot of sleep."

Interesting fact, he thought. Too bad it didn't answer his question. "Well, it's terrific. I love it." He'd love it even more when he found out she'd made it for *him*.

The timer beeped, and Honor started stuffing wrapping paper and ribbons into a trash bag. "Dinner's ready when you are."

She'd arrived at six, carrying half a dozen overstuffed plastic grocery bags and claimed she needed that much time to get the meal cooked and the table set. But the disappointed look on her face when she realized the boys had been up since five was all the proof he'd needed that the real reason for her early arrival had been her hope that she'd be there when they came downstairs and raced toward the Santa-delivered toys under the tree.

She hid the letdown well, though, and after letting the kids show her every toy and book and game, Honor put on an apron and got down to business. Now, as everyone scrambled for the best seat at the table, he watched her in the dining room doorway, chewing on a knuckle to keep the mist in her eyes from becoming more, and he was pretty sure that pride in her work didn't have a thing to do with it.

That's when it hit him: Honor needed this a whole lot more than the rest of them, and the insight gave him yet another reason to want to hurt Brady Shaw. By ruining her reputation, he'd made it impossible for her to meet and marry a man who deserved her, someone she could build a life and grow a family with. It seemed warped and weird—feeling a little bit grateful to Shaw—as he considered whether or not *he* could be that man.

He hadn't noticed until that moment that she'd moved into the dining room, where she stood, fingers gripping her chairback, waiting for him to catch her eye. When he did, she smiled and pulled out the chair. "There's no bird to carve," she said, "but you're still stuck with saying grace."

Stuck was hardly the word he'd use. Grateful. Blessed. Overjoyed. He could think of a hundred other ways to describe how he felt, standing beside her at the head of the table.

When everyone settled in and settled down, his prayer could have been a recording of the one he'd said on Thanksgiving, except for the short but heartfelt qualifier he uttered to himself: *If she's in Your plan for my life, I sure would appreciate a sign.*

When he opened his eyes and looked across the table, she nodded. Just once. But it was enough. He hoped the unbridled joy beaming from her face was the sign he'd prayed for . . . and not just wishful thinking.

15

Cash sniffed the base of a fat oak, then tugged at the leash. "Easy does it, boy," Austin said. "I've only got two legs, don't forget."

Matt laughed. "Just say the word if you want to hand over the leash, and I'll show you how it's done."

The dog chose that moment to stop and look over its shoulder. "Lookit that big doggy grin," Austin said. "I think he's trying to tell me you don't know one end of the lead from the other."

Matt barely heard him above the wail of a siren. "Man. What a day to need an ambo, eh?"

"I guess. You ever miss the SAR work?"

"Only every day. But the boys are well worth the sacrifice."

"Yeah, there's no rule that says you can't recertify when they're older."

"I'll let you in on a little secret. Already did."

"No kiddin'?"

"No kiddin'." Then, "So how'd you merit a holiday off? I figured they'd stick you with every crummy shift on the board, payback for taking two weeks for your honeymoon."

"Try and keep a good thought, why don't you?"

"Speaking of good thoughts, that was some present Honor made you guys."

"Surprised the heck outta me. I've known her for years, and never would've guessed she had that kind of artistic ability. And she's no slouch in the kitchen, either."

Matt patted his belly. "Bet I put on five pounds, just from that one meal."

"So what're you waiting for, man, an engraved invitation? Women like that don't grow on trees, y'know."

"I've only known her since the night that jet crashed on 95."

"Plenty of time, if your head's in the right place." He stopped, so Cash could sniff out a fire hydrant. "Never heard of night-flying geese before." He elbowed Matt. "You sure you got your facts straight, dude, 'cause how weird was that?"

It had been Matt's article that outlined the cause of the accident. Near as any of the experts could figure, the flock was headed in to roost when two birds got sucked into the plane's engines. "Rare," he'd quoted one wildlife expert, "but then, Canada geese can't tell time."

"*People* are to blame for that, not the airline or the geese. If folks didn't feed 'em, they would've migrated north, like they were supposed to, and all those people would be home today, celebrating Christmas with their families."

Matt nodded somberly, remembering that 41 had died and another 113 had been injured—some on the ground, others in the airliner—when the jet landed on the interstate. "I see fire and smoke like that, and first thing I think of is 9/11."

"Same here," Matt said. "That, and Iraq." Then he remembered that Austin's brother had died in the North Tower, setting off a years-long battle with alcoholism. "How're you doing these days?"

"That bottle's still in the companionway, with its seal intact."

"Good, good." He slid an arm across his friend's shoulders, gave him a quick, sideways hug, then put his hands back in his pockets. "Proud of you, dude. I know it hasn't been easy."

"I can't take all the credit. Mercy helped. More than she'll ever know."

"She's a good woman. You're lucky to have her."

"Don't I know it." Now Austin gave Matt a sideways hug. "Honor's a good woman, too."

"Don't I know it," he echoed.

"Then clue me in, dude. The boys love her, and it's as plain as the nose on your face that she's crazy about them. Heck, even Cash, here, is nuts about her. What's the holdup?"

"It's just . . . stuff."

"Not Brady Shaw stuff, I hope, 'cause if you believe that nonsense, you're even dumber than I thought."

"'Course I don't believe it. Never have. And neither does anybody else with a lick of sense. Problem is, a whole lot of people out there think if they see something on TV or read it in the newspaper, it's gospel. They don't bother to check it out, never ask if there's another side to things. Just swallow it whole, like brainless fish with a worm on a hook. That jerk Shaw told the story, but it was the idiots who believed it who turned Honor's life upside down."

"Singin' to the choir, friend. Singin' to the choir."

Matt told Austin about the research he'd been doing and that there were very few loose ends to tie up before he could make his move.

"Bet I could get a couple guys in the department to step up," he said, "maybe accidentally photocopy some reports." Austin shrugged. "If they blew off somebody's passenger seat and fell into the wrong hands, well, hey, stuff happens, right?"

"But you're getting married and leaving for London in a week. You can do all that by then?"

"I can sure give it the old college try." He shrugged again. "What've we got to lose?"

"You and me? Nothing. But Honor . . . she has a lot to lose."

"So let me get this straight. You're saying that once you've helped her unload some of that baggage, you'll make your move."

They turned the final corner in their walk around the block. "Yeah. I guess. Something like that."

"Well, sir," Austin said, clapping Matt on the back, "you've just given me all the incentive I need to get you those reports, aye-sap."

"Just don't do anything that'll implicate yourself or the other guys."

Austin struck a cool dude pose and swaggered up Matt's driveway. "Hey . . . do I look like somebody who was born yesterday?"

"No. Guess not."

"All right then, have a little faith, why don't you?"

Matt stood on the bottom porch step. "Much as it galls me," he said, clenching his jaw, "none of this will go before a judge, or help send Shaw to Jessup, where he belongs. Because it's all circumstantial."

"Not to mention every scrap of evidence was obtained without a warrant."

"That, too."

"Well, look at the bright side. Maybe when that lyin' sack of . . ." Austin growled. "Maybe when he sees what you've got on him, he'll end up in a *padded* cell instead of a prison cell."

"We can hope."

"You know what I regret?"

"That you can't be there when I grind Shaw under my boot."

Austin held open the screen door, and Cash planted both front paws on the threshold, waiting for the inside door to open. "You know me too well, brutha," he said, standing aside to let the dog and Matt pass.

They were hanging their jackets on the hall tree when Austin added, "I know you pretty well, too, y'know."

Matt snorted. "I'm almost afraid to ask what that means."

Austin peeked into the kitchen, checked the dining room, too, to make sure the coast was clear. "Sounds like everybody's in the family room. Good." He stepped up beside Matt, and, draping a big hand on the back of Matt's neck, said, "You know what they say about paybacks, don't you?"

"No, but I know what they say about mouthwash." He waved a hand in front of his face. "And you could use some."

"Dude," he said, "be serious for a minute." He snapped the fingers of his free hand in front of Matt's face. "Concentrate: I'm not doing this, ah, this *errand* for free. It's gonna cost you. Big time."

"Much as I hate divulging personal information of the financial kind, I feel it only fair to tell you there's only a hundred bucks in my checking account."

Austin grimaced. "That hurts, Matt. I don't want your money, you boob."

"Then what? Tell me. Fast. So I can find you a toothbrush . . . and ask Honor to go a little easier on the garlic next time she makes lasagna."

"Okay. Here it is in a nutshell: you," he said, driving his pointer finger into Matt's shoulder, "take it to the next step before I get back from London, or I'll be forced to take drastic measures."

"Ha. Like what?"

Eyes narrowed, Austin said, "Bet she'd love to hear about the time a hooker got her hair caught on your belt buckle."

"Hey. That wasn't my fault. She jumped into the cab at a red light, drunk as a skunk, and passed out cold in my lap. What was I supposed to do, kick her to the curb?"

"Not with her hair all tangled up in your belt. But I digress. Some of us who were there that night tell a slightly different version of the story."

"Hmpf. Accent on *story*, then."

Austin lifted his shoulders, extended his hands in silent supplication. "Oh, I'm reasonably certain that Honor will believe your version."

"Then why—"

"Because misery loves company."

"What?"

"Why should you be the last single man standing?"

Matt chuckled. "You're a jerk, Finley, you know that?"

"Yeah," he said, tapping his temple, "but I'm a smart jerk."

"Did you thump your head last time you were on a call?"

"No. Why?"

"Because you're not making a lick of sense."

"All I'm sayin' is, those kids of yours need a mother, and you need a wife. And Honor needs a family. So hunker down and do the right thing." He waved his hand, as if shooing a fly. "Get things moving along with—"

Honor stepped into the doorway and stopped him cold. "We're about to have some cheesecake, but Flora insisted that we wait for you guys to get back."

"She's such a sweetheart," Austin said.

Honor nodded. "So . . . get what things moving?"

"Oh, nothing." He winked at Matt. "Just guy talk." He grasped her elbow and led her into the family room. "What's this? A second dessert . . . in front of the TV? Be still my heart!"

Should he let on that he'd planned to move things to the next level with Honor, even before the comical reminder of that wild and crazy New York night.

Nah. Let the boy have his fun.

16

*T*hree days ago, when Baltimore area stations had started broadcasting blizzard warnings, news cameras panned empty store shelves that once stocked ample supplies of milk, bread, and the all-important toilet paper. Yesterday, the contents of grocery carts proved that TV viewers had stopped paying attention to the messages that crawled across their TV screens 24/7. Apathy, Honor had learned, killed more people than tornadoes, hurricanes, and floods combined.

Now, as she trudged through knee-deep drifts, she pictured the distraught face of the mother who'd given her children—boys ages nine and four, and a seven-year-old girl—permission to hike in the woods behind their house. "They've spent almost as much time out there as in the house," she'd cried. "I can't believe they could be lost . . ."

But lost they were.

That alone wasn't so scary; Rowdy had sniffed out a dozen or more kids who, even after a couple of days in the wild country, suffered little more than bug bites, rumbling tummies, and mild dehydration. Their dreams for the next few weeks had no doubt been peppered with scary visions of being lost and alone, but for the most part, they'd gone home none the worse for wear.

The difference here? The kids' winter jackets, gloves, and snow boots were still in the mudroom, right where they'd stowed them after school, day before yesterday. If Honor was cold to the bone in a downy parka and fleece-lined mukluks, after only a few hours' exposure to the biting wind and stinging snow crystals . . .

Perhaps their mother was right, and they knew the area well enough to find shelter in a cave or a hollow tree. And with any luck, they'd known enough to huddle together, as much to prevent one of them getting lost as to share body heat.

Years of bad endings to searches like this one told Honor that the chances of one live find were dim, but three? Her sigh of frustration formed a thick cloud of vapor in front of her face, and through it she saw a flash of red—Rowdy's rescue vest—then spotted his tail, like a fuzzy gold hand waving her onward. *You need to take a page from his book, she told herself. That dog never gives up hope.*

He was strong and tireless, and she knew from experience that he'd run nonstop for miles . . . if she let him. She couldn't let him, of course, because whether he realized it or not, he needed to stop, and often, for small bites of food and short drinks of water. Wait too long and he'd grow overeager and end up with gastric dilation or, worse still, torsion. She'd seen both happen to non-handlers' dogs after a long run or rough play; difficult as it was to turn down any much-loved dog, Honor would stick to the "just say no" policy where *hers* was concerned.

He'd earned every "He's the best I've ever seen" and "That's some dog" compliments, and she knew better than to take credit for it. True, she was a good trainer—of dogs and the people who handled them—but Rowdy was special in a hundred ways. Like the way he seemed to know when she was about to whistle for him and almost always spared her the trouble. "You're some dog, all right," she repeated when he got close enough to hug. "I oughta rename you Wilbur, like that pig in *Charlotte's Web*." He quivered from nose to tail, a sure sign that he wouldn't be happy until after she'd fed and watered him and he could plow through the snow again, in search of the missing.

"Patience, pal," she said, adjusting his booties, checking his ears and nose for signs of frostbite. Finding none, she pulled the Ziploc bag from her field pack, exactly as she had when they'd started out, hours ago. This time, it took only seconds for the icy wind and snow to stiffen the normally pliable plastic, and it crackled like cellophane as a tiny pair of Elmo mittens stored inside to preserve the scent, peeked from the opening. Rowdy's ears perked and he cocked his head in response to the unusual sound. "Find," she'd said, watching his head bob up and down, absorbing a noseful of scent. "Find!" And off he went, alternately nosing at the ground and sniffing the air.

Even for a well-trained natural like Rowdy, a day like this could prove confusing, even dangerous, for him and for her. She would never have admitted it out loud, but being off on her own, this far off and for this long was downright scary. However, flu season had laid several of the regulars low, and the weather had made it impossible for others to get out of their driveways, let alone make their way to the sector. It was one of those times when training and preparedness, coupled with stamina and a trusted canine companion, would have to provide the confidence to press on, even when the terrain got dicey and the weather grew fierce.

Marching along in shin-deep snow would have been exhausting, even without her pack. How had three little kids managed to get this far, dressed the way they were? Maybe the scent Rowdy was picking up wasn't theirs, after all. Because they could have made it this far from the house before the snow started, but in this mess?

What had their mother been thinking, letting them out here alone, even in good weather! The family had stubbornly— some might say greedily—refused to sell out to developers or city planners. The farm was the last of its kind in a three-state area, bordering state parks and county recreational areas that spanned miles.

And miles, she grumbled, tugging at the straps of her pack. She could reduce its heft by losing the bulky tarp, but given a choice between lightening her load and holding on to gear that could move a victim or become a makeshift shelter, Honor would choose the added weight of the tarp, any day. The coil of rope wasn't exactly lightweight, either, but like her trusty compass and radio, it was one of those things she wouldn't leave home without. She'd never put the thing on a scale, because she didn't want to think about what it weighed. Besides, it was a comfort to know that right on her back, she carried enough food, water, heat packs, and routine first-aid supplies, too, to support herself, Rowdy, and any survivors they might locate. As long as her batteries lasted, they'd be fine until help arrived.

Provided help could get to her . . . something else she preferred not to think about.

Rowdy's tracks veered right, then left and straight ahead. He'd been out of sight now for a good fifteen minutes. If there was a plus to searching in a place like this, it had to be the absolute silence; if he barked—and she hoped he would because it was the only signal she'd get of a live find—the sound would travel for miles, she'd have no trouble hearing him.

She struggled up a small knoll, using her poke stick like a ski pole. Not every handler chose to carry one, because they were clumsy and cumbersome, but Honor had always preferred to err on the side of caution. One story about a unit member who'd underestimated the depth of an avalanche victim was enough to convince her it was worth the aggravation of figuring out where to put it when it wasn't in use.

She held the field glasses to her eyes and did a slow turn, looking for Rowdy's vest. If she didn't see him soon, she'd have to call him in for another food and water break. This time, in addition to looking for frostbite, Honor would check his pulse and count every breath. He might well be equipped with a thick fur coat, but hypothermia wasn't out of the question on a day like this.

Though her peers voiced the usual complaints about winter assignments—numb toes and noses, the occasional case of frostbite, and trembling so hard from the cold that their muscles and bones ached—most preferred them to hot weather searches. Not Honor. She didn't like mosquitoes and snakes, heat and humidity, or maggots that feasted on fetid tissue any more than the rest of them—but even those things were preferable to being surrounded by an ocean of snow.

Worse, even, than far-as-you-can-see white . . . the strange and ceaseless moaning of the wind. Prior to the Brady Shaw story, cold-weather searches had provoked spine-chilling nightmares that were peopled by howling banshees and groaning ghosts. But even after Honor taught herself not to remember her dreams, she'd wake up dog-tired in a tangle of sweat-dampened sheets. She could mash the head of a snake with her boot or crush annoying insects with her palms and tell herself she had a little power over her environment. But this? There was nothing to do but prepare for the worst and hope for the best.

"Speaking of dogs," she whispered, "where's mine?"

Her perceptive pup must have sensed his mistress's restlessness because a moment later, he began to bark. Not the annoying yelps of a dog who wants to come in out of the cold or the high-pitched "gimme another treat" yips, but steady, persistent barking that told her he'd found something.

A chill that had nothing to do with the weather coursed down her spine. Too soon to celebrate, though, she knew. There were three children missing; he may only have found one. And talented as he was, Rowdy hadn't figured out a way to communicate whether what he'd found was alive or dead. In his mind, he'd accomplished what he'd set out to do, and it was up to the humans involved to take it from there.

But it was too soon to radio for help, too. He was a good dog, but he wasn't perfect; what if he'd made one of his rare mistakes, and cornered a rabbit or a squirrel, instead?

Beyond the next hillock, she caught sight of his vest, and as she got closer, Honor recognized that stance: hind legs slightly splayed and forepaws planted firmly, one slightly in front of the other, ears perked and tail up . . . alert, determined, and ready for whatever command his mistress gave him.

She palmed the compass in one hand, and radioed for help with the other. As she gave the coordinates, Honor noticed that behind him, deep inside the yawning hollow of a massive oak, a shadow moved. She couldn't see them, or what shape they were in, but she knew the kids were in there, alive. She knew because Rowdy *told* her with every huffy bark and stomp of his red-booted paws.

After adding that information to her report, she shed the pack, tucked the radio into an outer pocket, and dropped to her knees to peer into the hollow tree. And there they were, like crazy-eyed, trembling Keebler elves.

One.

Two.

Three.

Teeth chattering from fear and cold.

Huddled together like blue-eyed monkeys separated too soon from their mama.

But alive, thank God, *alive*.

Honor almost didn't trust herself to speak. She was the grown-up here. If her voice cracked, even a little, or she shed a tear of relief, it would only scare them more. Let their parents dole out the scoldings and reprimands. Let the cops ask how and why they got way out here. Let the doctors and nurses find out if their frostbitten little ears and fingertips and toes would soon get back to normal. Her job, now that Rowdy had found them and help was on the way: stay with them. Keep them as comfortable as possible. Offer gentle assurances that soon, they'd be home and in the arms of their parents.

Rowdy whimpered and paced behind her. "That's Rowdy," she said.

"Does he bite?" the littlest one said.

"Not unless you're a steak bone," she said, winking.

She patted the girl's sneaker. "My name is Honor. What's yours, sweetie?"

"Melissa."

"Well, Melissa, I know you're cold. And I've got just the thing for that. Heat packs. Ever used one?"

All three shook their heads.

"Oh, you're gonna love 'em. They'll get you all warm and toasty in no time."

From the looks of them, it would take a lot more than a couple dozen heat packs to accomplish that, but it was a start.

She fast-crawled to the pack, crawled back again, dragging it with her. No sense moving them out of the tree, because their combined body heat had raised the temperature by a good twenty degrees. Once the heat packs started working their magic, and she wrapped them in the tarp, it might feel downright balmy in there.

She focused on the biggest boy. "What's your name, sweetie?"

"Timmy."

"Okay, Timmy, I'm gonna unwrap these things, and you kids tuck 'em into your palms," she said, making eye contact with each, "like this, see, and hold on tight." If they noticed her checking for cuts and bruises as she passed out the packs, they showed no sign of it.

Rowdy was still pacing and whining. "Don't mind him," she told them. "He's just worried that I won't get you taken care of fast enough."

"My name is Greg," the youngest boy said. "And Rowdy is one silly dog."

"Yeah, what a nag!" She uncapped a water bottle. "One little sip, okay?" And as it made its way from child to child, Honor ripped into an energy bar and broke off three small chunks. "I'm not stingy, honest," she teased. "It's just that after all you guys have been through, you don't need to get a bellyache from eating too much, too fast."

Any minute now, reinforcements would arrive to whisk the kids off to the ER at Howard County General. Or Montgomery. Honor wasn't sure which was closest. But right now, she needed to take a minute and shower Rowdy with all the love and praise and admiration he'd earned. On her knees in the snow, she wrapped her arms around his neck. "Good dog," she blubbered, kissing his ears, the top of his head, the bridge of his nose. "*Good dog!* You're the best dog in the whole wide world. When I get you home, you're gonna get a full-body massage, and homemade biscuits, and I'll even let you sleep on the bed tonight."

A happy little half-bark that sounded something like "Hooray!" erupted from his chest.

"You can say that again," she said, nuzzling his neck. "I can hardly wait to get home and tell Matt and the boys all about our wild and wacky day!"

What she said didn't register until she looked into Rowdy's soft brown eyes, watched him cock his head, watched those little round eyebrows raise—right, left, right again. He gave her his best doggy smile, then planted a paw on her knee and *woofed.* And she would have sworn it had a question mark behind it.

"I know, I know," she said, a hand on either side of his beautiful, soulful face, "it's weird how Matt is the first person I thought to call."

"Is Matt your husband?" Timmy asked.

She heard the underlying, unasked question: if Matt were her husband, why would wanting to call him first seem weird? *Oh, from the mouths of babes . . .*

She adjusted the tarp that covered his sneakers, buying time to find a word that described Matt's place in her life. More than a friend, a whole lot more, but not a *boy*friend, exactly.

The whiny roar of snowmobiles, shuttling over the snow, saved her. Nobody—not the stocking-capped, goggled guys driving them or the kids they'd come to take out of here—cared what word she'd find, or if she found one at all.

But Honor cared.

And she knew she'd better find that word before she called him because it would describe a whole lot more than their relationship.

It would define their future—if they had one—too.

17

"Where did you get that stuff?"

Shaw tossed the folder onto his desk with enough force that it slid across the slick glass surface. If Matt hadn't stuck out his hand when he did, its contents would have ended up scattered across the floor.

He didn't know which pleased him more, the stark terror glittering in those baby blues, or the tremor in Shaw's usually velvet voice. "Don't you worry your pretty little head about that, *Brady*, because none of it will hold up in court, anyway."

He shoved back from his desk. "Then why are you wasting my time?"

"Because if that *stuff* got out?" He pointed at the folder. "You'd have to find a new line of work." Matt chuckled. "That could be a big problem 'cause the only thing you're good at is lying."

"I could sue you for slander. Libel. Defamation of character."

"The first two, maybe." Matt chuckled again. "But I think the prerequisite for a defamation suit is . . . the plaintiff has to *have* some character."

"Get out."

"Can't." He pointed at the file again. "Unfinished business."

Shaw grabbed the folder and jammed it into the mouth of the paper shredder beside his desk. When the grinding stopped, he gave a smug nod.

"Brady, Brady, Brady," Matt said, shaking his head, "I know you TV news guys think you're smarter than us beat reporters, but you don't seriously think I'm dumb enough to bring my only copy down here, do you?"

His smirk faded, telling Matt that's exactly what he'd thought.

"Get out, Phillips, before I call security."

Matt snorted. And leaning back in the chair, he propped both feet on the corner of Shaw's desk. "Call 'em. It'll be interesting to see how fast your cronies will line up to watch you self-destruct."

He ran a hand through his hair. "How much to make this go away?"

Matt got up and walked around to the other side of the desk. "Who uses a desk blotter these days?" he asked, planting his backside on its leather trim. "No, no," he said, a hand up to silence the anchorman, "no need to answer. That was a rhetorical question, genius." He leaned forward slightly to add, "I don't want your money."

"Then what? A job recommendation? The keys to my condo? *What!*"

Beads of perspiration glimmered on Shaw's forehead and the bridge of his nose. Matt plucked a tissue from the leather dispenser, and as the man took it, he said, "I want you to do whatever it takes to clear Honor Mackenzie's name."

He stopped blotting sweat. "Who?"

"I'll give you a minute." He tapped a forefinger against Shaw's temple. "The name's in there somewhere, though God knows it won't be easy to find, bouncing around that big empty chamber you call a brain."

"You're full of it, Phillips. Bluffing."

"Think so?"

"Know so."

Standing, Matt tugged at the cuffs of his favorite sweater, the cable knit Honor had made, just for him. "All-righty, then," he said, doing his best Steve Martin impersonation.

He was halfway to the elevators, wracking his brain, trying to figure out where he'd gone wrong. Had he given Shaw too much rope? Not enough? Matt ground his right fist into his left palm and cursed under his breath. "Idiot," he muttered, thumbing the Down button.

He was watching the little off-white numbers up above the doors light up . . . two, three, four . . . when Shaw walked up beside him. "Just how do you expect me to accomplish that?"

"You mean, because your whole house-of-cards career was built on that foundation of lies?" The elevator doors opened. "Not my problem, Shaw," he said, stepping into the car. "What was that our mamas used to say? 'You made your bed, now you sleep in it'? Well, maybe not your mama, 'cause if you're the product of her mothering . . ."

Shaw held the door open and said through clenched teeth. "Give me some time. Let me see what I might be able to do."

"*Might?* Not good enough, pal. You'll do it."

"If you file that story, you'll go down with me."

"I'm a lot more careful with my money than you are, hotshot. If I have to turn in my press badge, well," he said, shrugging, "it'll be the perfect opportunity to start that novel I've been talking about for years."

"You've got an answer for everything, don't you?"

"Yeah, pretty much." He laughed and removed Shaw's sleeve and hand from the door. "I'll give you a week. I don't hear from you by then, I break out the old typewriter."

"Typewriter?"

Matt pecked imaginary keys. "Novel? *Remember?*"

Whatever Shaw had opened his mouth to say was blocked by the elevator doors, hissing to a close.

Matt rubbed his hands together and did a little jig. He didn't know *how* Shaw would clean up his mess, but he knew that he *would*. Matt had hit a nerve, saying he didn't know what the guy would do for a living if the network moguls jerked the red carpet out from under him. Brady Shaw needed the lights and the cameras every bit as much as the celebrities he interviewed. It would kill him to go back to making up coarse little stories for the local market.

Yeah, he'd clean up the mess, all right, and he'd do it as fast as he could.

Two questions remained.

One, why hadn't Shaw asked for proof that Matt wouldn't come back to him in a week, a year, or ten, and make the same threat? *Probably because he hasn't thought that far ahead yet.* Which meant Matt had to come up with a ready response, when the accusation reared its ugly head.

And two, how could he guarantee, once Shaw's "clear the air" story broke, that Honor would never find out what part he'd played in making it happen?

"Guess you'll have to take a page from Scarlett O'Hara's book," he laughed to himself, "and worry about that tomorrow."

For now, the only thing he wanted was to see her gorgeous face.

18

I t's not happening, boss," she said. "Nosireebob. Not now, not a week from now, not *ever.*"

Elton shrugged. "I told 'em that's what you'd say, but you know how they are."

"*Do* I."

"I don't think they connected this to that Brady Shaw mess."

"Yeah, well, I'm not taking that chance."

"Can't say as I blame you."

Honor stood in the living room window, arms crossed and feet planted shoulder width apart. "They have a lot of nerve," she said, glaring at the news crew who'd parked their van in front of her house. "There were a dozen people involved in that rescue. Why single me out?"

"Oh, I dunno," he droned, "maybe 'cause it was your dog that found those kids, and you who trained him?"

As if on cue, Rowdy jumped up, propped his front paws on the windowsill and growled at the news truck. A second later, Rerun joined him.

"If I was one of their viewers, I'd rather find out why that goofy mother of theirs let three kids that young go out alone, that close to dark, with a blizzard in the forecast."

"Aw, now, don't be too hard on her. She was born to farming. Probably had to learn to drive a tractor and birth a breach calf before she was in high school. You don't keep a spread like that running all these years without making sure the next generation is as tough and capable as yours. And you can't do that by hovering and mollycoddling."

"I'd think it takes a good measure of common sense to keep a spread like that running, too. Seriously, Kent. You can't toughen up kids that young by sending them out into a—"

"Uh-oh. You start calling me by my last name, I know I've overstayed my welcome."

"Of course you didn't. I love having you around."

The dogs made a few laps around the coffee table, Rowdy going left, Rerun running right, before taking up positions in the window again. Only this time, they'd traded places.

"You oughta open that front door and let 'em have at it. By the time those yahoos out there realized these two wouldn't hurt a fly, they would've peed their pants."

Honor snorted. "Now *that* I'd pay to see."

Chuckling, Elton donned his Orioles cap. "Much as I hate to eat and run, darlin' girl," he said, putting on his Ravens jacket, "I've got places to go and people to see."

"I hope you're charging sponsorship fees," she teased, pointing at his coat and hat. "You look like a walking, talking, human billboard."

"Hey, don't mock team loyalty." He kissed her cheek. "The way they've been playing lately—or not playing, to be more precise—those yokels need all the support they can get."

She walked with him into the foyer. "Renewing your season pass this year?"

"You betcha. And if I can swing a few days off, I'm flying down to Sarasota." He rubbed his hands together. "Catch me some training camp games."

"Will Gladys be able to join you?"

"Nah. She's pretty much chained to her mama's bedside."

Honor nodded. The poor woman had been full-time caretaker of her elderly mother for years. "How's her mom doing these days?"

"Not good. Not good at all. Every day, there's a moment when we're sure that's it . . . she's breathed her last. And every day, she rallies, thanks to Gladys." He shook his head. "The woman is a better nurse than any I've seen in a hospital setting. And you and me both know that's sayin' a lot."

Honor had to agree. Over the years, he'd likely delivered hundreds of patients to ERs and trauma centers.

"Got more equipment in her room than you could shake a stick at, I tell you. Don't know how that wife of mine keeps from losing her mind, listening to that infernal beeping 24/7."

Meaning she'd moved into her mother's room. Poor Elton! "Gladys still won't consider hospice, huh?"

"Nope. I've talked until I'm hoarse, and she won't listen to her pastor, or anybody else for that matter. For some cockamamie reason, she's determined to do this, all on her own."

"Earning feathers for her angel wings."

"What?"

"Just something my mom used to say when people did good deeds." She smiled a little at the sweet memory. Sighing, she shook it off. "Well, take heart, boss," she said, squeezing his forearm. "If it was you in that bed, instead of her mother, Gladys would be just as dedicated to keeping you comfortable."

A slanted smile lit his face. "You're good people, Mack," he said, propping both hands on her shoulders. "Makes me wish I'd met your mama."

"Why?"

"So I could ask her if before you were born, she knew, some-how, what kind of woman you'd become . . ."

"Boss, you know that kind of talk embarrasses—"

". . . and if that's why she named you Honor."

Snickering, she waved away the compliment. "Knock it off, Kent, or I might be tempted to tell the guys about the time you crawled into a sewer to rescue a—"

"Any one of 'em would have done the same."

"Really."

"Really."

"Then why is your face as red as a tomato?"

Stuttering and stammering, he stepped back. "Because you set your thermostat at 100 degrees, that's why."

"Sixty-eight," she said, picturing the wily rat that had been hit by a car before disappearing down a storm drain. "Can't just leave it down there to suffer," he'd said. "Least I can do is put it out of its misery."

If that's what he'd done, she wouldn't have this remark-able, unbelievable story to tell. "Whatever became of Corky, the three-legged-rodent, anyway?"

Honor didn't think she knew another person who could frown and smirk at the same time.

"He had his usual supper one night, played on his exercise wheel, and keeled over, just like that."

She didn't know anyone who could save a gutter rat's life, turn it into a house pet, and get misty when remembering how it had died, either. "You're good people, Elton Kent." She gave him a playful shove, then opened the front door. "Now get out of here before you're late for all those people and places you need to see."

He was laughing as Rerun and Rowdy raced past him like two golden bullets, shot from a cannon, and headed straight for the news van.

"Rerun! Rowdy!" she hollered, pointing at the foyer floor. "Get back here this instant, before I—"

In the time it takes to blink, Honor heard the sound of screeching brakes.

Inhaled the scent of burning rubber.

Then, a dull, sickening thud.

And the sight of Rerun, jumping back with a terrified yelp.

"Rowdy," she whispered, "no, not Rowdy . . ."

Elton got to him first, and when she approached, he held up a hand. "It's bad, Mack. You might not want to see this."

Want to or not, she *had* to see it. She owed at least that much to Rowdy, who'd always, *always* been there for her. The instant she hit her knees, his eyes locked on hers and he tried to raise his head. "Easy," she soothed, stroking bridge of his nose, "easy . . ."

The guys from the news van had gathered around, but Honor was too busy giving Rowdy a quick once-over, hoping against hope that things weren't really as bad as they looked. She sensed, rather than saw, that not one held a mike or a camera, and said a silent prayer of thanks that Rowdy's last moments wouldn't become some sick and twisted YouTube craze.

"Good boy," she whispered, pressing her forehead to his. "Good dog."

"We cleared a spot for him in the van," came a voice from behind her. "We're five minutes from the vet's . . ."

But Honor had seen that look in human victims' eyes enough times to know they'd never get there in time. Even if the accident had happened *in* the clinic, there wouldn't have been time.

Rowdy was probably far enough gone that he'd feel no pain if they moved him, but she wouldn't take that chance. He'd die with dignity, and as peacefully as possible.

She didn't know how Elton managed to get inside and back again in the few minutes that had passed, but he knelt beside her now, gently draping Rowdy's favorite afghan over his body. The dog was beyond shock now, and Elton had known that as well as she did. But he'd also known that this small act of kindness and compassion would spare Honor having to look at all the blood—and there was *so much blood!*—and the obvious signs of a compound fractured rib.

"Thanks, boss," she choked out. And as he gave her hand an understanding squeeze, the driver of the car that had hit Rowdy knelt across from her. She had the look of a corporate attorney, or a banker, a real estate broker, maybe. *Careful, lady*, Honor nearly snarled, *or you'll get Rowdy's blood all over your high-priced power suit.* "Oh my God. Oh good Lord," the woman said. "I never saw him. He just came out of nowhere."

Bull! Honor thought. *You were going way over the limit, probably gabbing on your cell phone, when he—*

A big hand came out of nowhere and settled on the woman's shoulder. "Not now," said a deep, grating voice. "This isn't the time or the place for self-pity."

Sniffling, the woman got to her feet and let the man lead her away. *Good,* Honor thought, because no telling what vile insults might come out of her mouth if he hadn't.

Rowdy moved, not much, but enough to tell Honor he needed her to focus on *him*. She stretched out on the pavement beside him and tenderly held him to her. The heat of Rowdy's shallow, ragged pants warmed her cheek. Then he pushed a paw against her chest and, with a strength that belied his condition, forced her to back off enough to meet his eyes.

He was smiling, God love him, and through the film of her tears, she saw him bob his head, the way he did when searching for a scent.

One weak little woof puffed from his rubbery black lips—his doggy way of saying good-bye, before the telltale fog of death dimmed his once-bright brown eyes.

Honor figured they could probably hear her sobs all the way over on the next block. But she didn't care.

Her precious Rowdy was gone.

19

Matt's mood hadn't been this buoyant in . . . he couldn't remember when. Humming with the Garth Brooks song on the car radio and thumbs drumming the steering wheel, he glanced at the dashboard clock. If Honor hadn't picked up an extra shift, or offered to stand in for an absent coworker, she'd be in her kitchen by now, whipping up some sort of tasty feast for Rowdy and Rerun. *Those dogs eat better than you do*, he thought. But then, that was Honor . . . nothing but the best for those she loved, whether two-footed or four.

He should have called ahead, to let her know he was in the neighborhood. But with that mind-reading talent of hers, he couldn't risk having her know he'd driven out of his way to see her.

It just felt so *good*, knowing she'd soon be free of the rumors and innuendo spawned by Brady Shaw's all circumstantial, no-substance story, that he needed to see her face. No doubt a few of those who'd bought into the lie would keep right on cling-ing to the vicious gossip, but they'd be few and far between, and pressure from the rest would tamp their temptation to use the ill-gotten information to hurt her.

He turned onto her street, frowning at the sleek black Mercedes, parked in the middle of the road. Sometimes, he thought, the more money a person made, the more self-centered they became. Then, directly in front of Honor's house, he saw a news van. He doubted it had anything to do with the sedan, because its satellite wasn't extended, and that meant they weren't broadcasting. He hoped Shaw hadn't done something stupid, like going to Honor for ideas that would help him clear the air. "Nah. Not even Brady is that—"

What was Rerun doing outside, racing back and forth across Honor's yard? She never let those dogs out front, not even to load them into the car. Matt parked the pickup and reached into the dash for Cash's leash. He'd round up the dog and bring him back inside, then check the latch on the back gate and the ones on the screen doors.

It wasn't until he crossed the street that he got a clue about what was going on. There, at the side of the road and surrounded by half a dozen people, lay Rowdy.

Most animal lovers thought of their pets as family, but for Honor, Rowdy really *was* like her child. Every major accomplishment in her *Life After Brady* had a direct link to her work with that dog. Even Rerun, the smaller, sillier of her two Goldens, had come to her by way of Rowdy. She'd be a mess without him.

Too stunned to speak, Matt walked woodenly toward the group just as Elton covered Rowdy with a blanket. Then a woman in a black suit raced past him, crying, "Oh my God. Oh good Lord." He stepped aside as she hit her knees. "I never saw him" were the words she chose, but her tone said, "This is the *dog's* fault." Maybe she was blind. Or severely nearsighted and too vain to wear glasses. What else explained her failure to see that Honor's heart was breaking?

Caveman mentality rose up inside him, making him want to grab a handful of that perfectly coiffed and dyed hair, yank her to her feet, and drag her out of there. Instead, he put a firm hand on her shoulder. "Not now," he snarled, putting an end to her whining, "this isn't the time or the place for self-pity."

She was weeping full throttle by the time she got to her feet and did her best to wobble alongside him on too-high-for-human-feet designer heels. He pointed at the Mercedes. "That your car over there?" he demanded.

She glanced at the sleek, sedate sedan and gasped at first sight of the dented bumper, where Rowdy's blood and golden fur still clung to the chrome. Matt saw it at the same moment as she said, "Well *this* is going to cost a small fortune."

He didn't remember ever wanting to slug a woman, but he wanted to whack this one, good and hard. "Sheesh, lady, how fast were you driving!"

She pressed her lips into a thin red line and huffed toward the driver's door.

And Matt went after her. He slid the wallet from his back pocket as she buckled her seatbelt and emptied it of cash as she dug through her trendy handbag in search of her keys. "Here," he said, tossing the bills into her lap, "it won't replace the bumper, but it oughta cover the cost of having one of your *people* wash your guilt away."

The look she shot him as she slammed the door made his blood run cold. The car lurched forward so quickly that the rear tire nearly rolled over his foot. And when she chanced a glance in her rearview mirror, he hoped she could read lips: "I pity the fool who calls you his woman."

Matt took a moment to collect himself; he'd be no use to Honor in this angry, agitated state. But before he could go to her, he had to see that his boys were in safe hands. After explaining things to Harriet, he pocketed the cell phone.

Elton fell into step beside him. "Glad you're here." He nodded to where she lay, hugging the unmoving dog. "Mack would sooner die than admit it, but she's gonna need somebody to lean on tonight."

"Where's Rerun? I saw him running around out here earlier."

"Out back. Poor mutt's all freaked out. Nearly tore up the kitchen when I let him inside couple minutes ago." Elton described how the news van had riled up the dogs so badly, they'd burst through the door first chance they got.

"If you're gonna blame anybody," Matt said, scowling at the news van, "blame them."

"What goes around, comes around. Most important thing now is helping her make some tough decisions." Shoulders slumped, he blew a stream of air through his lips. "Maybe you can talk her into letting go of him. I sure couldn't." He removed his keys from his pocket. "I'd stay, but the wife's got a meeting with her mother's doctor, and I gave my word I'd keep an eye on the old lady while she's gone."

He couldn't take his eyes off her.

"Mack's tough, and she's survived worse than this. She'll be okay."

She looked anything but tough, huddled up with Rowdy that way.

"What about your boys?"

"Just called Harriet. She's already at my place."

"Good." He backpedaled toward his car. "If you can, give me a holler later."

"Will do."

His legs felt like rubber, the distance between him and her, endless. Finally, crouching beside her, he lay a hand on her shoulder.

She blanketed it with her own. "I love what you told that uppity shrew."

"Good thing she isn't a mind reader."

Honor levered herself up on one elbow, dragged the back of her hand across her eyes. "It all happened so fast. I don't think he suffered much. I hope not, anyway."

Matt had seen the dead and dying enough times to know that at the end, Rowdy was beyond feeling anything, at least on a physical level. He stood, helped her to her feet.

"Will you help me pick him up?"

The knees of her jeans, her jacket sleeves, the front of her sweater were covered with the blood that had seeped from Rowdy's mouth, and she stood shaking, from the shock of what she'd seen as much as the temperature. Honor had witnessed the entire thing, from impact to final gasp. That scene would flash in her mind's eye every time she closed her eyes, and the last thing she needed to add to the horrible memory was the image of her much-loved dog, limp and lifeless in Matt's arms. He took her hand, effectively forcing her to put her back to the grisly sight. "How 'bout if you go inside . . ." He wanted to say *get cleaned up,* "get warmed up. Put on a pot of coffee. Give Rerun some TLC, and let me handle this."

Honor looked up at him, boring into his eyes with such intensity he had a notion to check the back of his head for bore holes. He tucked her hair behind her ears, cupped her chin in a palm. "I'll be gentle with him, I promise."

"I know you will. It's just . . ."

She averted her gaze, just long enough to give him goose bumps, like the ones that pop up when the warmth of the sun is cut off by a cloud.

"It's just . . . I should be with him. I've always . . ." Eyes closed, she held her breath.

Her attempt at blocking a new stream of tears had worked, for the most part. "Yeah, you *have* always been with him."

A tear rolled down her cheek, and he caught it with the pad of his thumb. "Rowdy was oblivious to everybody else who was standing around when . . ." He swallowed, unable to make himself say *when he was dying.* "The only person he saw was you. Why, I doubt he even saw his best buddy, doing laps back and forth across the yard." Matt touched the tip of her nose. "And I think you know why."

She was crying softly now, nodding and smiling faintly and mmm-hmming.

"The minute you wrapped your arms around him, he calmed right down, took a deep peaceful breath, and sent you that big goofy dog grin."

"You saw it, too?" Honor met his eyes. "Oh, thank the good Lord. I thought maybe it had just been wishful thinking." She almost looked back at Rowdy but stopped herself at the last second. "I'll remember that moment for the rest of my life."

"I'm sure you will. That, and ten thousand other moments that made you laugh and smile and maybe even cuss a little."

"He was a stubborn pup, so yeah," she said, giggling softly, "there was some of that, too."

"You gave him the best life a dog could hope for, and he knew it."

When she pressed her cheek against his chest, Matt's arms automatically slipped around her. He couldn't remember when, exactly, but at some point since hearing about the Shaw fiasco, he'd said something about how the story and its fallout had gotten in the way of Honor meeting a man who deserved her. Well, he wanted to be that man. "I'll take good care of Rowdy," he said, stroking her hair, "you've got my word on it."

Her lower lip trembled as she said, "I know that." She stepped away from him, took a few steps, then faced him.

"Inside. Warm. Coffee. Rerun." Smiling sadly, she snapped off a half-hearted salute, and went inside.

Half an hour later, he walked into the kitchen, where the scent of fresh-perked coffee tweaked his nose and an enthusiastic dog gave him a friendly nose-bump to the hand. "Careful there," he said, crouching to ruffle the golden's ears, "or I might just get the impression you like me."

This time, Rerun nose-bumped his chin. "It's been some kinda crazy-awful day, huh? How you holdin' up, boy?"

The dog rested his chin on Matt's knee and emitted something between a groan and a whimper. "I know, I know, and you're lookin' at a couple of rough weeks ahead, yet. But you're like your mama. Before you know it, this awful day won't be anything but a bad memory."

Matt heard the sound of water running upstairs. *Good. Maybe a nice hot shower is just what the doctor ordered.* "So how 'bout a treat, pal? Think that'll make you feel a little better?"

Rerun sat on his haunches, head tilted, as if to say, "A biscuit ain't gonna cut it, dummy; you wanna make me feel better, get my best buddy back."

"And I thought *my* dog had an expressive face," Matt told him.

He opened and closed cupboards and drawers, looking for the one that held the dog biscuits. Halfway around the L-shaped kitchen, when he opened one where plates and saucers stood in tidy stacks, Matt began to notice a trend. "You're kiddin', right?" he said to the dog, reopening doors he'd already opened, where she'd put spices, breakfast cereal, canned goods, and pasta in A-B-C order. "She alphabetizes *everything*?"

Rerun's fuzzy round eyebrows twitched.

"Yeah, I'm getting a pretty good idea what your life has been like," he said, laughing.

Curiosity sent him to the foyer, where he peered into the closet. Sure enough, coats hung on the right side, jackets on the left, and she'd arranged each group in darkest-to-lightest color order. On the floor, a two-tiered shelf held sneakers and boots, and on the ledge above the rod, tidy stacks of scarves and gloves and a short stack of baseball caps sat side by side. "I won't tell anybody if you don't," he said, closing the door.

But even as he did it, Matt knew he had no room to talk. Dividers in his dresser drawers assured his tightly rolled socks wouldn't end up on top of the t-shirts and boxers. His canned goods weren't alphabetized, but he had stacked them with the labels facing out. And what about his tendency to put the salt shaker on the left of the pepper—even in restaurants—for no reason other than, "People say salt and pepper, not pepper and salt."

"Good grief," he muttered, heading back to the kitchen, "she's as loony as I am." But then, he had the Marines to blame for his "a place for everything" mind-set. What had turned Honor into an "everything in its place" girl?

"If . . . *when* we get together, the two of us are gonna drive the twins plum loco," he told Rerun. "Which reminds me . . . you haven't met Steve and Warner yet. Or Cash. We'll have to do something about that. You'll love 'em. And I *know* they're gonna think you're the best thing since—"

Honor's phone rang. Matt didn't feel it was his place to pick up, so he merely listened as the answering machine picked up. Four rings later, her recorded voice said, "This is Honor. Wait for the beep, then, you know what to do."

On the heels of the shrill one-note signal to talk, a grating cackle, followed by some of the most foul language Matt had ever heard—and he'd spent half his waking hours in a newsroom, where four-letter words were as routine as "The coffee pot's empty again." Shaw's broadcast had aired months ago, so what kind of loser was this guy, that he still got a sick thrill out of torturing her with yesterday's news? Matt remembered feeling sorry for Honor that day at T-Bonz, when a couple of the guys seemed more interested in raking her reputation over the coals than in toasting Austin's engagement. He'd watched as, in a matter of seconds, her expression flicked from friendly to fearful to forbearing, but until now, he hadn't understood the full scope of what that story had done to the rest of her *life*.

A powerful urge to wreak some good old-fashioned vengeance rose up in him, and he unclenched one fist long enough to grab the handset. Matt mashed the Talk button, determined to give the jerk a reason to think twice before dialing her number again. But when he put the receiver to his ear, all he heard was a quiet *click*.

"Yeah, well, if you think you can get off that easy, you've got a couple-a thinks coming . . ." Matt dialed star-69 and waited for the pervert's phone to ring. "Let's see how you'll react when somebody has the guts to identify himself, you lousy, stinking—"

The operator's sing-songing "We're sorry, but this service is not available in your area" made him want to pitch the receiver across the room. Punching End, instead, he slammed the handset into its cradle and hit the Play button, and as soon as the disgusting message began, he punched Erase. He had no business deleting it. This wasn't his house. Wasn't his phone. And Honor wasn't his girl, officially. But she'd been through enough today! If he had to step over every line of protocol and privacy ever written to protect her from garbage like that, so be it.

Thankfully, the robotic "Your message has been erased" recording had ended before she padded into the room on those tiny white-socked feet. The sight of her was enough to make his bad mood disappear, like the smoke from a spent match.

Matt thought she looked like a teenager with her face scrubbed clean of makeup and her still-damp curls pulled back in a ponytail.

"I thought you wanted coffee," she said, stepping up to the cabinet above the pot.

He noticed that every mug handle faced east, but Matt wasn't surprised. "I did want coffee," he stammered as she poured the steaming black liquid into one. "I do," he added when she held it out to him. "Thanks."

She sat at the table, and so did Matt. A minute ticked by, then two, yet she didn't ask what he'd done with Rowdy. Even if she asked, he wouldn't tell her how he'd stuffed the bloody blankets into a trash bag and tossed it into the bed of his truck, or that tomorrow, he'd pitch it into the dumpster at work. "I washed him up as best I could," *and put the bloody rags into the bag, too*, "and wrapped him in a quilt I found in a box in the garage."

"The one marked Goodwill?"

He winced. "Maybe. I, ah, never noticed. Sorry."

"It's okay," she said, reaching across the table to pat his hand. "I think the Goodwill people will agree that Rowdy needed it more than they do." She tucked in one corner of her mouth. "But I'm the one who should be sorry, for interrupting you. You were saying?"

"Well," Matt continued, "after I wrapped him up, I put him in a box." He stopped, trying to remember if there'd been anything written on *it*, and came up empty. "So, since I didn't know if you'd want him buried in your backyard, or at a pet cemetery, or if you had planned to have him cremat—"

"No." She shook her head hard enough to dislodge a curl from the ribbon holding her ponytail in place. "Definitely not that. I want him here."

He took a sip of the coffee. "Then first thing in the morning, I'll . . ." How could he say "dig a hole" without sounding crude and tactless? "Anyway, I'll take care of that, too."

"It's the weirdest thing," she began, "because as much as I loved him, you'd think I *would* have had a plan, wouldn't you?"

"Hey, I've written articles on that topic, so I know that most people go to their graves without anyone having a clue as to how they'd like to be buried, or even *if* they want to be buried. I could recite the stats, but it's late, and I'd probably bore you to sleep." He took another swallow of coffee. "But here's *one* example for you: when Faith died, I didn't know what I was supposed to do. We were young. Stupid. Thought we were invincible. Never gave a thought to dying, or drawing up a will, or anything like that. Heck. I was so uninformed I couldn't even put together an intelligent question to *get* information about any of it."

Her face wrinkled with an "Aw gee" expression. And then Honor said, "I'm sure the whole thing was hard on you, in a thousand different ways. Especially with a job and two infants to take care of."

Hard barely cut it. Matt remembered spending a couple of hours in the hospital chapel, crying his eyes out, trying to wrap his mind around the fact that one minute, he had a pregnant wife, and the next, he had a dead one . . . and two helpless infants. He sang the line "I Get by with a Little Help from My Friends."

She balanced an elbow on the table, rested her chin on a fist, and stared. After a second or two, he said, "No way I've got spinach in my teeth, 'cause I never touch the stuff."

"Really? But it's delicious, and so good for you!"

"So are a thousand other things. I think I'll stick with those, if it's all the same to you."

Honor continued studying his face, and it unnerved him in ways he couldn't even describe. "What?"

"Your eyes are bloodshot."

Because I blubbered like a baby out there in the garage, that's why.

"And puffy."

Blubbering like a baby will do that to a guy. "Like I said. It's late."

"Fair warning . . ."

"Of?"

"I'm liable to blubber like a baby with no advance notice. Happy and smiling one minute, bawling like a calf the next."

And so she'd done it again. If Matt could figure out *how* she managed to penetrate his thick head, and read his thoughts, maybe he'd have a ghost of a chance at blocking her.

Her mouth slanted with a small sad smile. "I think it's sweet, for what it's worth."

"What is?"

"That you cared enough about him to shed a tear or two."

A tear or two? *More like a* thousand *or two*!

Out there in the garage, washing Rowdy, wrapping him in a favorite blanket, gently laying him in the box that would be his coffin, Matt was reminded of all the deaths he'd been too proud, too macho, too *Marine* to fully mourn. Seeing the dog in that condition whipped him back to Manhattan, where even the thick gray ash wasn't enough to soak up the blood that had pooled in the skeletal shadow of the South Tower. Matt pictured fellow rescue workers, crushed as they dug for signs of life amid twisted metal and pits of still-burning debris. He remembered the comrade in arms, deployed to Afghanistan on the same transport plane, who deliberately threw himself onto an IED one dusty, sunny morning to spare others in the unit. Rowdy's whole life had been made up of moments like those, and like every other heroic first responder—cop or fire-fighter, EMT and SAR member—he'd been willing to sacrifice himself, if that's what it took, to get a hard job done. Almost as heartbreaking as Rowdy's death, itself, was acknowledging how much more he would have contributed to the world, if not for a crazy, unexplainable, irreversible moment in time. And *that's* what had opened the blasted floodgates!

"You can't dig a hole tomorrow," she was saying. "The ground's frozen solid."

Matt pinched the bridge of his nose and stared at the ceiling. Of course, she was right. Why hadn't he thought of that? "Maybe if I get an early start, I can—"

"Matt. No. You could wrench a muscle. Or catch your death. I'll call Rowdy's vet. Maybe he'll have a suggestion."

Aw, babe, he thought, looking into her lovable, freshly scrubbed face, *yer breakin' my heart.* One of the things that first attracted him to her had been the music in her voice. She had a talent for finding a note in every vowel and consonant that gave each word its own Honor-written melody. And the warmth and wit that beamed from her eyes, whether she was talking or concentrating on a task or off in la-la land, daydreaming. He missed both, mostly because he knew how much effort she'd put into the standoffish façade, designed to keep heartache at bay.

He wondered if she had any idea how much effort *he* was putting into staying on this side of the table, when the only thing he wanted to do was scoop her up and carry her off to a place where sorrow and shame didn't exist. But Elton had been right; Honor *was* strong and tough, and in time, she'd get through this heartache with the same grace and dignity she'd come through everything else.

When it was just the two of them, she stripped off that façade. A big risk, because what if, like so many others, he'd use her vulnerability? He loved her all the more for trusting him. So why was he sitting here, folding and refolding a paper napkin until it felt like the chamois cloth he used to polish his car?

He got up and, on his way to her chair, tossed the napkin into the trash can. When he turned to face her, she stepped into his outstretched arms and tucked her face into the crook of his neck. "Thank you," she whispered.

No, thank you.

She stepped back, then took his hand and led him into the living room, where Rerun had sprawled out on the couch. "Poor thing," she said, leaning into Matt's side. "This will be harder on him than it is on me."

Leave it to Honor to consider a dog's feelings over her own. She was right, of course, because Rowdy's rescue missions were pretty much the only times they'd been separated.

"He probably thinks Rowdy's out on some SAR business, that he'll be back in a few hours, same as always."

Yet again, she'd echoed his thoughts, but the hitch in her voice when she said Rowdy tugged at his heart, and he gave her hand a little squeeze. "Your fingers are freezing," he said, sandwiching her hand between his own. "How 'bout if I build you a fire?"

In place of an answer, Honor more or less shoved him into the gigantic overstuffed chair beside the woodstove. "No, you'll burn the house down."

"Hey, I know how to build a safe fire. Been doing it for—"

Honor climbed into his lap. "I haven't used it in forever. God only knows how much creosote has built up in that stovepipe." She put her head on his shoulder and sighed.

"This . . . ," she patted his chest and snuggled close, "this is better than a fire, anyway."

"I'll say."

"I wonder if they talked about it, afterward."

Maybe this mind-reading stuff was contagious because Matt knew exactly what she was talking about. He rested his chin in her curls. "I can almost hear Rowdy, giving Rerun an accounting of the day's events, with Rerun going 'No way!' and Rowdy saying 'Yuh-huh!'" He chuckled to himself. "Remember that old cartoon, with the goofy little dog and the big grumpy-lookin' one?"

Honor laughed softly. "'Where y'goin', Ralph, what'cha doin', Ralph, can I come with ya, Ralph, huh, huh, huh?'"

"All while the little guy is jumping back and forth over the big one's back."

"And he puts up with it because secretly, he *likes* the little one." She shook her head. "Yeah, that pretty much describes it, all right."

Small talk. Chitchat. Usually, he hated it. But this? This felt as normal and natural as breathing.

In the comfortable silence that followed their cartoon talk, he wondered if Honor would get another dog to replace Rowdy. Would it be a puppy, or some mutt rescued from the pound . . . not that any dog could take Rowdy's place. It wasn't likely she'd put Rerun to work as a service dog. He did the dog math and frowned because, at thirty-five, Rerun was considered too decrepit for rescue work. He thanked God *humans* didn't measure a man's usefulness that way because he only had three years on the mutt!

Sooner or later, one of her SAR pals would announce that their rescue dog was about to deliver a litter. Would Honor adopt one of those and train a Rowdy Number Two?

Way too soon to talk about that now, but he'd have time, later.

Her soft, steady breaths puffed warmth into the hollow of his throat, and Matt realized she'd fallen asleep. He leaned his head against the back cushion and closed his eyes, wondering what would Harriet would think when he rolled in, rumpled and disheveled and needing a shave.

If Honor woke up before morning, she'd have to do it on her own. No way he intended to disturb her, not even if his arms and legs went so numb he couldn't feel them at all.

Yeah, he had time.

Plenty of it.

He had the rest of his life.

20

"I hate to admit it, but if I hadn't given Mercy my word, I'd stay home tonight."

"I guess that's understandable." Rowdy had only been gone three days, and as far as he knew, Honor hadn't left Rerun's side for a moment. "But it'll do you good to get out, take your mind off all the sadness for just a little while, focus on something joyful."

"You're right. I know that. I just feel weird, leaving him alone so soon after losing his lifelong pal."

If Matt was there with her, instead of on the phone, he'd give her a hug because boy, she sure sounded like she could use one. "He'll be fine, and so will you."

"So what did Harriet say when you dragged yourself in after sunup yesterday morning."

He had to laugh. His helpful neighbor had gone to bed after the 11:00 news, as usual. The minute he walked in the door, he heard her up there in the guest room, snoring like a chain saw when he rolled in at dawn. How the boys managed to sleep through the racket, he didn't know, but it sure made him yearn to be ten years old again. "She said I was a thoughtful and considerate young man for getting up early—without waking her or the kids—to get breakfast started."

"You mean you cook, *too*?" Honor sighed. "What did you make?"

Why the extra emphasis on the word *too*? he wondered. "Not so much what I made," Matt said, "as what I *did*. I set out bowls, spoons, napkins, and the kids' favorite cold cereal. I was sitting at the table, drinking coffee, and reading the paper when she came downstairs, and she never even asked what time I got in."

"Not to be disrespectful, but it really isn't any of her business."

"I guess."

"And she's right, you know."

"About . . . ?"

"You *are* thoughtful and considerate. I can't believe you sat there all those hours under my bulk."

"Bulk. Don't make me laugh." Although memory of the way his left arm had gone completely numb was enough to make him flex his fingers. At one point, an hour or so into her nap, Matt considered the possibility that he'd suffered permanent nerve damage, and how ridiculous he'd look, trying to explain to his doctor how it happened.

"I still don't get it. Why didn't you wake me up?"

Because it felt good, knowing you trusted me enough to fall asleep in my arms. Too soon to admit something like that? Matt groaned because he'd never known a woman who roused more emotions in his heart or more questions in his head. "I dozed off myself, that's why." And he had . . . for a second here, and a second there.

"Is Harriet staying with the boys again tonight?"

"No. They're invited. Austin says he can't get hitched if his two favorite kids aren't there."

"Oh, I'm so glad. It'll be good to spend time with them again."

"Yeah. They're looking forward to it. It's their first wedding."

"I can't wait to see them in coats and ties."

"Better look fast, then, because I have a feeling that stuff will go flying before the preacher says 'You may kiss the bride.'"

Honor laughed—not quite the lyrical sound he'd grown to love, but close. "So we'll pick you up at three."

"I'll be ready and waiting. But really, wouldn't it be easier if I just met you there?"

"For you?"

"Of course not, silly. For *you*. If I drive myself, it'll save you coming all the way over here and—"

"Whoa. Ten whole minutes out of my way. Careful. With gas prices where they are, I might be tempted to charge you for the extra mileage."

"Matt . . ."

Laughing, he said, "Honor, . . . we're not gonna start this again, are we?"

He heard her sigh but pretended he didn't. "Be there in two hours," he said and hung up. He understood why she'd been hovering over Rerun, but she needed a break from the whole Rowdy incident. Besides, the forty-five-minute drive there and back gave her and the boys an additional hour and a half together—important if this Matt-and-Honor thing was going where he hoped it would.

It took longer than expected to get the boys into their suits, which made him glad he'd started getting them ready an hour ago. Matt couldn't decide which was the bigger challenge, keeping them still long enough to make a Windsor knot in their matching blue-striped ties or flattening their stubborn cowlicks. *Well*, he thought, grinning into the rearview mirror, *at least the ties look good . . . for now.*

"What do you bet she'll be on the front porch when we get there?" Steve said.

But Warner disagreed. "Maybe if Rowdy hadn't got runned over, but—"

"Hadn't been run over," his twin corrected.

"What. Did you write the dictionary or something?"

"The rules of grammar are *not* in the dictionary." Steve tapped his temple. "Some things, you just *know*."

"Then what are those little slanty letters for, huh, genius? Dad says they tell you what part of speech the words are. Like . . . like the *n* is for noun and *v* means it's a verb." He frowned, then met Matt's eyes in the mirror. "What's a verb, Dad?"

Steve exhaled a sigh of frustration. "It's an action word, dummy."

Matt watched Warner's eyes narrow.

"Oh, you mean like, when I say, 'I'm gonna punch your lights out,' *punch* is the action that makes it a verb?"

Now Steve was frowning, too. Some days, Matt thought it best to let them work things like this out on their own. This wasn't one of those days. "Knock it off, you two. And I don't want to hear any of that nonsense at the wedding, either, you hear?"

Warner leaned closer to Steve and whispered into a cupped hand, "Then I guess I'll have to make sure Dad doesn't hear it when I call you a stupid-head."

"Warner, don't make me stop this car." As he braked, Matt nearly laughed out loud when the boy's eyebrows arched. If he hadn't seen Honor's front door open, he probably would have said, "But Dad, you already stopped the car."

Steve pointed at Honor's picture window. "Hey, Dad, is that Rerun?"

"Yeah, but don't say a word about how he's behaving. Honor's still pretty broken up about losing Rowdy. If we pay too much attention to paws-in-the-windowsill Rerun, she might just change her mind and skip the wedding."

"She'd never do that," Warner said.

"How do you know, stupid-head?"

"Da-a-ad, he called me—"

"Steven. Enough." Then, "How do you know Honor would never cancel plans to go to the wedding?"

"Because she's nice. And nice people don't break promises. And she promised Mercy that she'd be there."

Honor was locking the door as Matt thought *from the mouths of babes.*

"Wow," Steve said, leaning around his twin to get a better look.

Warner pressed his nose to the rear passenger window. "She looks real pretty, doesn't she, Dad?"

He'd seen her hair pulled back into a ponytail and stuffed under a baseball cap, but that glamorous twist was a first. "Sure does." Matt wished Austin and Mercy had decided to wait until summertime to get married because Honor's long black coat hid her dress. She'd look gorgeous in something gauzy and formfitting, but because of the season, Mercy had probably opted for velvet and lace. *Who do you think you are all of a sudden*, he thought, getting out of the truck, *Christian Dior?* The closer she got, the more his nerves jangled, and Matt didn't know if he liked feeling like a some snot-nosed boy, come to take his best girl to the senior prom.

As he opened the door, she leaned into the pickup's cab and said "Y'know, I think you're the three most handsome fellas I've ever seen in person."

"What do you mean, *in person*?"

"Well, you know, the movie and TV stars and—"

"Sorry I asked," he said, laughing as she buckled her seatbelt.

And once he'd done the same, Honor said, "I sure hope this weather will clear up. From what Mercy says, there's barely room in the cabin of Austin's boat for just the two of them."

"How many people will be there, Dad?"

"I think Austin said twelve, Steven, not counting himself and Mercy. And the pastor, of course."

Warner whimpered. "Not the one from Austin's old church I hope, who gives those long, *long* sermons."

Matt chose to overlook it and immediately wished he hadn't, because it freed Warner up to say, "Are you feeling any better, Honor, about Rowdy dying, or are you still real sad?"

Times like these, Matt almost wished he were a bit more like his dad, who would have reached back and whacked him for making a comment like that. Almost.

"It's pretty tough," she said, "but thankfully, I have Rerun to take my mind off it. Sort of."

"Sort of?" the boys said.

"Well, it's weird, you know? One minute he does something funny or cute, and I totally forget about what happened to Rowdy. And the next minute, I look at him and realize he's all by himself. That's when it's hardest."

"I'd probably cry a couple of buckets if Cash died," Steve admitted.

"Yeah," Warner said. "At least."

If Matt could guarantee all small talk would be as productive as this, he'd never complain about it again, because it was forging a bond between his boys and Honor. Since meeting her, they talked about her every time they saw a pizza commercial. "Hey, Dad, remember how Honor used a pair of scissors to cut the pizza slices in half?" Amusement park ads were followed by, "Can you believe Honor has never been on a roller coaster?" And if they saw a woman with long, curly hair or green eyes, she was immediately held up for comparison to Honor. It told him they liked her enough to miss her, almost as much as he did, when she wasn't around. And that was a very good thing, if—

A cold chill snaked down his spine. She was fond of them. That much was evident in the way she the way she looked at them—especially when they didn't *know* she was looking. It was clear from that easy, natural way she had of talking with them, too. But what if the affection was surface stuff and nothing more? Matt had convinced himself she'd wanted him to see glimpses of her true self, shining through a carefully woven façade. But what if he'd been dead wrong, and she hadn't let her guard down because she trusted him and the boys?

Heart pounding, Matt's hands began to sweat and his ears grew hot. He'd never introduced them to any of the women he'd dated before, not to see a movie, not even to wolf down a hamburger at the local fast-food joint. They were good, big-hearted kids who gave 100 percent to everything, and he wouldn't risk having them hurt simply because their lonely dad took pity on a brokenhearted woman. He knew Honor needed him . . . for the moment. But the twins were *ten* and needed him more. Matt gripped the wheel tighter: starting now, he'd be a whole lot more careful about how much they saw of her.

Because much as he cared for her, he cared for his sons more. *Lots* more.

21

The groom stood near the galley doorway, tugging nervously at the cuffs of his dark suit.

"When's it gonna start, Dad?" came Warner's raspy whisper.

"Any minute now, son." Matt didn't remember being this nervous on his own wedding day, and he knew the tension had nothing to do with the ceremony that was about to take place. One of the first questions he'd ask on the other side of the Pearly Gates was why he'd been cursed with such an analytical mind. If that crazy thought hadn't popped into his head during the drive over here, maybe he could enjoy himself. Or at the very least, put on a good show of it.

Flora, who'd been assigned to hit the button that started the music, fumbled with the switch for a moment before *The Wedding March* boomed from a robotic-looking stereo no bigger than a boot box, and Bud snapped a few pictures with his ancient Polaroid. Matt stood up straighter and glanced at Austin, who'd started to sweat, thanks to being crowded into the tiny cabin with ten of his dearest friends.

Honor rounded the corner first and walked slowly down the companionway, followed by Mercy and her brother, Leo.

Despite his earlier decision to ratchet things down a notch or two, Matt had to admit that the maid of honor looked far prettier than the bride. Shimmering, pale-green velvet skimmed her feminine figure and fell in soft folds just above those perfect knees, and even from this distance, he could see the color reflected in her big eyes. She'd painted a thin swath of deeper green shadow on her eyelids, and it shimmered in the candlelight and the flash of Bud's camera . . . but not nearly as much as her eyes themselves.

Then a burst of white caught his eye—the cuff of Austin's white shirt, rising as he ran a finger around the stiff collar. And Matt hung his head, thinking that if they gave prizes for fool of the year, he was a shoo-in, for falling so hard and so fast that he hadn't given a thought to how it would affect the boys or himself or even Cash. And what came next? *Same ol', same ol', that's what.*

Reverend Patterson had earned a reputation for long-winded sermons, peppered with jokes and clichés intended to entertain his congregants, and today was no exception. Matt's mind wandered, and only a word here and there seeped through . . . something about the ceremony that had brought them all here on this bitter-cold New Year's Eve. And unless he was mistaken, a word or two about how a couple needed to learn to roll with the punches in much the same way they'd coped with the crummy weather that forced them down from the tugboat's top deck.

All Matt could concentrate on were the cramped quarters where the foursome stood shoulder to shoulder in a small, tight semicircle facing the pastor and forced him to face Honor head-on.

She'd worn jewelry, something he'd never seen her do before, but if the sparkly bracelet and earrings thought they could compete with that smile or those eyes—

Knock it off, you big idiot, he groused. *This whole keep-your-distance thing will be tough enough without going all weak-kneed, just because she looks . . .*

Bud ducked in and out, the quick, *click-whir* of his camera a physical demonstration of the emotions snapping away inside Matt's mind. Unlike the flash-induced halos, dancing in front of his eyes, the feelings would hover in his heart for a long, long time.

Patterson cleared his throat, opened his weathered Bible, and, balancing it on one upturned palm, looked toward the companionway . . . as Matt recognized the feeling and gave it a name: mourning.

Ashamed, he frowned. Stared at the toes of his Marine-shiny shoes, lest the pastor or Honor or, God forbid, the bride or groom get an eyeful of the self-pity that was no doubt written all over his face. He should feel guilty, and ashamed, because what kind of man compares the grief of losing his wife to the *potential* loss of a relationship that had never begun! He'd hidden his grief from everyone during those first, awful months after Faith hemorrhaged, giving birth to the twins. The crying jags went from a dozen times in a twenty-four-hour period to once daily, then weekly. In time, he could talk about her, could even look at her picture, without choking up. *That* kind of grief was normal. Expected. It made *sense.*

But this? This made *no* sense.

"Wilt thou have this woman to be thy wedded wife, to live together after God's ordinance in the holy estate of matrimony? Wilt thou love her, comfort her, honor her, and keep her, in sickness and in health, and, forsaking all others, keep thee only unto her, so long as ye both shall live?"

He looked across the small space that separated him from her. *I would. In an eyeblink,* he whispered in his heart, *even though I think you'd break my heart.*

"I will," Austin said, taking Mercy's hand.

Now Patterson faced Mercy and repeated the stiff and formal questions. "What token of your love do you offer?"

It took a moment of fumbling, but Matt produced the ring as Austin let go of Mercy's hand and plucked it from between his best man's thumb and forefinger.

"Place the ring on Mercy's finger, and repeat after me."

Austin's hand shook; Mercy's trembled even more as the plain gold band slid onto the third finger of her left hand.

"With this ring," Patterson said, "I thee wed, in the name of the father and of the Son and of the Holy Ghost, Amen."

Austin's voice wavered as he echoed the oath, and Matt wondered why he hadn't seemed as anxious on his own wedding day. Which should he credit for that undeserved calm, he wondered as Mercy repeated the phrase, the oblivious stupidity of youth, or a love that was too unripe to seem scary on any level?

"Bless, O Lord, this ring, that he who gives it and she who wears it may abide in Thy peace, and continue in Thy favor, unto their life's end, through Jesus Christ our Lord, Amen."

Austin lifted Mercy's gauzy veil and, slipping his arm around her waist, pulled her close and pressed a lingering kiss to her lips. When at last he stood back, he looked at Patterson. "Well, preacher," he said, beaming, "what're you waitin' for? Get on with the 'I now pronounce you' part!"

Laughing, the reverend obliged him. "Forasmuch as Austin and Mercy have consented together in holy wedlock and have witnessed the same before God and this company and thereto have given and pledged their troth, each to the other, and have declared the same by giving and receiving a ring and by joining hands, I pronounce that they are man and wife, in the name of the Father and of the Son and of the Holy Ghost, Amen."

Next, the official first kiss. When Austin came up for air, he tenderly cupped his new bride's face in his hands. "Are you happy, Merc?" he rasped.

"Only totally and completely." She kissed his chin. "And finally."

Is this what a Peeping Tom feels like? Matt wondered as a vague sense of longing swirled in his heart. If he hoped to get a handle on this—whatever it was—he'd better fill every waking hour with activities to sidetrack his Honor-centered thoughts. Maybe find a way to get back into search and rescue that didn't put him in the position of leaving his boys without any parent at all.

Fortunately, Bud served as the distraction now, stepping up to snap photos of the newlyweds, of Honor handing over Mercy's bouquet, of the small gathering that encircled the happy couple to offer hugs and congratulations and blessings.

He caught Honor's eye as she let go of the spray of flowers. Was Honor just another one of the thousands of women who typically cried at weddings . . . or had she read his mind, again?

22

I don't get it," Steve said.

"Oh good grief," Warner groaned, rolling his eyes. "What *now?*"

"Why did Mercy's brother come all the way over here from London for a couple of hours if he was just gonna see her again on the honeymoon?"

"Because he wanted to walk her down the aisle," Honor explained. "Leo is all the family she has in the world."

Steve nodded, a thoughtful frown etching his young brow. "She's got Austin now."

"And when she has kids, she'll have them, too."

"Good point, Warner," she said, ruffling his hair.

"Hey, Dad," the boy said, "why don't we buy the boat?"

Honor looked over at Matt, who'd been quiet in an almost-grumpy sort of way since she got into his car earlier, half expecting him to bite Warner's head off.

"We've been over that ground before, son. There isn't time to give her the TLC she deserves. But more important than that, I'd have to dip into your college fund to pay for her."

"College! I'm *ten*, Dad. You have a whole . . ." He screwed up his face and did the math in his head. "You have eight years to make more money for that."

"I'd just as soon stick to the tried and true."

"What does *that* mean?"

"It means," Steve said, "that it's better to leave that money right where it is, in case of an emergency." He looked to Matt for confirmation and, getting none, added, "Right, Dad?"

Matt had been picking up paper plates and cups, left over from the reception. Without looking up from his work, he said, "Close enough."

Honor couldn't think of a thing she'd said to put him in that gruff, arms-distance mood. Couldn't come up with anything the boys might have done that would explain it, either. It left her with one reason: the wedding reminded of his own and made him miss Faith. Well, either that, or he'd finally figured out that Honor was way too high maintenance for his taste. No surprise, really, because only God in heaven knew what sort of things he'd heard about her. But then, why should that enter into it? As an award-winning journalist, surely he'd checked her out, thoroughly, and whatever he'd dug up hadn't stopped the sweet smiles and looks of longing he'd sent, *every single time* they'd been together . . . until today.

He'd held her so tenderly that she'd drifted right off to sleep on the night Rowdy died, and in the morning, Matt cooked bacon and eggs that she couldn't eat and cleaned up after himself while she sniffled and blubbered and wondered what to do with the dog's body. Once she'd finally decided that cremation made the most sense, Matt made all the arrangements, then delivered her precious Rowdy's remains to the vet and paid the bill, which included a black velvet sack and polished mahogany box that now sat on her mantle. And it had been

Matt who'd found a silver-framed photo of the vest-wearing, grinning Rowdy to stand beside the container.

With a full-time job, two young boys, and a dog of his own to care for, her neediness had probably scared him. He hadn't known her long enough to figure out that Honor wasn't a wallflower, so how could he know that what seemed like all-consuming, bottomless grief was only a temporary condition?

"Why so quiet?" he wanted to know.

When she looked up, Honor saw him standing in the middle of Austin's tiny galley, holding the big black trash bag that he'd filled with empty foil food containers and Styrofoam cups. "Hard to believe a woman so into 'going green' would use a product that isn't recyclable." *There. Proof positive that I'm on the road to recovery!*

"Wasn't much she could say about it. Austin put the Sullivans in charge of the reception."

Of course. Now that he mentioned it, Honor did recall Mercy saying something along those lines. She glanced at the brass ship's clock across the room. "Guess they're in the air by now."

"Scary," Warner said. "My friend Timmy went to Ireland for his summer vacation, and he said they flew over the Atlantic Ocean at night, and it was just a bunch of black out the window of the plane."

Steve added a few paper plates to Matt's bag. "Yeah. Scary."

"But once you're on the other side," Honor pointed out, "you're in a whole new place, starting a whole new adventure." Would he see it as *more* proof that the healing process had begun? Not if that detached expression on his face was any indicator. Honor sighed. Some days, she thought, it just didn't pay to get out of bed.

"So what kind of dog will you get," Steve asked, cutting a cautious glance at Matt, "when you're ready, I mean?"

"It'll depend, I guess, on a lot of things. Like what kind of dogs are having puppies, and whether or not it's a nonaggressive breed."

"Why is that an issue?" Matt asked.

Oh, she thought, so you haven't lost your voice? "Because," she began, "this time around, *Rerun* will be the alpha dog. I don't want him feeling any pressure to go all macho on me, establishing his turf. He's the man of the house now, y'know?"

"Why not just get a female? I hear they train quicker, anyway."

His tone reminded Honor a little of her own, during those first turbulent weeks after they'd met. She saw no reason to go the tit-for-tat route, but it might be a good idea to curb her enthusiasm an iota or two. "It's certainly within the realm of possibility." Honor shrugged. "It'll depend on first impressions, I guess."

"You mean when you meet the puppies," Steve said. "We never got to pick one, 'cause Cash was already three when we got him."

She remembered only too well the story Matt had told her about how he and the twins had saved the Pointer from years of constant abuse. "A rescue dog of a whole different kind."

"Yeah," Warner said, "'cause he was res*cued* instead of being the rescu*er*."

"So are we done here yet, Dad?"

"Pretty much. Just need to catch the lights and lock up."

"Catch 'em," Warner said, giggling. "I didn't know they were running."

"Ha-ha. I'm raising a comedian."

Well, Honor thought. *It's good to know he hasn't forgotten how to smile.*

"Where's Harriet?"

"Right here," she called from the galley. "Can't let all this wedding cake go to waste, so I'm wrapping it up for you boys and Honor." She laughed. "And for me, too, of course."

Honor could have kissed the woman for providing a legitimate excuse to leave the cabin. "Need any help?"

"Not unless you know how to keep plastic wrap from sticking to frosting."

"Toothpicks?" She grabbed a few and poked them into the cake as Harriet stood by.

"So what's up with Mr. Happy today?" the woman asked.

"You noticed it, too?" Honor breathed a sigh of relief. "I thought it was just me, being overly sensitive."

"Just between you and me," she whispered, leaning in close, "today, he reminds me of the way he behaved when he and the boys first moved in next door to me." Harriet put down the roll of plastic wrap and hugged herself. "Oh, they were *such* gorgeous babies. And really, can you believe how different they are? Why, if a person didn't know better, they'd never believe they're even related, let alone twins."

She reminded Honor of her grandmother, happy and helpful . . . and easily distracted.

As often as not, Gran's chocolate chip cookies came out of the oven flat as crepes because she'd forgotten the baking powder, or bitter as bile due to double doses of baking soda. Where Harriet was going with this little side trip was anybody's guess, but Honor didn't have the heart to put her back on track. "Yes, they're adorable."

"Oh, but listen to me, going on and on. Why, if a person didn't know better," she repeated, "they'd think I was a little kid with ADD or something!"

Harriet's warm, robust laughter bounced from every surface in the tiny room, attracting two curious boys . . . and their cranky father. "Goodness gracious sakes alive, Matthew," she said, "you look as though you've swallowed a cupful of lemon juice. Mixed with vinegar no less! What *is* your problem today, Mr. Grumpy?"

The twins giggled as Matt's brows rose slightly. "I don't have a problem."

But that quick glance at Honor said otherwise. She wondered, not for the first time, what she might have done to offend him. And—not for the first time—came up empty. She busied herself, wrapping the cake. Anything to keep from looking at him.

The boys entertained Harriet with rapid-fire knock-knock jokes while Honor rearranged the contents of Austin's tiny fridge. Any day now, an agent would start bringing potential buyers onboard the boat, and the scent of spoiled food surely wouldn't seal any deals. A perfect place, she thought, moving eggs, milk, and lunchmeats to a cooler, to hide from Matt's chilly, distant looks . . . and the painful, exasperating truth:

Sometime between those sweet moments when she'd slept in his arms and when he picked her up today, he'd heard or read something about her. Or Elton or even her former boss, Buzz, had told him about the whole Uncle Mike mess. She wasn't so naïve as to believe he hadn't researched every facet of the scandal that toppled her career—he was an award-winning reporter, with friends in high places and access to information the average Joe didn't have—so maybe *that* tidbit had been the proverbial last straw. She'd allowed herself to believe that he was different, that he possessed the backbone and thick skin required to stand up to the onslaught of judgmental, self-righteous finger-pointing, and name-calling. She believed that now, too. The irony: this man who'd built his career on a foundation of honesty and ethics loved his boys too much to expose *them* to the ugliness. *Talk about your double-edged swords,* she thought, because it only made her love him more.

The soft slap of waves against the boat's hull might have been calming and restful, if not for a thought far more disturbing . . . not that he'd leave her, but that he *wouldn't*.

Matt hadn't so much as hinted at a future with her. Hadn't said that he cared for her. Hadn't even kissed her. But he wanted to. Honor knew it just as she knew that Warner and Steve would continue trying to top each other's knock-knock jokes and that Harriet would laugh at every silly word. It wasn't vanity or arrogance, but Matt's very nature that made her so certain. He was part white knight, part protective dad, part investigative reporter; together, those traits would compel him to dig deep inside himself, until he found the resolve to hang in there, despite the taint that clung to her like moss on a north-facing tree . . . and a way to justify exposing his innocent young boys to it.

He'd do it for no reason other than he believed she needed him to, even though it could destroy his career *and* subject the boys to all manner of insult and innuendo. Why, even dear sweet Harriet would suffer, watching it unfold, because she cared for them.

No decent person would allow anything hurtful to happen to innocent bystanders, especially those who'd come to mean so much to her. From where she stood, there appeared to be only one way to protect them.

And come morning, she'd orchestrate a plan to get them all out of the line of fire.

23

$\mathcal{H}$onor's nerves jangled as she reread the e-mail from her pal at Homeland Security. The department was in the process of training dogs to aid in searches at all ports, rail stations, airports, and courthouses in White Plains, New York . . . and they needed qualified personnel to train the dog handlers.

The job was a godsend. Not only would it get her out of town—and away from Matt and his terrific twins—it would allow her to continue working with dogs and exercise her training expertise.

Buzz invited her to call, any time, to discuss the position and provided his new office and cell numbers. She glanced at the clock. Knowing Buzz, he'd still be up, watching the evening news.

"Well as I live and breathe," he said on the first ring. "If it ain't li'l Honor Mackenzie." Muffled rustling told her he'd palmed the phone. "Honey," she heard him say, "it's Mack."

His wife picked up the extension. "If I wasn't so happy to hear from you, I'd come down there and kick your butt. What's wrong with you, girl, letting so much time go by without getting in touch?"

"Give it to her good, Rosie."

Honor smiled at the reminder of Buzz's pet name for his wife of thirty years. "Sorry, Rose." Honor ignored her guilt and the embarrassment that caused it. The last time she'd seen the couple, they'd been visiting Baltimore for an anniversary trip. The night before they were to head back to New York, Brady Shaw's story broke. Communication had been spotty, at best, in the many months since. "Life's been . . . busy."

"That's a lame excuse," Rose said, laughing, "but I'll let you get away with it. This time. So how are those four-legged geniuses of yours?"

Honor swallowed. "Rerun is fine." And at the mention of his name, the golden ambled to her side and lay his chin on her knee. "But Rowdy was hit by a car a few weeks ago." She quieted Rerun's whining with a gentle pat between his ears.

Buzz said, "That's awful." And Rose added a high-pitched "Oh, no."

"It was quick," she explained. "I don't think he suffered."

"How's Rerun handling it?"

"I'll bet he's just the saddest li'l puppy . . ."

She gave the dog another pat. "He's coming around. So how are the kids?"

"Fine. Happy. Getting—"

"Smart-mouthed," Buzz tucked in. "But at least they haven't ended up in jail."

Or on the 6:00 news . . . every night for weeks.

Grinning, Honor pictured Eli and Brigit, who'd moved in with their grandparents after their parents were killed in a car accident. Honor had met Buzz and Rose at the junior high school's holiday pageant and remained close to the whole family, right up to the Brady mess.

"But you called to talk about this opening up here in White Plains, right?"

Rather than admit that was the *only* thing that could have prompted her to reconnect with the first people to react to the scandal, Honor said, "There's just one opening?"

"To do what *you* do, yeah. Just the one. The world has been a very different place since 9/11. Everybody bellyaches about being searched, but they demand security, everywhere. Can't have one without the other. But we're hoping the use of scent dogs will add a level of security, without adding to travelers' discomfort."

"Makes perfect 'scents' to me," Honor said.

Laughing, Rose said, "Sweetie, it's good to hear you're still 'punny.'"

"Sometimes I worry about you, Rose," Buzz said.

"Why?"

"Because you think things like that are . . . ," he cleared his throat, "punny."

Honor didn't find any humor in it, and neither would the Turners, if they'd known how much she'd surprised herself with the pun. Lately, she much preferred quietly blending into the woodwork than attracting any sort of attention to herself. The only place she seemed comfortable making noise was during SAR missions, when the occasional wisecrack lightened the tension.

"Well, you two," Rose said, "if you're gonna talk business, I'm outta here." She laughed before adding, "Good hearing from you, Honor." Then, "Buzz? You make sure to lock her into a date when she can come see us, you hear?"

"Will do, sweet face."

Buzz's affectionate nickname made Honor wonder if God ever intended to answer her prayers for love that remained warm and affectionate for years, despite the highs and lows life threw at them. Fortunately, she didn't have to dwell on the fact that *no* was an answer, because Buzz said, "Before I get into job talk, I want to remind you that we, that Rose and I, that is, we never believed a word of that story. It's as full of holes as Brady Shaw's big bloated head. Anyone with a lick of sense knew it back then, and they know it now, too."

Honor's life would be a lot different . . . if only that were true. "Thanks, Buzz" seemed a shallow and paltry thing to say, but since more effusive, complimentary things sounded phony, even in her own ears, she said it anyway. "So when will they start interviewing?"

"Not they. Me. And I know exactly the kind of candidate I'm lookin' for. How soon can you get up here?"

Honor had sent a card, congratulating him on his promotion, but for some reason, it never occurred to her that he could influence *this* decision. Sure it would sting if her resumé was rejected during the selection process, but if *Buzz* was the one doing the rejection? Even more disconcerting . . . what if he hired her? "Wow. Well. Gosh. I-I only just started the search for a new job this morning. Sent out a few e-resumés. Got a few 'out of the office' replies. I've barely had time to wrap my mind around hearing from you, especially this soon, let alone think about when I might be ready to come up for an interview!" After getting all that out in the open, Honor wished she'd been talking to one of those voice mail recorders that allows callers to replay and erase messages because she'd said way too much and laughed far too loudly.

"Mackie, you're more than qualified for this job slot. Fact is, you're probably *over*qualified, and I think you know I'm not the type who'd say a thing like that if I didn't believe it. And, you know I'm not the type to show partiality to one applicant over another for personal reasons. The interview is a formality, nothing more, or I'd hire you right here, right now. You know the old saying 'You can't fight city hall.'"

She'd heard the phrase, but didn't see how it fit into their conversation.

"Step by step, inch by inch," Buzz said, answering her unasked question. "If we follow the rules, nobody can say I was playing favorites, hiring you."

"How many other applicants have you interviewed?"

"Six, maybe eight. In a couple of years, a few might be as good as you. Right now?" He harrumphed. "You're it, girl. *It*."

"So you're not concerned that my, ah, history will make problems for you?"

"Not at all. Like I said, the resumé and interview are policy, plain and simple. Infuriating as it is, red tape is what greases the bureaucratic wheels. So don't give that Shaw mess another thought. Nobody up here knows about it, and in the off chance they did get wind of it, it's ancient history by now. You don't think I'd drag you all the way up here if I thought you'd end up dealing with the same swamp, do you?"

"No. No, of course you wouldn't." *At least, not consciously . . .* "So how soon are you looking to get the new hire on board?"

"Not 'my new hire.' *You*. And I needed you yesterday. Day before, even. If I thought for a minute I could manipulate time and make it happen that fast, you'd be here already."

Buzz had never been one to beat around the bush. Didn't like wasting time, either. Both traits worked in her favor because if things fell into place well, she could have a new job and address by summer. To meet administrative requirements, she'd need to update and revise her lecture notes and handouts, and it probably wouldn't be a bad idea to photocopy articles that had mentioned her. Citing quotes from the mayor and high-ranking police and fire department personnel who'd benefited from her SAR work should make it easier for Buzz when he slid her file in front of his superiors. She'd start praying tonight that they'd share the attitude of prospective employers who, after reading quotes from Baltimore's mayor and high-ranking police and fire department personnel, extended job offers. Honor had politely turned them all down with a straightforward "I love being a firefighter." After Brady's story broke, her response to the handful of offers that came in had been dramatically different. "I like having the freedom to make my own hours" wasn't entirely factual, but guilt born of the fib was far surpassed by relief at hiding from the ugly truth.

The thought awoke a jaw-dropping question. "Oh my gosh, Buzz . . . what do you think they'll want to hear, you know, to fill the gap on my resume? I mean, if I don't list my years with the fire department, I'll look like I'm trying to hide something. Which I am! But if I list them, well, won't that look even worse?"

He concluded the nerve-wracking pause with, "How 'bout if you just let me worry about all that, okay? Dealing with stuff like that is all part of my job. Now, I hate to repeat myself, but how soon can you be here?"

"Well," she thought, stroking Rerun's velvety nose, "I'll need to find someone to take care of the dog. And unless my boss is short-handed, getting time off from the office shouldn't be a problem, because I—"

"Okay. Okay. I hear ya. Lots of items on the old To Do list to check off. So how 'bout let's do it this way: You line up all your ducks and then get back to me. Just don't piddle around too long. I need somebody, approved and in place, by the first."

Ironic, she thought, that her new life could very well begin on April Fool's Day. "I'll be in touch, soon. You have my word."

"So I take it things haven't settled down any, thanks to that sleazeball's news story . . ."

"Actually, that has settled down, quite a lot." Except for a few furtive glances and the strange "somebody's watching me" sensation that came over her when people stopped whispering the instant they saw her walk into a room, life had pretty much returned to normal. Or, as normal as it could be for a person whose job involved typing up hospital bills when she was trained to put out fires.

"Then why the big push to get outta Dodge?"

Honor had never said she hoped to leave the Baltimore area, soon. But then, Buzz's perceptiveness no doubt helped him get *his* job. "Just . . . things," she said.

"Ah, man troubles, eh?"

She pictured Matt and the boys the way they'd looked, weeks ago, at Mercy and Austin's wedding. The yearning was so deep and complete that it nearly put tears in her eyes. "Sort of. No, not really."

"Y'know, the older I get, the more convinced I am that y'all hold secret meetings and read from a book called *The Woman's Guide to Men*," he teased. "I asked a simple question, and I get an answer that's a riddle. Wait. Don't tell me: that's from the chapter titled 'Keep Him Guessing'?"

"Soon as we hang up, I'm getting online to see if it's available in paperback!" She smiled in reaction to his hearty laughter. "Far as I know, there isn't any such book, and there isn't a guy in my life, either. At least, not one who's . . . It's just, he and I . . . Oh, I don't know, it's . . . complicated." Honor exhaled a huge breath. "Let's just say things ended before they began." A little truth, a little evasion should satisfy this overprotective father alternate.

"Guess you don't agree with that old 'running away never solves anything' adage, then."

"I'm not running away. It's more like I'm . . ." There didn't seem much point on completing the sentence.

"And you know the one that goes something like 'you should never leave town because of a broken heart'?"

"No, can't say as I've heard that one, but really, Buzz, my heart isn't broken and I'm not running away." Half a lie was better than a whole one, right?

"Hey. Give it any name that makes you feel better about the decision."

Now Honor conjured the image of Matt and the boys on movie night—happy, carefree, comfortable, and thriving in their three-man household. She'd do anything to protect that and felt more certain than ever that this move was the right thing, for her *and* for them.

"You can't see me, but I'm rolling up my sleeves. I can be there in four to five hours, tops. Want me to kick some butt, see if maybe I can set that fool straight? Talk him into treating you right?"

Smiling, Honor said, "No, but thanks. He's treated me very well." *Too well, and that's the problem.* She told Buzz about everything he'd done on the day Rowdy was killed. "He's a good guy, really."

"Except for being—what's that phrase you women like to use?—a commitment-phobe."

"He's a widower, so no, I don't think commitment phobia is the problem."

"Aside from Rose and my own beautiful girls and grand-daughters, you're the most perfect 'other half' I can name. Which tells me he heard The Story, and it's messing with his head."

His overemphasis of the words made her smile a little because Buzz had referred to it exactly that way, ever since it aired. "I can't speak for Matt, but I know it's messing with mine." She'd never been comfortable, talking about herself, even when the subject matter was positive. But when the Shaw story was involved, it made Honor want to go off someplace and disappear from sight. "But enough about me. What's Brigit doing these days?"

"Still working at the hospital."

"Children's ward?"

"Yep. I don't think she could do anything else, if you want my honest opinion. She loves 'em all, big and small. You should have seen her at the survivors' reunion couple months back." Buzz laughed. "Why, you would have thought every Big C survivor was her very own."

Honor pictured the freckle-faced blond who'd been her sidekick all though junior high and high school. The friendship was yet another item on the list of losses that began racking up after Brady's story aired. "And what about Eli? Last I heard, some high-profile Wall Street firm lured him away from the bank."

"That's true. He and Lizzy barely passed the nine months married mark before li'l Eli came along."

"I'm so glad. I miss them, and you and Rose, too."

"Well, then, when you come up for the interview, let's get together. Rose will jump at the chance to get you all around the dinner table again, just like in the old days. Give you and the kids a chance to catch up and . . . Say, you haven't met Eli's wife, have you?"

"No, but I'm sure if he chose her, she's lovely."

"That she is," Buzz agreed. "And wait until you meet that li'l grandson of mine. Cuter than the Gerber baby, I tell you. Rose would love nothing better than to see you all around the dinner table again, just like the good old days."

Strange . . . but no mention of Brigit's personal life. Just as well, since it would only wake prickly memories of their last conversation. The last time she'd visited the Turners, Eli had put up his dukes, feinting and jabbing and mimicking

Rocky. "Lemme at da big galoot. I'll teach him what happens to guys who spread lies." Brigit, on the other hand, put the full blame for Honor's woes on competitiveness, not Brady Shaw. "Remember that time when you didn't sleep for three days straight, trying to get your science fair entry *just perfect*? And what about that bake-off at the church picnic?" she'd said, rolling her eyes. "Why, I thought you'd faint, waiting for Mrs. Griffin to pin that blue ribbon to your shirt." In other words, Bright believed not only that Honor was capable of sleeping her way to the top, but guilty of exercising poor judgment *and* poor taste by complaining about the consequences, as well. So, as much as she'd love to see the Turners, a family dinner wouldn't happen if it meant facing Brigit's disapproval. Life didn't offer many opportunities to avoid the harsh glare of censure, but when it did . . .

"When you get back to the office," she said, neatly sidestepping the invitation, "maybe you can shoot me a quick e-mail, let me know if there's a day or time that works best with your schedule, and I'll arrange things around that."

"Sounds good. But don't book a hotel room. You're staying with us."

Even as she said her good-byes, Honor knew she wouldn't accept that invitation, either. If a few innocent visits to the lieutenant's house were enough to supply Brady with the ammo to shoot down her career, she didn't even want to think about how much damage an overnight stay might provide. In all likelihood, she wasn't even on Brady's radar any longer, but Honor couldn't—wouldn't—take that chance.

24

*H*er grumbling stomach and a faint headache reminded her that she'd skipped supper. And lunch, too. Honor rummaged in the fridge for something quick, nutritious, and filling. A cold slice of pizza caught her eye. Not exactly gourmet cuisine, she thought, sliding it into the microwave, but it would quiet the noise. Not exactly the healthiest supper, either, so she washed down a multivitamin with a glass of tomato juice.

Rerun sat beside her, ears perked and eyes shining, ever alert for the bit of cheese or crumb of crust that might fall to the floor. "Let's not make a habit of this," she said, feeding him a pepperoni slice.

He smiled up at her, as if to say, "Why not?"

"Because you'll get spoiled," she answered, giving him a second slice, "and I'll get fat."

Still munching, he padded over to the French door and pawed its levered handle.

"Okay, Mr. Subtle, I'll let you out." She opened the door as the phone rang. "Back in a flash," she told him as he thundered down the back porch steps.

She'd barely got the word hello out of her mouth when a familiar voice said, "Not the smartest thing you ever did, siccing Matt Phillips on me."

Paying for caller ID didn't make much sense if she wasn't going to use it. But then, if she hadn't answered, she wouldn't know that something connected Brady Shaw and Matt Phillips. "I'm old news, Brady. You must be desperate for a story to be calling me."

"Desperate?" He laughed. "Hardly."

"Why else would you climb back down into the sewer with the likes of me?"

"*Back* down into the sewer . . . ?"

It made her smile, knowing he'd picked up on her obvious reference to the slimy quality of his reports. "What's wrong? Did you miss your li'l rat buddies?"

"Don't try to change the subject. You're the reason Phillips is threatening me. What I don't know, is *why*."

Good question, Honor thought. "Even if I knew the answer to that, why would I share it with you?"

"Because maybe you can talk your sweetheart out of it, spare him the expense and humiliation of a lawsuit. Besides, it's the decent thing to do."

Talk him out of what? she wondered. "Guess they got your number and demoted you, eh? I'd say 'crossword editor,' but since you don't even know the meaning of the word *decent*, that isn't very likely."

"What're you babbling about?"

"You seem to enjoy talking in riddles. Thought I'd do the same."

"Whatever. Just tell him for me he doesn't need to pay another visit to my office. I'm calling his bluff."

Calling his bluff? "Just so I'm clear, *which* office visit are we talking about?"

"Wasn't aware he'd stopped by more than once."

Neither was I, she thought. But at least now she had something to blame for the peculiar behavior that had begun at about the same time.

"Interesting," Honor said, hoping to pry more details about Matt's visit from Brady.

"You're pretty good at playing dumb, I'll give you that," he snorted, "but okay, I'll play along. For now. Phillips delivered a file, pages of trumped-up charges and other garbage he and his pals dug up. Told me if I didn't run a retraction story, one that clears your name, he'd . . . Wait just a cotton-pickin' minute. Why am I telling you all of this? Like I said, who else would put him up to a stunt that could land him in court, defending himself against slander and libel and charges of securing evidence without search warrants?"

Honor smirked because his slip of the tongue told her Matt had something on Brady, something big and career-damaging. He was gambling, with this phone call, that her connection to Matt was strong enough to influence what he might do next.

"So what does Phillips have that you need? Can't be money; he's a *Sun* reporter." He underscored the sarcastic comment with derisive laughter. "Can't be power; he works for that goofball—"

Disgusted, furious, ashamed—though she really had no reason to be—Honor hung up. And after letting Rerun inside, she locked up and began to pace. What was Matt thinking, digging into Brady's background? He might as well step into a hibernating bear's cave or stick his hand into a hornet's nest!

This time when the phone rang, she looked at the caller ID block.

Matt. She hadn't talked with him in weeks. Was it mere coincidence that he'd called on the heels of her conversation with Brady? Honor intended to find out.

"The boys nagged me into calling," he said when she picked up. "They're worried about you, since you've been out of touch for so long."

The boys were worried. The qualifier stung but couldn't have come at a better time. It would be a lot easier, leaving now. "I'm fine," she said, wondering whether or not to even bother telling him about Brady's call.

"Okay. Good. I'm—"

"How *are* the boys?"

"They're fine."

It was good to hear his voice. But she couldn't let herself focus on that. Far better to wonder if he'd tell her about his meeting with Brady. "Good." Then, "So what have you been up to lately?"

"Working. Running the boys back and forth to Scouts. And soccer practice. School." He cleared his throat. "Same ol', same ol'."

Honor thought back to the first time she'd noticed the change in his demeanor, on the evening of Austin and Mercy's wedding. He'd looked so handsome, dark hair slicked back and smiling in his dark suit and starched white shirt that she couldn't help picturing him in a tuxedo. Would his behavior have changed so dramatically if he *hadn't* discovered something unsavory about her while scrounging for dirt on Brady? Something that he just couldn't overlook, especially when the boys were so directly involved?

One more thing to make leaving easier. And his answer to her next question would make it easier still, no matter how he answered it. "Had any interesting meetings lately?"

"Meetings . . . ? No. Just the usual stuff."

Honor didn't know whether she felt more hurt or betrayed by his evasiveness. "Really."

A long, silent moment passed before he said, "Obviously, you have something to say. So just say it, Honor, and save us both a lot of time and aggravation."

"Brady Shaw called me, not a half hour before you did."

"*What?* Tonight? Why would he call you!"

"To ask me to give you a message. He's calling your bluff. And that's pretty much an exact quote."

Another lengthy pause preceded his raspy sigh. "Aw, for the luvva . . . *Sheesh.*"

She could almost see him, raking the fingers of his free hand through his dark waves. The same hand that had so tenderly laid Rowdy to rest, then held and comforted her as she cried herself to sleep in his lap.

Honor gritted her teeth and stiffened her spine. If she let her guard down now, how could she summon the guts to go to New York? "So it seems Brady has booted you out of the sandbox, without letting you take any of your toys. I guess that pretty much limits the control you'll have on my life now, doesn't it?" If she sounded sarcastic and sanctimonious to herself, Honor could only imagine what she sounded like to Matt.

"How's Rerun?"

Well now, *that* was out of left field, she thought. "He's doing very well, all things considered."

"Still walking around the house, looking for Rowdy?"

She didn't remember telling him about that. But how else could he know such a thing? "Yeah, sometimes," she admitted, "but I try and keep him distracted. Toys, games, long walks, anything to get his mind off *then* and onto *now.*"

"You're a natural with dogs. And kids." He paused. "Correction. You're good with people in general."

It felt so wonderful, hearing the warmth in his voice again, that Honor was tempted to invite him over, so she could lose herself in the comforting circle of his arms. But she couldn't, not if she hoped to protect him and the twins from any more of the fallout connected to her past. "So what have you been up to," he asked, "aside from telephone conversations with the devil's right-hand man?"

"Between doing his bidding, you mean, and work and training sessions? Why, there's barely time for eating and sleeping."

"I didn't mean it like that, and you know it."

It didn't matter what he meant or didn't mean. Didn't matter that he cared enough to call and check on her. Or that he'd gotten himself embroiled in who knows what with that sleaze, Brady Shaw, mostly likely on her behalf.

Or was it?

Only one way to find out . . .

"So tell me, what was the *point* of your meeting with Brady?"

"No point, if he's serious about calling my bluff. Because I don't have a leg to stand on. Every shred of evidence was obtained by less than ethical means. I'd do more harm to the guys who helped me get it than to Shaw, and he knows it."

"How self-centered is it for me to think you did all of that on my behalf?"

"It isn't self-centered at all. That's *exactly* why I did it."

"Okay, then how ungrateful am I to wish you hadn't? Because I don't like knowing that you see me as this weak, pathetic little thing who's incapable of protecting herself, or—"

"Whoa. Back up there for just a minute. Do you mean to tell me you *could* have put up a defense against Shaw's story?"

She didn't owe him an answer. Didn't want to rehash it all. But once she started talking, Honor couldn't seem to make herself stop.

A year ago, she told him, after giving things a lot of thought and prayer, she made a conscious choice to take it full on the chin, alone, without Lieutenant Hoffman's knowledge or approval. "If Wyatt had known anything about it," she continued, "he would have squashed my plan before I had a chance to put it into motion" . . . and paid for the selfless action with his job, the family home, and the respect of his peers, not to mention what mayhem his wife and kids would have been forced to endure. "But I wasn't married, didn't have kids or any other family to speak of. What did I have to lose?"

"Oh, gee, I dunno," Matt put in. "Only *your* job. *Your* dignity. *Your* standing in the community. I realize you think Wyatt Hoffman was every bit as innocent as you were, but you had to wonder why he took that transfer to the boonies and *let* you shoulder the burden, alone."

"I didn't give him a choice, remember? I—"

"Bull," Matt interrupted. "Think about it, Honor. I did."

She'd worry over what he meant by "I did" later. For now, Honor would have to be satisfied knowing that whatever his investigation had uncovered left him uncertain of her innocence and suspicious of her motives. That would help make the move easier, too.

"Oh, lest you think I'm suffering from some sort of martyr complex, let me set the record straight. There were times, *lots* of times, when it seemed as though things would never right themselves. Believe me, I felt plenty sorry for myself, wondering 'why me?' Asking myself why I hadn't let *Wyatt* take the heat. And I'm ashamed, even now, to admit that most of those times, I wished I *had*."

"I don't know anybody who'd feel differently under circumstances like that."

"Doesn't make it right. I'm supposed to be a Christian."

"Honor, listen to me. Hoffman had family to support him. Not just a devoted wife and kids who adored him, but parents, in-laws, siblings, even friends and coworkers who thought he hung the moon. Who had *your* back? Who was there for *you*, saying 'hang in there,' 'you'll land on your feet,' 'just ask, and we're there for you'? Nobody, that's who. You know what ticks me off? At every stage of this thing, Hoffman knew what was going on. If he'd been lily white, he would have stepped up with the evidence he'd gathered on Shaw. But he buried it to save his own skin."

"What do you mean?"

She heard his frustrated sigh.

"What I mean is this: Hoffman's dirty, too. In some ways, dirtier than Shaw. He isn't guilty of arson—at least, not that I know of—but there's a list of cover-ups and payoffs and bribes nearly long as my arm."

"Wyatt? I-I don't believe it."

"Oh, you can believe it, all right. How do you think he could afford that big gorgeous house, an Ocean City condo, two pricey cars? Jennifer is a housewife. No way he could afford all that on his department salary. And don't tell me he inherited the money, because I looked into that, too, and he *didn't*."

She didn't know what to say. Or think. Or feel. If Matt was right, it meant she had thrown away her career and her reputation to protect a man with even fewer scruples than Shaw. The fact that she *hadn't* wondered how the Hoffmans could afford their upper-class lifestyle on a middle-lass income not only made her feel gullible, but foolish as well.

"I know what you're thinking, and you're wrong."

"Oh, so I'm *not* a brainless twit?"

"If searching out the good in everyone you meet makes you a brainless twit, then I think the good Lord should have included that in every human's DNA. It's an area where *I'm* completely deficient."

"That's crazy talk." Honor believed in his goodness to the core of her. "There must be some explanation for everything because Wyatt's a good person."

"Greed is a powerful motivator."

Images of her time with the Hoffmans flashed through her memory. Holiday dinners. Backyard barbecues. Birthdays. Relaxing, leisurely afternoons around the pool. "But he was so kind and generous. Brought me home, introduced me to his family . . . Jennifer and the kids became my cheering squad, counting every sit-up and push-up and lap around the track, and never once complained when his pacing interrupted their favorite TV shows as he drilled facts and figures into my head. I passed the endurance tests. Passed the written tests, too, because of them."

"You would have made it on your own. In time."

"No. I wouldn't. The guys at the department nicknamed me Rocket, because I shot to the top so fast."

"Greed's a powerful motivator," Matt said slowly, "and so is indebtedness."

"If you mean he thought I'd look the other way when he stepped out of line, out of some cockeyed sense of loyalty . . ."

"That's exactly what I mean. But somewhere along the line, you must have done or said something that told him you'd do the right thing, no matter what."

"So he threw me under the bus."

"Right. Because Shaw barely uncovered the tip of the pro-verbial iceberg with his pathetic little exposé. I never had any intention of dredging all this up for you. I just thought if I could pave the way toward clearing your name, maybe . . ."

An exasperated huff sighed into her hear. "Look," he said, his voice barely a whisper. "Honor. I'm sorry. I honestly believed if I dug up the right evidence, I could talk Shaw into retracting the story, so you could put the whole mess behind you, once and for all, get your good name back. I had no idea how big this was, and—"

"But Matt, don't you get it? If Brady *had* gone back on the air with a retraction, it would have looked bogus. People would've wondered who I'd slept with *this* time to clear away the last mess. And Wyatt . . . I don't know what to say about that, except . . . poor Jennifer would have been forced to wade through the quagmire all over again. And the kids. They're a whole year older. They'll understand more."

"But at least the truth would be out there. Wouldn't that give you some real satisfaction?"

"I already know the truth. That's enough for me. Besides, as you so astutely pointed out, because of *how* you came by the information, good, hard-working people would get hurt far worse than Wyatt or Brady."

"You only know the half of it."

"Then fill in the other half."

He hesitated a tick before saying, "They're both nothing but common thugs. Carousing, lying, stealing . . . Shaw burned down five houses, Honor, *five*—counting his Ocean City condo—and a brand new car. And do you know why? So he could pay off his gambling debts with the insurance checks."

She filled Rerun's water bowl. "You actually have proof of all that."

"You bet your big gorgeous eyes, I do. I can prove every word I said about your precious *Wyatt,* too. Correction: I have evidence on the both of them, but because I didn't come by it in what you'd call a 'constitutional rights' kind of way, they might just get away with it. I just hope for your sake, that lousy investigator Shaw hired only made one set of photographs."

"Photographs? Of *me*?"

"Of you and Hoffman in some pretty compromising positions."

"But . . . but that's impossible!" This was the first she'd heard of any such thing. It was good to know, finally, what had initiated Matt's change in attitude toward her. Not so good, though, hearing that he'd seen photographs of . . . only God knew what. "How can there be pictures when nothing improper ever happened between Wyatt and me? Why, the two of us were never alone together. Jennifer and the kids were . . ."

And then she remembered three or four weekends when Jennifer and the kids had driven to Philly to relieve her older sister, who'd been taking care of their stroke-victim dad. Honor's heart pounded. Okay, so she and Wyatt had gone through the same workout routines and exercises during those weekends, and they'd hit the books long into the night, too. But he'd never so much as looked at her in anything but an older brother kind of way. "I'd like to see those pictures. They had to be Photoshopped. *Had to be.* Because we never got closer than . . ."

And *then* she remembered all the times Wyatt had steadied her as she struggled to hold the proper form during push-ups and how he'd kept her from clattering to the floor a couple of times when her arms turned to jelly, trying to squeeze out the required number of pull-ups. If Brady really had hired somebody to get a few candid shots, it wouldn't have been a difficult task, since the rear of the Hoffmans' house was constructed of curtain-less sliding doors and windows.

Honor explained all that to Matt, adding "See? See how dirty they're willing to fight? They'd destroy anyone who got in their way."

"In a heartbeat."

"And yet you aren't afraid what might happen now."

"If either of 'em had half a brain, they might be scary, but they're both as dumb as a box of rocks."

Troubling questions continued to plague her, and with each one answered, another took its place. "Matt. Those pictures . . . do you think Brady showed them to Wyatt?"

"Not a doubt in my mind. But that isn't why Hoffman dropped the arson charges."

Honor almost didn't want to know why he *had* dropped the charges.

"Shaw had pictures of some important people, coming and going from the Hoffman house at odd hours. And fat wads of cash changed hands."

Now Honor wished that when she moved away, she could take Matt and the boys with her. "Will you do me a favor, Matt?"

"You know I will."

"I need you to promise me something."

"I'll try."

" 'Do or do not,' " she said, " 'there *is* no try.' "

He chuckled quietly. "Okay, but first, tell me what I might be locking myself in to."

"You have to drop this. All of it. Forget about everything related to the whole Brady Shaw-Wyatt Hoffman mess. Get back to writing about plane crashes and autism and all the other in-depth stories your editor assigns. Focus on your boys and their soccer games. Be a friend to Austin and Mercy now that they're thinking about becoming parents. Forget about those awful pictures and the documents and the file and everything else and—"

"Hey, lighten up a little, will ya?"

Tears filled her eyes, and she knuckled them away. "Do I have your word?"

"Honor. Knock it off. You're starting to scare me."

"Promise?"

"This is starting to sound an awful lot like good-bye . . ."

She could not, would not say those words, even though that's exactly what this was . . . what it had to be, especially now that she knew that he'd willingly sacrifice himself—and those innocent boys—for her.

"Please, Matt. This is important to me."

"Okay. I promise."

"I know you're a man of your word. So you'll drop it. All of it. right now?"

"You're crying. Honor, what's wrong?"

"Nothing!" she all but shouted. "Except that I can't get you to make one little promise!"

"It's not so little, but okay, all right. I promise. You have my word: I'll drop it. All of it. Right now."

Honor sunk onto the seat of a kitchen chair. "Thank God. Thank *you*, Matt," she said.

And then she hung up and wept like a scared little girl.

Because that's exactly how she felt.

25

*T*he last time Matt felt this way, he'd been eleven years and one day old.

That day, from his seat on the top porch step, he'd tried to ignore the conversation taking place on the other side of the screen door. But nothing—not the drone of Mr. Miller's lawn mower or the squeak of Amber Wilson's saxophone—drowned out the angry voices. He hadn't looked up as his dad thumped past him, dragging that beat-up, old suitcase down the stairs. The last thing he'd learned in science class was how peripheral vision enabled people to see, even when things weren't right in front of their faces. And that's what told him his father had chucked the big bag into the trunk of his car.

He'd seen it all before, eighty-two times, to be precise. He knew, because he'd kept track of every departure and every return of his dad, the traveling marketing manager. That day, as he balanced a saucer of birthday cake on bony, scabby knees, he choked down a sickeningly sweet frosting flower, wishing all the while that math hadn't been his best subject. Because he'd never have attempted to scratch out the problem in frosting, using the tine of his fork: at eleven years old, he'd lived a total of 4,015 days, and of those, his dad had been gone 2,047.

When his dad trudged back up those gray-painted steps, Matt had put the cake plate aside, nodding and doing his best not to cry as his dad sat beside him and tried to explain. "This isn't your fault," he'd said. "Your mother and I just need some time apart." He'd promised to call every day. Said he'd come to get him for overnight visits, at least once a week. Then he drove off without so much as a wave or a smile, without even glancing in the rearview mirror.

Matt carried the cake inside, thinking he'd finish it at the kitchen table. That way, if he let go and a few tears fell, nobody would see and nobody could call him a whiny girl. Not Mr. Miller or Amber, and especially not that bully Harry Sanderson. But his mom had been in there, sobbing and wheezing into a paper towel, so he scraped the cake into the trash can and let the dog lick the plate clean . . . and hadn't eaten so much as a bite of birthday cake since.

He didn't know why, exactly, Honor's good-bye had hit him so hard. If he added up all the hours he'd spent with her, they probably wouldn't add up to a forty-hour workweek. He'd never kissed her—though he'd wanted to a couple hundred times— and physical contact had been limited to a hand to lead her here, an arm slung over her shoulders there, a half dozen hugs . . . and that one memorable night when she'd fallen asleep in his arms. *Aren't you the pathetic clod,* he thought, shaking his head, *holding on to that as your brightest moment with her.*

He'd tried, but Matt couldn't connect a moment like that to his years with Faith. He remembered crazy, scattered things, like the way he'd rub her hands when they came in from shoveling snow or the way they took turns refilling each other's coffee mugs on leisurely weekend mornings. She didn't like action-adventures, and he couldn't stomach chick flicks, which pretty much limited nights out at the movies. He loved Italian cuisine, her favorite was Asian, so they often laughingly thanked the good Lord for inventing good old American restaurants.

But a moment like that one with Honor? Nope. Not a one. Matt felt like a heel, downright awful, and guilty, because hadn't Faith earned a memory like that? He'd tried justifying it with half-baked rationale. He'd been too busy juggling a job and two kids. There hadn't been time for fluff like that, not with double diapers to change and two feedings every couple of hours. Then they started to crawl, and he'd spent every spare second and each ounce of energy keeping buttons out of their mouths and making sure they didn't take a header down the stairs. And once they were on their feet, toddling, then running like sprinters, well, it was all that, multiplied by a thousand.

Shouldn't he have felt something after he'd sopped up the bath bubbles and stuffed them into antileak diapers and patted the last burp from their round bellies? Or while he walked around picking up toy trucks and rubber balls and teddy bears? Matt knew he *should*. So then, why *didn't* he?

Just one reason he could think of, and because it made him feel even more like a heel, he did his best to drive it from his mind. A little more resentment toward Honor, he decided, might be just what the doctor ordered. Because before meeting her, he'd never given such things a thought. Now here he was, battling the ache of guilt because he couldn't come up with a single sweet Faith-memory to compare to those soul-stirring, heart-pounding hours, watching Honor sleep.

Watching her sleep!

He'd lost a big chunk of his mind since meeting her. It was as simple as that. Nothing else made sense, because not only did she have him thinking goofy, schoolboy thoughts, but she'd inspired his dogged determination to go after Shaw, and in the process, Hoffman, a decision that could have cost him everything and put his boys at risk, to boot. "Crazy," he muttered. "You've gone completely insane."

"What, Dad?"

Matt had worked hard to put on a good front for the boys' sake, but his heart sure wasn't in it. "Nothing, Steve. Just thinking out loud, that's all."

"Is there Alzheimer's in our family?"

Even in his present state of mind, Matt understood what had prompted the question. He'd been distracted, and on a couple of occasions, they'd caught him staring into space and called him on it. And now, he was talking to himself. "Not that I know of," he said, gently knuckling his son's blond head. "There's a lot going on at work."

Warner nodded. "Yeah. Sometimes it helps to work stuff out, out loud."

Steve giggled. "Only if you're, like, *retarded*," he said, elbowing his twin.

Matt knew the signs: if he didn't intervene, they'd be wrestling on the floor within minutes, and what started out as playful roughhousing would quickly turn into more serious brawling. And because Warner outweighed Steve by a good ten pounds, *some*body might get hurt. Matt was *almost* tempted to let them have at it, to teach Steve a lesson about buttoning his lip, and buy himself a few minutes to regain his composure.

"Don't even think about it," he warned. "It's too close to bedtime to get into it."

Warner narrowed his dark eyes. "First thing in the morning," he said, grinning as he aimed a forefinger at Steve, then himself, "you. Me. Here. Fight."

Steve's blond brows rose high on his forehead, and he sighed. "It's about time you got around to reading that chapter about Neanderthal man in your history book." He did his best to mimic his twin. "Ugh. Oomph. Duh. Doh."

Warner was about to smack him when Matt said, "Steven. Upstairs. Pajamas. Toothbrush. Now."

"Oh, no-o-o," he droned, clamping a hand over his eyes. "I'm *doomed*." He came out from hiding and took one look at Matt's stern face. "All right, okay. I'm going," he mumbled, heading for the stairs. On the landing, he stopped and draped himself over the railing. "I just have this to say: I know *exactly* what I'm gonna ask God for when I say *my* prayers tonight."

Don't fall for it, Warner, Matt thought. *It's a setup . . .*

"What?"

"That whatever is responsible for making you two talk like cavemen isn't hereditary, that's what."

He thundered the rest of the way up the steps as Warner flopped onto the sofa beside Matt. Slumping against the back cushions, he said, "Can I just slug him, Dad? *Please?*"

Matt drew the boy into a hug. "Not today, son."

"Tomorrow?"

"We'll see." He kissed the top of the boy's head and said his own prayer of thanks, for the blessing of two silly, lovable boys who filled his life with so much joy and laughter . . . and much-needed distraction.

∼⊘∼

Her new post paid well, far more than any to date, but it hadn't been as fulfilling as Honor had hoped it might be. This phase of the job involved hours of nonstop paperwork, the tedium of filing, making countless phone calls, and fact-checking every item on her lengthy To Do list. "Keep your eyes on that light at the end of the tunnel," she'd chant every morning as the subway clattered down the tracks connecting

Queens to the City. The tired old cliché didn't make the commute any easier, but at least it gave her something to focus on besides the dreary indoor tasks that kept her chained to a desk, instead of out in the field, doing the work she loved best: training dogs and their handlers.

Another major disappointment had been finding out that her base of operations was in New York, and not White Plains. Her salary would have added a considerable sum to her savings account every week . . . if she didn't need it to pay rent and buy subway tokens.

The one sunny spot in her otherwise dreary new world were Rerun and the ancient little house they called home. It wasn't such a bad little place, as houses go, but an all-concrete backyard, surrounded by an eight-foot privacy fence, made her feel like she lived in a shoebox. And Rerun made no secret of the fact that he wasn't crazy about doing his business on hardscape. What had taken minutes back home in Baltimore now ate up huge chunks of time. So Honor's priority, once she'd unpacked her meager personal possessions, was constructing a six-by-eight-foot-deep box. She filled it with store-bought dirt and planted an entire bag of Kentucky bluegrass seed. "Just be patient," she told him every time they went outside, "and in a few weeks, you'll have your own private bathroom." There wasn't a doubt in her mind that he'd understood every word because the dog kept a close and wary eye on his tiny plot of lawn, and woe unto any bird or bug that dared to land on the seed-protective burlap blanket.

While waiting for the grass to sprout, she searched hardware and department stores for an old-fashioned push mower, like the one her grandpa used. Mothers' Day had come and gone before she found one, and oh, the curious stares she inspired, rolling it home from the flea market. It took two days of scrubbing to remove years of neglect, and an entire Saturday afternoon to hone the blades to a shining-keen edge. She managed to get half of the plot mowed before the skies opened up, and didn't close again for eight straight days.

Fortunately, there was plenty to keep her busy, inside. After securing the permission of her landlady, Honor painted the pea-green kitchen cabinets bright white and replaced the black wrought-iron hardware with brushed nickel. In the powder room, she laid a checkerboard of shiny black and white tiles atop fading red linoleum, and the hall bath's walls went from Miss Piggy Pink to a soft sea foam green. She squeegeed every windowpane and hung fresh new curtains, then shampooed the living room rug and upholstery. By the time the rains stopped, she was more than ready to get outside, where she wire-brushed the cement slab in preparation for a coat of acid that turned it from dull gray to a soft russet that matched the cushions she'd bought for her high-backed redwood chairs.

She learned which shops carried the best produce, and where to buy quality pork chops and steaks to grill on her miniature hibachi. On occasion, Honor treated herself to a bouquet from the fanciful flower cart she passed walking home from the subway. Her neighbors were friendly and helpful and respectful of her privacy, and with the exception of elderly widow Nunzia Gelichi, no one asked "Why a *precioso* woman like-a you is no *casado*, eh?"

"I'm just not the marrying type," Honor had said, laughing. But alone, as night descended and sleep eluded her, she admitted the unhappy truth: she'd lost her fiancé at Ground Zero and left the only other man she'd ever loved in Baltimore. During her twice-weekly talks with Elton, she asked how Matt and the boys were doing. If Matt had moved on, her pal and former boss had the good grace not to mention it. Which put Honor in an awkward position: she meant every word of the prayers she sent heavenward, asking the good Lord to watch over him, to keep him safe and happy, but Honor had no desire to hear, firsthand or otherwise, that her prayers for his romantic contentment had been answered.

Now, sipping iced tea and paging through the Sunday paper, Honor sent a silent thanks to the grumpy Rottweiler that lived on the left side of her yard because his grizzly-like growls and persistent attempts to tunnel under the fence by pawing at the concrete helped distract her from thoughts of Matt and what might have been. "Too bad we can't help Beast find his way into Matilda's yard, isn't it?"

But he only stared at her. "You're right. That does seem a bit extreme, even if Matilda's nonstop yapping *is* maddening."

Summer was grinding to a steamy, sticky close, and still the place didn't feel like home, not to Honor, and certainly not to Rerun, who missed his big grassy yard and the cool basement tiles where he liked to sprawl on days like this.

Not a day went by that she didn't think of Matt. Or his boys. Or all three. She remembered making the bet with herself: putting her house on the rental market, packing, starting a new job would divert her attention, help her miss them less.

"Good thing you're not a gambler," she mumbled, heading into the air-conditioned house, "because you would have lost your shirt on that one."

26

As the tenth anniversary of 9/11 loomed on the horizon, every faction of the entertainment industry was working hard to get a fresh new slant on the story, Matt's newspaper was no exception. Even before he sat down in Liam's office, he had a pretty good idea why he'd been summoned.

Liam propped his red high-top Converse shoes on the corner of his desk and leaned back so far in his chair, Matt wondered what kept it from toppling backward.

"So how fast can you make arrangements for the twins and hop a train to New York?"

"Why don't we skip all the bush-beating and get to the point. When do you need me up there?"

"By Monday."

Matt glanced at the three-by-five calendar behind his boss's desk, where fat black scribbles noted story headlines, bylines, and deadlines. It shouldn't have surprised him, seeing his initials in the middle of five connecting boxes, but it did. "You're kidding, right? The anniversary celebrations don't get under way for weeks, yet."

"Hey, you oughta know by know that *this* old buzzard lives by the 'early bird gets the worm' philosophy." He leaned forward and propped both forearms on his desk. "I want the lowdown on what's gonna unravel and who'll pull that first string." He wiggled his eyebrows and snickered. "By the time those so-called network reporters deliver the obvious, folks will already know what's what." He pointed at Matt. "'Cause you're gonna tell 'em."

He hadn't been to New York in years. Ten, to be precise. He'd followed the progress being made by construction crews at Ground Zero, but only peripherally. Every line in every story only served as a black-and-white reminder of what the country lost that fateful day. Matt mentally ran down his list of friends killed in the line of duty and a fellow reporter who'd been in the South Tower, waiting to interview some hotshot Wall Street banker when the first plane hit.

Now Liam pointed due east, to bring Matt's attention to the bullpen. "Anybody out there would jump at the chance to write this one. You 'n' me both know that."

Matt followed the line of Liam's finger, gaze resting on the determined faces of coworkers . . . and competitors. His boss was right: any one of them would head north at a moment's notice. So why was *he* hesitating?

In a word: Honor.

She'd been gone five months, and the only contact he'd had with her in all that time had been occasional conversation from Elton, who talked to her several times a week. Whether she'd confided in her old SAR leader or he'd figured things out on his own, Matt couldn't say. But he was grateful as all get-out that the man kept finding legitimate excuses to call and update him.

Last Matt heard, she'd slogged through the paperwork aspect of the job and stood front and center for in-person training sessions. It surprised Matt to hear she wasn't happy up there because if anybody was cut out for work like that, it was Honor, who all but crackled with excitement at every chance to teach someone how to train a rescue dog.

"I'm sending you up there to work, not to schmooze. So you can wipe that hang-dog expression off your face."

Matt looked up so fast, a lock of hair fell across one eye.

"Just because she's there and you're there is no reason you have to see her." He chuckled, then added, "But if you do, you might want to spend a half hour in a barber's chair." That pointer finger wiggled in the air. "You're lookin' a mite ragged around the edges, if you don't mind my sayin'."

Matt finger-combed the hair back from his forehead. "Been busy. The boys. Scouts. Stuff, y'know?"

"Yeah. I know."

And if that expression was any indicator, Liam really *did* know. Having lost his wife of thirty-two years six months earlier, the grizzled editor was probably the only person in Matt's circle of friends and acquaintances who understood how big a hole Honor's leaving had carved in his life.

"So you can get Harriet to stay with the twins, then?"

"I'll have to check."

Liam shoved his phone closer to Matt's side of the desk and, with a wave of his hand, said, "Well?"

Matt had been calling Harriet's number for so many years, his finger could probably peck out the right keys in his sleep. She picked up on the second ring, her musical "Hello" so effusive that Liam winced and drew back as if blasted with a bucket of ice water.

"The answer is yes," she said, laughing.

"I haven't even asked the question yet!"

"You're calling to see if I'll mind those darlin' boys of yours, right . . . ?"

"Well, yeah, but—"

"Then the answer is yes."

"—but I'll need you for nearly a week. Round the clock at my place."

"And that's an issue because . . ."

Matt laughed, too. "I guess it isn't an issue. Liam's sending me to New York."

She gasped. "To cover the grand opening of the memorial at Ground Zero?"

For a gal who claimed not to like the news, she sure was up on the latest. "Yep."

"I can hardly wait to read what you'll write. You have such a wonderful way with words, Matthew."

Eyebrows raised, he said, "If I hand the phone to Liam, will you repeat that?"

"You'd better not."

"Uh, what?"

"I'm sure that poor man has a mountain of work on his desk. If I get started, singing your praises, he'll still be sitting there at midnight."

"Put on a pretty dress, Harriet Ruford. I'm taking you and the boys out for dinner tonight."

"Don't have any wine with dinner," Liam said as Matt shoved the phone back where it belonged. "You're leaving first thing in the morning." He handed Matt an Amtrak envelope. "Wouldn't want to be fuzzy-headed and miss the 10:10 train, now would you?"

Matt pocketed the tickets and thanked Liam, then hunkered down at his desk. He had two stories due by end of business. One, a 350-word piece on a new artist, exhibiting her paintings at The Gallery in Ellicott City, and the other, a 750-word feature about a kid with terminal cancer who spent his free time painting comic book heroes on his fellow Hopkins patients' forearms. If I hoped to do justice to either—and get them turned in by deadline time—I'd better get his mind off of New York . . . and a certain gorgeous gal who now called the Big Apple home.

⌒⌒

The familiar voice, spilling from the answering machine, greeted her the minute she opened the front door. Heart racing and pulse pounding, Honor's hands shook so hard she could barely get the key out of the lock.

"*. . . four days,*" he was saying, "*and I'm hoping you'll let me take you to dinner one of those nights.*"

She let Rerun out back, then kicked off her shoes and stood trembling from her rain-dampened head to panty-hosed feet. "How did he get your number?" she wondered aloud. And then she said, "Elton." The man had consistently delivered news about Matt and the boys, twice weekly—sometimes more— since she'd arrived in New York that last week of March. Nearly every night, she'd heard his DJ-like baritone in her dreams. Hearing it now, *almost* live-and-in-person, jarred her more than she cared to admit.

Rerun scratched at the door, and she let him in, then played the message again. And again:

"*Hey, Honor. It's me, Matt. I know, I know . . . long time no talk to, eh?*"

Her fingertips slid slowly over the telephone's keys as he laughed. Oh, how she'd missed the sound if it!

"*Liam's sending me to New York. Ground Zero story. I'll proba- bly be there before you even have a chance to listen to this message.*" He rattled off the name and number of the hotel where he was staying near Ground Zero. "*I, ah, I'm hoping you'll call me when you get in. I'd, ah, I'd really like to see you while I'm in town. I'll be there for four days, and I'm hoping you'll let me take you to dinner one of those nights.*"

⌒ *197* ⌒

Eyes closed, Honor held her breath. Rerun recognized his voice and, resting his chin on the edge of the end table, nudged her hand. "Oh, boy. Aren't you the master of subtlety," she joked, ruffling his fur.

But the dog just sat there, smiling up at her with that expressive amber-eyed face.

"You think I should call him?"

Rerun's whispery *woof* startled her enough to make her hit the Play button again.

". . . I'm hoping you'll call me when you get in . . ."

Well, what could it hurt to call? He'd probably be out and about, anyway, scouting out facts for his story. She'd leave a message, and he'd respond to it while she was at work tomorrow, and so it would go until he went back to Baltimore. *Where he belongs.*

She wondered if this was how Mercy had felt, when she opened her door in that Chicago apartment building and saw Austin standing in her hallway. Mercy had freely admitted that back then, she'd been a die-hard atheist who'd refused to give God a try, even to ease Austin's mind. He'd already lost so much, Mercy said, before they'd met: he was still in grade school when his dad was killed in a convenience store robbery, a hotshot young cop when his brother vanished into the smoke and rubble of the North Tower, then cancer took his mom. Losing his job as a New York cop had been final blow, and started him on a downward spiral that continued until Griff, his AA sponsor-turned-friend, introduced Austin to Christ. He'd been holding on—just barely—when a stray bullet, fired into a ghetto soup kitchen, took Griff, too. Honor remembered how it put tears in Mercy's eyes, remembering Austin's confession: he didn't want to choose, but if she forced him to, he'd choose God.

And yet by some miracle, Mercy and Austin got past stubbornness and bitterness and attitudes born of past hurts. Reason enough to hope that she and Matt could overcome the things separating them?

Maybe . . . if she could make herself step out in faith, as Mercy and Austin had done.

"If," she said, handing a biscuit to Rerun, "the biggest little word in the English language."

☙

Matt lathered up his face and stood shirtless in the mirror. Hard to believe, he thought as he stared at his reflection, that he'd been in town two days already and still no word from Honor.

He aimed his chin at the ceiling and dragged the razor from collarbone to jawbone. Ironic, he thought, as the blades *scritch-scratched* across his skin; if his nerves could make noise, that's exactly how they'd sound.

A few mid-afternoon thunderstorms had blown through the area; maybe she'd lost power and didn't get his message. But if she had, and he called again, how would that make him look?

"Like a man who's desperate to know where he stands," he said, stretching his mouth as far left as it would go. After shaving the right cheek, he moved to the left, rinsing the stubbly foam from the razor after just a couple of swipes. "Give her until tonight," he told himself. "Then go home and write your story."

An old Milt Kellum tune played in his head: *Got along without ya before I met ya, gonna get along without ya now.*

"Yeah, well, that's a whole lot easier said than done."

And then his cell phone rang, startling him so badly he nicked his jaw. "Blast," he said, dabbing at the bloody spot with a balled up tissue. "Who in blue blazes—"

"Hi, Matt. It's me, Honor. Too early to call?"

As if she needed to identify herself. He'd recognize that voice in a rush-hour crowd at Penn Station. "No, no. 'Course not." He sat on the edge of his mattress, alternately looking at the tissue and pressing it to his cut. "My first appointment isn't until noon. Lunch thing with the mayor. I don't need to leave here for a good thirty minutes yet." He groaned to himself. "I'm glad you called. Thought for a while there maybe you didn't get my message. That was some storm blew through here yesterday."

"Yeah. Knocked out power for a lot of folks."

"So how's the new job?"

"It's . . . it's fine, just fine. I'm calling from work, actually, so if all of a sudden I have to hang up, I'll call back."

"Gotcha."

"How are the boys? I'll bet they've each grown a foot since I saw them at the wedding."

"They're good. Great, actually." Had it really come to this? Would they spend the rest of their lives swapping weather stats and other trivia? *That,* he supposed, *depends on whether or not you stay in touch.* "Are you out in the field yet, or do the bureaucrats still have you all bound up with red tape?" She laughed, and the delicious sound of it trilled all the way down to his bare toes.

"I'll admit, those first weeks were about as exciting as watching dust collect on the coffee table. I can't tell you how many times I nearly packed up and went home out of sheer frustration and boredom . . ."

I wish you had, he thought, wondering if she realized that she'd called Baltimore *home.*

". . . but eventually, I slogged through the mountain of paperwork, and came up with a plan that appeased the higher-ups. And now, I'm happy to say, I get to play outside with all the big kids."

Aw, Honor, he thought, *do you have any idea how much I've missed you?* "I want to hear all about it, but if I don't get a move on, I'll be late."

"Oh. Right." She giggled. "Can't keep the mayor waiting, now can you?"

"Well, I could, but I won't. At least not until after I get some decent quotes."

"Sure. I understand."

"So, are you free for dinner tonight?"

Even the slight hesitation unnerved him enough to curl his toes. Literally. He flattened both feet on the pilled carpeting, waiting, waiting for her answer.

"When do you go back to Baltimore?"

"Day after tomorrow. On the 8 a.m. train."

"That's wonderful! Not that you're leaving, of course, but that you have some time before you do. I don't have any plans, but—"

No, not a but, he thought as his toes curled up. Again.

"—but where are you staying?"

"Times Square. Why?"

"Well, I'm thinking maybe it would be easier if you took the subway here, and I fixed dinner for us here. I only live a block from the Main Street Station."

"No kidding? I used to live near there. I remember lots of good restaurants. Wouldn't you rather eat out after working all day?"

"Wouldn't you rather have a home-cooked meal after eating out all week?"

"Oh, you can't tell *you're* Irish . . . answering a question with a question . . ."

"I hate to be picky, but Mackenzie is Scottish. It means Son of Coinneach," she said, emulating a thick brogue.

"It also means fiery and handsome, so I guess there's something to this name-picking stuff."

"So what's your preference? I can throw steaks or pork chops on the grill, or—"

"Fix whatever you'd make if I wasn't coming over. My mom used to say she could put salt and pepper on a rock and I'd eat it, so you can hardly go wrong feeding me."

She started reciting her address and phone number when he stopped her with, "Whoa. Slow down. Let me grab a pen. And paper." Matt rummaged in the drawer beneath the phone and found both, and after he'd written the information down, she told him to stop by any time after five, and he hung up wishing she'd said four.

But who was he kidding? He wouldn't have been happy unless she'd said *now*.

27

"Nice place," he said, nodding approvingly as she hung his sweatshirt jacket on the hall tree.

"Oh, it'll do. Keeps the wind out of my hair, what more can I ask?"

"Something smells delicious . . ."

"Veal Parmesan."

"You must be a mind reader. I've been craving Italian for weeks."

Rerun padded up and sat beside her, then edged forward when Matt held out his hand. "Better watch it. Once this big lummox decides he likes you, you're stuck for the duration."

Squatting, Matt stroked the dog's ears. "That's okay. He'll help me miss Cash less."

All day, she'd been too nervous to concentrate on anything, and rather than wait for one of the guys to notice her jitters—and ask what had caused them—Honor had left work early. After getting supper started, she'd tidied the house, wondering with nearly every step how long it would take, once Matt arrived, for the tension to wear off. Their last conversation hadn't exactly ended on an up note, after all. But the instant she opened the front door and saw him standing there on her porch, smiling that *smile* of his, the worry just melted away. And what a relief to know that, if they couldn't be a couple, at least they could be friends.

Honor peeked at the tiny digital timer, clipped to her apron pocket. "Three minutes before the pasta's done. Just enough time for a tour, if you're interested."

"You bet I am."

Honor pointed at the scatter rug beneath his feet. "Foyer." She did a half-turn and gestured toward the sofa. "Living room." Another half turn. "Dining room." Then to the end of the hallway, where she opened the narrow, six-panel door. "Bathroom. And notice, if you will, the beautiful condition of the claw-foot tub and octagonal tiles." Now she pointed to the door beside him. "That's the guest room, and this is the master bedroom." Arms akimbo, she added, "Voila!"

"I like it," he said as she led the way to the kitchen. "It's very . . . *you.*"

"I was just putting the finishing touches on dessert when you rang the bell. Can I get you anything to drink while I top it off? Soda, iced tea, lemonade . . . ?"

"Iced tea sounds good." But Matt didn't wait for her to serve him. Instead, he helped himself.

"How'd you know exactly where to find the glasses?"

He winked. "Oh, I have my ways." He patted Rerun's head. "Isn't that right, boy?"

She pulled out a kitchen chair, then went back to chopping vegetables for the salad. "Make yourself at home."

"So was it tough," he said, taking a seat, "adjusting to big-city life after living in the Baltimore suburbs for so long?"

"Does anyone ever fully adjust to it?"

"Now that you mention it, I suppose that would explain why New Yorkers talk so loud."

"So you didn't have any trouble finding the house?"

"Not a bit. You gave me some great directions. Besides, I lived in Flushing for years. Until . . ."

Honor put the salad bowls on the table. "Until 9/11?"

Matt nodded.

They'd done a good bit of talking, prior to tonight, about his boys and his work, about the Brady Shaw fiasco, and Mercy and Austin's roller-coaster relationship, but this was the first time that particular date had come up. The very mention of it made him look at least as uncomfortable as she felt, and so she changed the subject. "I've lived all my life in Baltimore. Except for my time at St. Johns, that is."

He got up and washed his hands, then opened the drawer beside the sink and gathered up two forks, two butter knives, and two spoons. "No kiddin'," he said, arranging them on paper napkins, "you went to college here in Queens?" He went back to the cabinet for plates. "What was your major?"

"I enrolled in the EMS program, you know, to become a paramedic?" She did her best to abbreviate the story of how she'd quit school when the active, alert grandparents who'd raised her grew suddenly frail, as if they'd decided to wither and die, together. During the months she cared for them, conversation revolved around medications, adult diapers, and what time "that nice Irish boy, Conan O'Brien" came on. Her grandfather passed first, and within weeks, her grandmother followed.

"Gee, Honor. I'm sorry."

"Water under the bridge," she said, dumping the pasta into the colander.

"If I'm not being too nosey, why did they have to raise you?"

"Long, boring story. In a nutshell, my folks died in a car wreck." She soaked the noodles with thick red sauce, then discharged a burst of nervous laughter. "And my grandparents had the space."

Matt winced. "How old were you? When you moved in with them, I mean?"

"Eleven."

"That's how old I was when my dad moved out."

She met his eyes, saw the pain that still glittered there. One more thing they had in common, it seemed.

"You must have some genuine Italian in you."

"On my mother's side." She put the pot on the table. "With a name like Mackenzie, how'd you figure that out?"

"I dated a girl in high school. Whole family was Italian." All four fingertips touched his thumb. "This, this-a how *real Pisanos*, they eat-a the pasta."

Laughing, Honor laid the veal cutlets onto a plate, poured the leftover sauce into a bowl, and put both onto the table. "Well," she announced, "it's ready. *Mangiare!*"

Matt filled her plate, then filled his own, and they spent the next hour talking about her job, about the story Liam had sent him to New York to write. He told her that Steve had figured out how to download photographs from their digital camera onto the computer, and turn them into slide shows. And Warner? "He wasted no time figuring out how to mess it up, just to bug Steve."

Laughing, Honor started the coffeemaker, then submersed their plates and flatware into soapy dish water.

"What, no dishwasher?"

She wiggled her fingers. "With just one of everything, I don't really need one."

They spent the next hour in the living room, sipping coffee and nibbling at the fudge brownie cake she'd made for dessert, Matt slouched at one end of the sofa, Honor sitting cross-legged at the other.

"So you were saying, about your grandparents?"

"Oh. Right. So anyway," she continued, "Gramps and Gran made my fiancé and me promise to give all of their clothes to Goodwill. So there we sat one sunny morning, surrounded by cartons and bushel baskets and stacks of old clothes, watching TV as we stuffed cardboard boxes with corduroy slippers, flannel PJs, and initialed white hankies. We were holding up a pair of underpants big enough to sail a boat, laughing our fool heads off, when the screen flashed . . . and we saw the first jet collide with the first tower. Then the second one hit. We sat there for hours, just watching, like somebody had glued our shoes to the floor. By the time he reported for duty that night, the terrorists had already claimed credit for the attacks. John called me from the station—he was assigned to Engine Company 42—and said that half of the guys were in tears when he got there, and the other half were crazy-mad and talking revenge. All of them, he said, felt like they just had to *do* something, but they didn't know what."

Matt was sitting forward now, elbows balanced on his knees, clenching and unclenching his hands in the space between.

"And that," she continued, "is when *John* came up with the bright idea to go up there."

"To Ground Zero."

She nodded. "To help with the search for people buried in the debris."

A heavy sigh escaped Matt's lips. "Yeah. I remember digging until my hands bled, trying to help Austin find his twin." Eyes closed, he shook his head. "Everybody was looking for somebody . . . cops, firefighters, Port Authority guys, paramedics . . ." He reached out and grabbed her hand. "So what happened to John and the guys from 42?"

"They all came back, some a little banged up and bloody, some with broken fingers and toes . . . except John." She sighed. "John never came home at all."

He reached across the center cushion and gave her hand a little squeeze. "That's rough. *Really* rough, and I'm sorry as I can be."

"He's the reason I became a firefighter. I wanted to do something to honor his memory, and his sacrifice. He's the reason it was so hard, giving it up when . . ."

Now Matt was beside her, one big hand on her shoulder, the other cupping her chin. "Hush," he said, looking deep into her eyes, "I think we've talked enough about 9/11, and John, and Austin's twin." After pressing a brotherly kiss to her forehead, he got to his feet. "I could go for another cup of coffee. How 'bout you?"

"There might be enough for half a cup each."

Honor had no reason to feel such disappointment about that kiss. She'd told herself the job change, the move to New York was a sound, rational decision, made after careful thought and heartfelt prayer. But the truth was she hadn't hit her knees or opened the Bible or anything of the kind. Instead, she'd jumped online to see what jobs might be available and, seeing the quick reply from Buzz as some sort of sign from above, rode the wave of events until one day she found herself unpacking boxes of clothes and Rerun's favorite toys in a tiny old house in Queens, wondering why anyone in their right mind would slap thick pea-green enamel anywhere, let alone on kitchen cabinets.

She hurried into the kitchen, knowing even before she slid two mugs from the cabinet shelf that the reason her legs felt like rubber and her feet as heavy as blocks of wood was that if she'd been honest with herself, they might just have had a shot at the same kind of happiness Austin and Mercy had found.

Now, what chance did they have, with him in Baltimore and her all the way up here in Queens?

"I'm in the mood for cake," she said. "And you know what? I think I'd rather have milk instead of coffee." Turning to ask if he'd like that, too, Honor nearly crashed into him. "Goodness," she said, fumbling to regain her balance, "I think you need to start wearing a bell around your neck." The heat of a blush started somewhere at the mid-calf point and crept slowly upward, until her cheeks felt hotter than if she'd spent hours outside in the midday sun. "You move like a cat," she laughed nervously, wincing inwardly at the harsh, high-pitched sound. And good old solid-as-a-rock Matt just stood there, calm as you please, aiming that gorgeous, slanting half smile at her.

"Sorry," he said, relieving her of the mugs. "Didn't mean to scare you."

Well, you do *scare me,* she thought, taking the milk from the fridge. *You scare me to death.* Her analytical left brain saw the logic of picking up and moving hours from the only place she'd ever called home. Her right brain wanted to go with her gut—or, more accurately, with her heart—and throw herself into his arms and admit that despite her best efforts *not* to, she'd fallen crazy in love with him anyway.

He'd filled both mugs and slid them into the microwave before she closed the refrigerator door. "What's that for?" he asked when she put the jug onto the counter.

"I, ah, gosh." Another round of ridiculous giggling. "I really have no idea, because I know you take yours black, same as me." Honor put the milk away, wishing she could climb onto the shelf beside it and *just chill out* before she came right out and said something totally inane, like, "Kiss me like you mean it, you big goof, because I love you like crazy!"

"Hey, wait a minute," he said, pressing the Stop button in the microwave. "You said you wanted milk, not coffee, didn't you?"

"Um, yeah, come to think of it, I did!"

And there he stood in the middle of the kitchen, one ceramic mug in each big hand and nose wrinkled like a kid who'd just tracked mud onto his mom's clean kitchen floor. "You're not one of those people who saves leftover supper coffee for breakfast, are you?"

"Um, no, I'm not."

"Okay to dump it, then?"

She felt like the little plastic dachshund that used to sit in the back window of her grandfather's Oldsmobile, head bobbing with every bounce and bump of the car. "Sure. Of course. And just leave those mugs in the sink. I'll wash them later." *After you're back in your hotel room, and I'm here alone, looking for that place in the floor that's supposed to swallow people whole when they act like* complete idiots!

"Well, no need to dirty two more glasses. I'll rinse the mugs while you slice the cake."

It wasn't until she uncovered the cake plate that she noticed the time. "Oh, my gosh," she said, pointing at the clock. "Not that I'm rushing you, because I'm not. Honest. I'm enjoying this visit a whole lot more than you know." What *was* it about him, she wondered, that made her run off at the mouth this way! "It's been great seeing you, really it has, but I wouldn't want you to miss your train. I mean, I know the daytime subway schedule by heart, but—"

He stepped up and dropped both hands on her shoulders. "Honor . . . ?"

"Matt."

"Uh-oh." A smile tilted his mouth and crinkled at the corners of his eyes. "We're not going *there* again, I hope."

"Evidently, we already did." He'd cut himself shaving, she noticed, looking up into his face. Gently, Honor touched a fingertip to the tiny scrape. "What happened there?"

He wrapped her hand in his and shuffled forward a half step. "Got a phone call while I was shaving this morning. Startled me."

"Not my phone call, I hope."

A quick shrug was his answer.

"Oops. Sorry."

If he heard the apology, Matt showed no signs of it. He seemed way too busy, searching her face for . . . Honor would have paid a high price to know the reason for his intense scrutiny.

When he broke eye contact, it was as if a light went off. She watched him tilt his face toward the ceiling, Adam's apple bobbing as he swallowed, then gave her hand a slight squeeze. "Guess I'd better skip the second dessert," he said, tapping the face of his wristwatch. "If memory serves, the trains run all night, but what if I'm wrong?"

It seemed pretty cut and dry to her: if that happened, he'd just have to come back and bunk down on the sofa. He might see it otherwise, but she could think of worse things than falling asleep, knowing he was just a few yards away. Honor wondered if he snored. Or talked in his sleep. Wondered, too, why it felt as though she might burst into tears at any moment.

Honor took a careful and deliberate step back. "Well," she said, testing her voice, "if you get there and the last train has left the station, promise me you won't take a taxi back to Manhattan."

He chuckled. "You sure are a demanding little thing."

Honor would have asked what he meant—if she didn't already know the answer. "Sorry," she said again. "I didn't mean to come across as difficult, but I honestly believed it was best for all concerned if you put that whole Brady-Wyatt thing to rest." She shrugged. "Fact is, I still believe it."

"Well," he said, shrugging into his sweatshirt jacket, "I'm nothing if not obedient."

He had his back to her, so she couldn't tell if his retort had been sarcastic, or if it only sounded that way.

Matt patted his wide sweatshirt pocket and withdrew a silver-wrapped package. "I can't believe I forgot to give this to you," he said, handing it to her. "Sort of a combination house-warming, congratulations on the new job, thanks for dinner kinda thing."

Her hands were shaking when she accepted it, and those threatening tears seemed ever closer now. "Matt, I-I don't know what to say."

"You don't have to *say* anything," he teased. "Just open it."

Honor left the stick-on silver bow in place and peeled off the wrapper to expose a shiny black box, slightly bigger than a paperback novel. Under its lid, a blanket of white tissue paper that hid a weathered old book. "I don't believe it," she whispered, following the contours of each bold letter, etched deep into the worn brown leather. "*White Fang*," she read aloud. And inside, just as she suspected, proof that what she held in her shaky hands was a first edition of the classic novel. When Honor looked up, she could tell that he was smiling, even through the misty fog of her tears. "Oh wow, Matt, it's . . . it's just . . . it's *incredible*."

"So you like it, then?"

Hugging it to her chest, she bit her lower lip and nodded. When at last she found her voice, Honor said, "Like it? I *love* it." *And I love* you, *for knowing that of all the books out there, this would be the perfect choice.* "Thank you seems a pretty lame thing to say after unwrapping a gift this special, but thanks, Matt. I'll treasure it, always."

Rerun sat on his haunches, head bobbing as he sniffed the air around the book. "Times like these, I wish dogs could talk." Crouching, he gave the golden a sideways hug. "What historic trivia could you tell us, based on what that amazing nose of yours is telling *you*."

Standing, he wrapped his hand around the doorknob. "Well, thanks for supper. Everything was delicious. You were right. This was a whole lot better than a restaurant meal."

"I'm glad you enjoyed it."

"You've ruined me, though. I'll never order Veal Parmesan again. No way any chef could top that meal."

"Please. Stop. You're making me blush."

He chucked her chin. "You want me to stop, you'll have to stop standing there looking so gorgeous, all pink-cheeked and blinking those big green eyes of yours."

"You know what?"

"No, but I have a sneaking suspicion you're about to tell me."

"I think you enjoy embarrassing me."

Matt's smile faded slightly as he opened the interior door. "The truth shouldn't embarrass you, Honor." One hand on the screen door's latch, he squinted and rubbed his chin. "What's that old saying?"

"The truth shall set you free," they said together.

"Yeah. That."

And then they laughed.

"I don't want to make you late for your train," she said, "but before you go, do you mind answering one question?"

"Shoot."

"*White Fang* is one of my favorite stories, ever. And in my opinion, Jack London is just about one of the best writers who ever lived—present company excluded, of course."

He bobbed his head and assumed a haughty expression. "But of course."

"How did you *know* all of that? I don't remember discussing books or authors with you."

One beefy shoulder rose in a quick shrug. "Y'know, I don't think I can give you a satisfactory answer, because the truth is, that baby found me, not the other way around."

Honor hummed the *Twilight Zone* theme music.

"No. Seriously. I was standing in line, waiting to pay for that antique platter and bowl set I gave Austin and Mercy for a wedding gift and saw it on the top shelf behind the counter. I could see right away what it was, in spite of the cobwebs. So while the girl wrapped them up, I asked to see it. Sneezed for half an hour after blowing the dust off its cover, but the instant I opened it up," he said, standing at attention, oath hand in the air, "it called your name."

"You mean to say you've had this since . . ." Honor did some quick math. "You've had it for *eight months?*"

"Closer to nine, but yeah. I wanted to clean it up a bit, give it plenty of time to breathe, so that when I finally gave it to you, it wouldn't stink of mold and mildew." Thumb and forefinger nearly touching, he said, "Half a dozen times, I came *this* close to mailing it to you. After Elton told me you were in New York, I mean. I shopped and shopped for the right card to go with it and came up dry, every time. Now, I'm glad Hallmark hadn't figured out to say, well . . . Let's just say it was worth the frustration, because if the U.S. postal service *had* delivered it, I would've been deprived of seeing that *look* on your face when you opened the box."

She didn't know which was harder to believe, that it had been that long since the wedding, or that he'd known her well enough to choose just the right gift.

"I wrote a little something inside," Matt said, stepping onto the porch, "but now it's *my* turn to enforce a promise."

"Oh?"

"You have to promise not to read it until I'm out of sight. Completely."

"Okay. I promise."

He had one foot on the top step, one on the second when he turned. "Oh. And another thing . . ."

"*Two* promises?"

"You got two. Why not me?"

"Can't argue with logic like that, now can I?"

It took just two long strides to put him back in the foyer. "For the luvva Pete," he said, gathering her so close that the corners of the book dug into her ribs. Then he cupped her face in his hands and bored into her eyes with an intensity that sent a shudder of warmth down her spine. His lips grazed her jaw and her eyelids, her cheeks and her chin, and when at last they touched her lips, there was nothing brotherly or "just friends" about it. The kiss seemed to go on and on, and yet it ended entirely too soon, leaving Honor breathless and wobbly-legged and wishing she'd had the presence of mind to bank every touch and breath and sigh to memory, so that when loneliness descended, she could withdraw the lovely memory and revel in its sweet warmth.

It took him a moment to untangle himself from her arms, and when he did, Matt raked both hands through his hair. "Two promises, remember?"

Smiling, Honor nodded, for she couldn't for the life of her remember what he was talking about.

He held up one finger. "Don't read the inscription until I'm out of sight." His index finger joined the first. "And for the luvva Pete, Honor, do a better job of staying in touch, will ya? Please?"

Then he turned on his heel and jogged down the steps and out of sight.

Honor slumped onto the sofa and hugged the book tight. He wouldn't have needed to elicit that second oath, because even if she'd peeked inside the instant his size-twelve shoes hit the sidewalk, her tears would have prevented her from reading his inscription.

28

*D*uring that first week following his visit, Honor picked up the phone no fewer than half a dozen times a day. Mostly, she just stared at the buzzing receiver before slamming it back into the cradle. Once she'd dialed all but the last digit of his cell phone number, and then pushed the flat gray disconnect button.

She didn't have to wait long, as it turned out, to get back into the swing of things. Classes had started, and no one anticipated double enrollment in every session. "If I'd known we'd be such a hit," she teased Buzz one busy afternoon, "I'd have added a couple of zeros to my salary requirement."

"You're Irish," he'd shot back, "so consider Murphy's Law: if you had, the bottom would've fallen out of this thing, and you'd be collecting unemployment instead of gray hairs."

The department had given her permission to hire a secretary, to be shared with Buzz. He kept her so busy, typing and filing and photocopying, that Honor took pity on her and carried her own workload alone. Surprisingly, that load lightened, thanks to Buzz's new assistant. Not so surprisingly, it didn't lighten enough to take her mind off Matt.

He popped into her head at the most peculiar moments. Once, while collecting quizzes, she called a female student Matt, simply because her eyes were the same shade of brown as his. While daydreaming about him at a red light the other day, the light turned green. The guy behind her leaned so hard on his horn that it got stuck . . . and she'd heard the annoying blare for blocks. Then, yesterday, she dialed the front desk to ask the security guard if the package containing her new cell phone had been delivered, and said, "That book is my all-time favorite present" instead.

Somehow her work got done, despite her woolgathering. But she was torn: hearty enrollment meant good things for the future of the program, but as the only qualified teacher on the roster, her work seemed never-ending. She watched her students closely, searching out those who had what it took to certify *and* become competent instructors. It took weeks to find two capable candidates, and within weeks, Honor felt comfortable leaving them to share the lectern for short periods of time.

Now, as she dialed Matt's cell, her star pupils were running the show in Classroom B. She didn't expect to leave them there for long. It had taken less than a minute to leave every other message in his voicemail box. Why should this call be any different? Yawning as she counted the rings, Honor tapped a fingertip on her desk. She'd recited the same information so often, *she* felt like a recording.

"Well, it's about time," he said.

Hearing his voice delighted—and terrified—her. "You're a hard man to reach."

"Said the kettle to the pot." Matt laughed. "So how are things?"

"Busy, but I'd be hard-pressed to name someone who isn't saying that these days."

"And that goofy mutt of yours?"

"I took a chance on him, finally, and he's doing great in the rescue program. I believe one day soon, another K-9 hero will be living under my roof."

"I can almost see him now: 'I want to thank the American Rescue Dog Association for this beautiful medal . . .'"

Laughing, Honor shook his head. My, but it was good to hear his voice, and not a crackling recording of it. "So what are the boys up to these days?"

"Working hard at hardly working. I threatened to take a coal shovel into their room the other day and toss everything I found on the floor into a trash can. Trouble with that is, I can't afford to replace all those school clothes and toys."

"Aw, don't be so hard on 'em, *Dad*. Christmas isn't that far off. I'm sure Santa will come through for you."

The mention of the holiday made her remember last year's celebrations and family dinners. She'd no doubt get an invitation to join Buzz, but even if she said yes—which wasn't likely—it wouldn't be as good as last year. "So what's this I hear about you getting back into the field? I thought you gave that up, because of the boys."

"True on both counts—and have I told you how great it is to hear your voice?"

"Funny. I was thinking the same thing a minute ago."

"Well, now, that's a silly thing to say. You hear your voice all the time."

Honor groaned, and Matt said, "Sorry. Too much time around eleven-year-olds, I guess."

"Did they like what I sent them for their birthday?"

"I'll say. They've seen three movies in three weeks and, thanks to that generous gift card, took a pal with 'em each time. But you know what? They would have preferred having you here to a present."

"I know. And I'm sorry. I would have loved to be there. But I'm glad they liked the gift cards. They're growing up so fast, it's hard to know what they'll like."

"Tell me about it. One thing they like is *you*. I'll bet not a day goes by that one of them doesn't mention you or ask about you. Which reminds me, they wanted me to find out what you're doing this Thanksgiving."

Honor automatically turned to the November page in her desk calendar. She didn't know why, because of course she couldn't join them. "I have classes right up until the Wednesday before, and after a short break, they pick up again the following Monday."

"What time does your last class end on Wednesday?"

"I'm usually home by eight, eight-thirty. Why?"

"Because if you made a reservation now, you could catch a train late Wednesday and stay right through Sunday. The kids would love that."

I'd love it, too.

"And so would I."

"But I don't have anyone to take care of Rerun."

"So? Talk to your vet. Get him to prescribe some tranquilizers and crate the big boy. He'd love it here, with Cash and the boys and a yard to run around in. The guest room has its own bath. You could think of it as a mini vacation."

"Let me see what I can arrange and get back to you."

"Oh . . . Harriet says to tell you hi. Same goes for Bud and Flora, and Mercy and Austin. And hey, speaking of whom . . . breaking news: Mercy is pregnant."

"What? Pregnant! No kidding? That's fantastic! I'll bet Austin's chest is so puffed up, he's popping all the buttons off his shirts."

"Yeah. He's pretty psyched, all right."

"And Mercy? Is she all right, too?"

"Well, sure. Far as I know. Why wouldn't she be?"

"No reason." Honor remembered that long conversation she and Mercy had last Thanksgiving, when an emergency pulled Austin from the dinner table. She must love her man a lot to risk losing him *and* risk being left to raise a house full of little Finleys, alone.

What about you, Honor wondered. *Could you step out in faith that way?* It was certainly something to think—and pray—about. "When is the baby due?"

"Mid-November, I think."

"Do they know yet if it's a boy or a girl?"

"Didn't think to ask."

"Men."

"What can I say? We have more important things to worry about, like whether or not our favorite girl will come home for the holidays."

Home. Oh, but that sounded wonderful! She tried not to focus too intently on the favorite girl part of his comment. "Well, it's something to consider."

"Something to *seriously* consider."

"Okay, seriously." She smiled. "I'll call you."

"Soon, I hope."

"Yes, soon."

"And with any luck, you won't have to leave a message." Then, "By the way, have you had a chance to read the book?"

"*White Fang,* you mean? I've paged through it, but I'm a little afraid to actually *read* it. The pages are so delicate."

"Books are meant to be enjoyed, Honor. Read it. Trust me, it's stronger than it looks, sorta like you. Besides, who knows what you might find on those delicate pages that you never saw before."

It had been her favorite novel ever since Mrs. Lester made it required reading in the seventh grade. "I guess it can't hurt to read the story a nineteenth time."

They said their good-byes, and she made the obligatory promise to try and spend Thanksgiving in Baltimore . . . then closed her calendar and quoted Thomas Wolfe as she headed for the classroom: "You can't go home again."

29

*H*onor got the call in the dead of night: a little girl, barely older than Matt's twins, reported missing from her bed.

"I know you've put in a full day," Buzz said, "but this guy's a friend. Closer than a friend, really . . . more like a brother. He'd be obliged, *I'd* be obliged, if you and Rerun could get out there, join the team to see what you can find." He trusted her more than any SAR team member he'd ever worked with; if she couldn't come up with something, he said, here probably wasn't anything to come up *with*.

It had been tough, saying good-bye when Buzz moved the family north, but times had been tough and good jobs even tougher to find, so Honor said and did what it took to keep the lines of communication open. If she'd done things differently, Buzz wouldn't have hired her, and she wouldn't be in New York right now, taking a call from one of the best . . . and a man she admired.

It had been a while since she'd been shaken out of bed by a "get up, go now" call. Fortunately, old habits die hard, and the tablet and pen on her bedside table were within easy reach when Buzz rattled off the search coordinates. Her sturdy canvas-and-leather pack hung, fully loaded, on a hook beside the front door, too; two minutes after hanging up, she was dressed, and in three, she and Rerun were out the door.

Sleep hadn't exactly been a friendly visitor these past few months, so drowsiness and exaggerated yawns at her desk hadn't surprised her. But a thing like this had the power to energize Honor like nothing else could. A missing child? Who didn't get revved up by the possibility of finding and returning her to the loving arms of her parents?

Honor tried and failed to drive the speed limit and rolled up in record time. The intersection Buzz mentioned wasn't marked by a street sign, but the strobes of police cars slicing into the blackness made it pretty clear she'd arrived at the right location. As she strapped on her pack and snapped Rerun's vest into place, Honor spotted the search manager right off . . . a big bulky man with a clipboard and a no-nonsense attitude. He stood, feet shoulder-width apart in the center of a circle of trackers, half who tugged at the straps of their own packs while the rest held tight to their dogs' leashes.

Intensity lined every grim face as the cops took turns reciting what little they'd gleaned from the family, from neighbors and friends who formed an outer circle around the first, hoping to overhear a bit of news. These were the people Honor least trusted, because for all their outward sincerity and despite their teary, worried faces, they always seemed more interested in grabbing the spotlight—at least for as long as it took to deliver their ill-gotten tidbits—than in seeing the missing and lost brought home.

There weren't enough photographs to go around, so dog handlers got pictures and those without were told to pay attention:

Macy Carson, age twelve, had long brown hair and brown eyes. She stood 4'8" tall, weighed 110 pounds, and wore pink braces. The vital statistics were recent and accurate, her near-hysterical mother insisted, because she'd just enrolled Macy in a new dance class, and the litigation-fearing administrators required full physicals before a girl could participate. Mom and Dad were divorced a year ago, the team was informed, but this wasn't a case of parental abduction; the distraught father shook his head and muttered as he paced in the halo of a street lamp.

The place last seen? Macy's bedroom, where now, shadowy figures walked back and forth on the other side of a window shade that glowed golden, thanks to the bright bulb of a table lamp. The parents felt certain she hadn't run away, because only yesterday her music teacher informed Macy that she'd won the lead in the school play, and she'd been singing *My Favorite Things* pretty much nonstop since getting the news. It was a Friday night, but there were no parties going on—at least, none the cops had heard anything about—and no slumber parties scheduled. She'd never had a boyfriend, never got a grade lower than a B, never mistreated her cat, and only rarely bickered with her little brothers.

Rerun and the two other rescue dogs were encouraged to inhale as much scent as the quickly closing window of time would allow. It was cold, and pitch black on this early-November night; Macy owned two coats, and both still hung in the closet behind her mother's front door. A light rain had begun to fall, increasing the odds she'd suffer exposure out there, while decreasing the dogs' chances at following a trail.

The plan: work wide sweeps in a "hasty search," and see what the dogs could pick up, then narrow the scope, gradually. This time of night, there hadn't been much foot traffic in and around Macy's yard, meaning her scent wouldn't be buried by layers of other humans' scents. Rerun struck a pointer pose, tail out and head erect, head bobbing as he drew new things in through the sensitive sensors in his nostrils. The eye shine of a raccoon, racing across the driveway, sparkled, but Rerun paid it no mind. "Good dog," she said. "Way to go."

She hadn't given him enough credit. Rowdy had been such a natural, such a ham that he'd stolen the limelight. But if he'd seen one of the masked critters darting through the dark, it was just as likely he'd chase it as not. Rerun? He kept his nose to the ground, huffing and woofing and whining.

"Rerun's on to something," she said softly into her radio.

A minute, maybe two later, a pack of investigators showed up to point other dog handlers in the direction Rerun had gone. An hour after that, the dogs were agitated and so were the handlers. By daybreak, exhaustion and frustration raised tempers and voices and blood pressure. It seemed they were going in circles, because that's exactly what they were doing, and still no sign of Macy.

The same ugly word was in everyone's mind, but no one wanted to say it: abduction.

As much as Honor loved this work, she hated endings like this ten times more. She loaded Rerun into the car and pitched her pack into the trunk. Nobody involved with SAR missions believed every search could end positively. But the ones involving kids? Nobody involved wanted them to end any other way.

"Buzz," she said to his answering machine, "it's me, Honor. It's 9:04 and I'm on my way home. If this stupid dashboard clock is right, I'm already four minutes late for work. Well, guess what? You can just add twenty-four hours to that, minus the four minutes, because I won't be in today. Give me a couple hours to shower and catch a nap and I'll tell you all about our little after-hours search party."

Then she peeked into the rearview mirror at Rerun, still alert and upright on the backseat. "How'd I get so lucky?" she whispered. Some would say it was because she knew how to choose a puppy. Others would credit her teaching skills. But Honor knew better. The 20 percent of rescue dogs that retired, old and gray after years of successful SAR missions, weren't good at what they did solely because of skilled handlers. Search was in their DNA, and she'd lucked onto two dogs that would have been naturals, no matter who had trained them.

"Oh, you're gonna get a whole lot more respect from now on," she said.

Rerun yawned, then stretched out on the seat.

"Unimpressed with my shallow generosity, are you?" Maybe he'd see her as more sincere if she made a spot for him at the foot of her bed. And after feeding him something special for breakfast, she'd climb up there with him, and pray to sleep like the living dead, so she wouldn't have to think about . . . anything.

Not many people would understand the disquieting feelings rumbling in her head. "Shrug it off," they'd say. "It's over. Just pick up where you left off."

Easier said than done. Lots easier. And it might be easier still if she had someone to talk to, someone who knew what it was like to come home, elbows scraped and knees banged up and every toe blistered, knowing that, despite it all, you'd *still* come up empty. She wanted to commiserate with someone who'd shouted a single, specific name into the dark, only to have it echo back, awful and empty. Matt understood what it felt like to drive home from a mission, hounded by guilt. If the team had hung in there just one minute more; if they'd thought to look around this corner instead of that one; if they'd arrived sooner, or later, or at a different starting point, then maybe, just maybe, Macy would be home with her mother and bothersome little brothers right now.

Second-guessing herself had never helped before, and it wouldn't help now. If Honor had an inkling how to put a stop to the haunting conviction that because they'd failed last night, it was Macy's *body* they'd find, not a girl too cold and terrified to answer when they'd called her name.

Matt would help her stare down that horrible truth, and he'd pep talk her into believing she could do it again, the next time a girl like Macy went missing . . . if she called him.

There was something wrong with her, something that went bone-deep and far beyond the Brady Shaw-Wyatt Hoffman story she'd been hiding behind. Oh, it had made her miserable, to be sure, and cost her plenty. But it had been old news for months now, and any power it might have had to harm Matt and his boys had long ago fizzled. Until, *unless* she could give the illness a name, what hope did she have of finding a cure?

30

On his way into town, Matt stopped by the small cemetery where his young wife was buried. Years ago, he'd constructed a fence around her grave; white pickets and a black-latched gate, for no reason other than she'd asked him to. She'd asked for a statue of Gabriel the archangel, too, and though it had been a struggle to find and afford one, Matt had given her that, too. Down on one knee, he plucked a few weeds the caretakers had missed and, tossing them aside, read the simple inscription carved into white marble:

FAITH WARNER PHILLIPS

BELOVED WIFE AND MOTHER
8 JANUARY 1974 – 15 NOVEMBER 2002

The wind whispered through the grass and mingled with the soft hiss of traffic that buzzed on the highway beyond the big iron gates. He hadn't known what lesson God was trying to teach, making him a widowed father to twin boys at the tender age of twenty-eight, and all these years later, he still hadn't figured it out.

"Don't know why I'm here now, either," he whispered.

But that was a bald-faced lie.

Matt had come here today to say good-bye.

Those first trips up the steep and narrow road that spiraled toward St. Paul's church had been pleasant enough, thanks to manicured lawns on the tree-lined street. But with each visit, the ancient oaks looked more gnarled than grand, and once-stunning architecture began to remind him of the *Psycho* house because all he could focus on was the bitter and barbaric sight that awaited him at the top of the hill.

If there was any truth to the "she joined her Maker in the twinkling of an eye" verse Pastor Rafferty had read, ten years ago today, Faith wasn't here. Had never been here. Her parents and his had guilt-tripped him into monthly visits "to pay respect to the dead." But they were gone now, so why was he still going through the motions?

Surely not for the boys. What they knew about Faith came by way of anecdotes, one for every picture in the photo album. He'd never brought them here, because, well, what would he tell them? That he'd shoved their pretty young mother into a box and planted her under a garden sculpture? If that wasn't the stuff nightmares were made of, Matt didn't know what was! Far better for them to hold on to the image of her walking carefree down the gold-paved streets of heaven.

He'd first conjured the image as friends and relatives paraded by, sniffling and red-eyed as they placed long-stemmed white roses on the lid of Faith's coffin, because it was better than admitting she'd harbored some sick, secret fixation with her own funeral. How else was he to explain the way her eyes blazed with intensity as she wrenched promise after promise from him—this kind of tombstone, that kind of ceremony, a piper to squeeze a demented, wheezing version of "Amazing

Grace" as her loved ones gathered round the grave—when all he wanted was to hold her for as long as possible.

If she'd put half as much effort into holding on as she'd spent on letting go, could she have summoned the strength to live?

The question had nagged at him for ten long years, and he was tired, so tired, of beating down the resentment it roused. It was time to let it go, once and for all, and maybe grab a molecule of the peace Faith had found on those gold-paved streets of heaven. How much brighter would his life be once he let himself take comfort from knowing she was right where she'd always wanted to be . . . no more vacillating between anger at God for taking her, and anger at her for so willingly, eagerly leaving him.

Matt took a deep breath and let it out slowly. "So I guess this is it, then," he said.

But the stone stood cold and silent against the slate-gray sky.

Matt pulled another weed, then got to his feet and traced the curlicues flanking the cherub's head above her name. A rush of warmth wrapped around him as he closed that white picket gate, and he took it to mean it was okay with Faith if he never opened it again.

He wondered, as he drove away from the cemetery, what she'd think of Honor. It was such a wacky, out-of-left-field thought that it made him laugh a little. As the chuckle dimmed to a smile, he pictured her. She'd been on his mind a lot these past few days. Yesterday, in particular. Matt almost called her, more than once, but decided against it. Just because he'd gone completely loopy over the woman didn't mean he had to show it every minute of the day. It especially didn't mean he had to show *her* how completely over the top he'd gone.

Besides, any day now, she'd call to let him know about Thanksgiving. If he didn't hear from her by week's end, *then* he'd call. Finding out how soon he needed to get the guest room ready wouldn't make him look desperate, right?

At the top of the next hill, a sharp left would put him on her street. Talk about desperate. And a stupid waste of time. Because of course Honor wouldn't be there; she'd rented the house to a couple who were expecting their first baby. Soon, from the looks of the woman's round belly. The first time he'd driven by, Matt told himself that any good friend would do the same, to check things out, make sure the tenants were taking good care of the place. Seeing the tidy yard should have given him peace of mind. Instead, it felt like a sucker punch to the gut and made him miss her all the more.

If he knew what was good for him, he'd pop the question on Thanksgiving. "Pass the pumpkin pie and the whipped cream. Oh. And by the way, will you marry me?"

He didn't have to ask the question to know that the only thing that could hurt more than the empty, ache of missing her was if she said no.

31

Sorry to call so late," Matt said, "but tomorrow is the Wednesday before Thanksgiving, and—"

Honor hit Mute as Rerun cocked his head. His chin bobbed, the way it did out there on the trail, when he was gathering scent in those sensitive nostrils.

"What, you sense stupidity, do ya?"

A silent, breathy bark was his answer.

"Don't look at me that way," she said, hugging him. "I feel bad enough as it is." She padded into the kitchen, the dog on her heels. "If I give you a biscuit, will you knock it off?"

Doggy grin in full bloom, he accepted the bribe, then followed her back to the living room and picked up right where he'd left off. Groaning, Honor hit the phone's Erase button and flopped onto the couch and hid behind her treasured first-edition copy of *White Fang*. She managed to block the golden's quiet stare but not the dizzying list of emotions that tumbled in her head. Cowardly had to come first, and because she'd been too spineless to pick up the phone and do the right thing, guilt rang in at a close second.

Telling him she'd think about riding down on the train to spend Thanksgiving with him and the boys had been an irrational thing to do. Promising to let him know by tonight whether or not she'd actually do it had been foolish. Not making the call had been gutless. And ignoring him just now, well, that had been out and out rude.

Why he hadn't erased her from his phone book was anybody's guess because from the moment of their official meeting, that night of the plane crash, she'd been nothing but troublesome.

Matt, on the other hand, had been anything but. Thanks to him, she'd found reasons to laugh, and hope, and dream again. How sad that because she'd let her life turn into such a muddled mess, she couldn't do all of it *with* him.

"I can feel you," she muttered to the dog, "still staring at me."

Sure enough, when Honor lowered the book, she saw Rerun, sitting like a tiny, blond version of the Sphinx, his brown eyes fixed to hers. She was about to go back into hiding when a sheet of ivory paper fluttered to the floor. "What's this?" she wondered aloud, bending to pick it up. Instantly, she recognized the bold lines of Matt's powerful script.

Born in silence and weaned on ice, his heart beat, beat, beat with strength. His voice keened, long and low, deep into the night. Up it rose, like warm steam that rode upon the air, and floated in the streams, its echo reaching, seeking, touching every corner of the earth; a call, a plea, a prayer that he might find the one who would love him, just love him . . . when the time was right. When life grew bitter and cruel, though he taught himself to mirror the meanness, his strong and honorable heart wasn't in it. After the battles, he stood proud in his high place, looking, listening, waiting for the one who would love him, just love him . . . when the time was right. Then, at long last, he had found the one who loved him, just loved him . . . for now, the time was right. This was the one for whom he'd fight, to the death if need be, for he was White Fang, who was loved fiercely because he loved fiercely. The spirit of this wolf-dog lived in Rowdy, and lives in Rerun, and in the heart of their mistress, who is loved fiercely because she loves fiercely.

It wasn't signed or dated, like the inscription he'd made her wait to read "For Honor Mackenzie—who lives her name—a book about a wolf that did the same. Always, Matt."

She used her shirttail to dry her eyes as Rerun moved into the tight space between the sofa cushions and the coffee table. And Honor hugged him . . . fiercely.

ॐ

The twins, Austin and Mercy, Harriet and the Sullivans, even Liam asked about her, but because Matt didn't know how to explain Honor's behavior, he didn't even try.

It hurt, knowing she'd rather spend a family holiday alone than with him. But he hid it well, laughing and joking, eating too much, and dozing as the Ravens played their hearts out to put points up on the scoreboard.

If he was keeping score, the tally would read Honor 3, Matt 0.

But he'd learned to live with loss when Faith died, and he'd manage again. He'd been blessed with the best sons a man could hope to have, and friendship, a job he loved. Cash walked up beside him and nudged his hand, as if to say, "Hey, what am I, chopped liver?" He patted the pointer's head and sneaked him a bite of breast meat. It hadn't escaped his notice that, yet again, the dog sensed his mood and dispensed his own fuzzy brand of TLC.

Had it really been a year ago that he'd sat at Mercy's table, looking across at Honor, who knew with a glance what he was thinking even before he did? It seemed much longer than that. And it seemed like only yesterday.

"That Was Then, This Is Now" hadn't become a song and a movie and a book because it *didn't* resonate with heart-gripping truth. When he called her house the night before last, Matt sensed that she'd been home, that she'd been standing right there, listening as he left his rambling verbal montage . . . and yet she hadn't picked up. Not when he said, "Call me, any time, I'll wait up," or any of the half dozen other inane, borderline-humiliating things he'd said, not even when he finished up with, "I'm probably crazy to admit it, but I miss you like crazy, Honor Mackenzie."

Even if he'd been wrong, and she hadn't been home when he'd blathered on like a love-sick fool, wouldn't a message like that have provoked a quick return call once she got in, to tell him, at least, not to bother changing the sheets on the guest bed?

Evidently not.

Austin plopped down beside him, grinding an elbow into Matt's ribs. "What's eating you, pal?"

Matt only shook his head. "Ate too much, I guess."

"Save the pretense for those jokers you interview." He got up and with a nod of his head said, "Looks to me like Cash wants to take a walk."

At the mention of his name, the dog lifted his sleepy head.

"He'd rather just stay right there, dozing in front of the fire."

"I'm surprised you don't know him any better than that. After all these years together? Please." Austin hunkered down and tousled the dog's floppy ears. "Wanna go for a walk, boy? Should we go outside?"

On all fours now, Cash nuzzled Austin's neck. "See? He's rarin' to go, man. I hope you brought his leash."

"It's in Warner's jacket pocket," Steve called from across the room.

"Thanks, buddy." Austin flung open the door to the hall closet, grabbed his jacket and Matt's, and found the leash, balled up in Warner's pocket.

"Reminds me of that old joke," Matt said, putting on his coat. " 'Here's your hat, what's your hurry?' "

He flung open the door. "Speaking of which . . ." He bowed, one hand pressed to his jacket's thick, bronze-colored zipper, the other moving in an exaggerated wave that effectively invited Matt to pass by.

"I'm not in much of a talking mood," he said once they hit the sidewalk.

"So I've noticed."

"I know you mean well, but I'm not much in the mood for wisecracks, either."

"Understood. So you won't mind then, if I spout wise while you listen."

Cash glanced over his shoulder and grinned at Austin, as if to say, "Give it the old college try, buddy."

"Have at it, friend," he said, grinning despite himself. "Good luck with the 'wise' part of that, though."

"Oh. So you can crack wise, but I can't? I like *that*. But I digress. I'm sure you've noticed certain, ah, similarities in the personalities of our ladies . . ."

"Thought you were going for *wise* not *eeze*."

"Huh?"

He shook his head and chuckled. "Never mind. Sorry to interrupt your train of thought."

"Not hard to do, what with my one-track mind and all. And FYI, I caught your pun: similari*ties*, personali*ties*, la*dies*. What I'm referring to is, Mercy was a mixed-up mess, Honor's still a puzzle. Have faith, Matt. Don't give up on her just yet. She might surprise you and come around."

"I dunno . . ."

"Look. She's up there, minutes from where her fiancé died. No family, no friends to speak of, nothing but work and more work to keep that amazing brain of hers occupied. Too much time alone is a dangerous thing. Ask me how I know."

Matt remembered only too well what happened when Austin pulled back from friends. Those were dark and dangerous months, and for most of them, he wondered if the "old" Austin would ever resurface.

"She has some great holiday memories, thanks to you. So give her some rope. Let her sit this season out and think on that. If she hasn't come around by, say, Valentine's Day, you can bombard her with roses and chocolates and poems. And if that doesn't work? *Then* you can throw in the towel, and nobody who loves you will blame you a bit."

He'd already written her a poem. Poured out his heart in it, and Honor hadn't so much as mentioned it, let alone commented on its intent. But maybe Austin had a point. Time, distance, and a chance to compare her life in Queens to what she had here in Baltimore. He nodded. "It's worth a shot, I guess." All except for the poetry. He'd wrung himself dry on that one.

"So any day now, eh, buddy?"

Austin whistled. "Hard to believe, ain't it? Me. A dad. A *dad*."

"That's gonna be some lucky kid."

His lopsided smile gave him a youthful quality that reminded Matt of a much younger, far more innocent Austin Finley.

"Y'think?"

"Are you kidding? The way you throw yourself into everything you do? You're gonna be the best dad ever . . . with one exception."

Austin harrumphed. "If you say so."

They climbed onto the porch of the Finley's Fells Point condo. Any day now, Mercy would go into labor, and she and

Austin would descend these same brick steps; when next they stood here, she'd be a mother and he'd be a father. Older and wiser than he'd been when fatherhood fell into his lap, Matt knew they'd do just fine. In fact, they'd probably find a couple thousand ways to improve upon the tried and true systems parents had been employing for centuries.

Important work, he thought, hanging up his jacket. More significant work, even, than training surgeons or missionaries, teachers or world leaders. And it wasn't always easy, raising a child to become a productive, caring, God-fearing citizen, especially in today's bustling world.

Matt was proud of his boys. They'd fare well, if they stayed on this path, not only because their hard work had produced stellar test scores and the respect of their teachers and peers, but because they proved every day that the *heart* was every bit as important as the head. They needed, no, *deserved* a mother substitute who'd give as good as she got. And sadly, that wasn't Honor. At least, it wasn't Honor right now.

She'd never hurt them on purpose, but in her present state of mind? Honor could do all kinds of emotional and mental damage.

If Austin was right and with the upcoming holidays, if she opened herself up to an epiphany, well, *then* maybe they had a shot at this family thing. Until and unless that happened, he'd stand firm and shield them from disappointment and regret.

Because if her rejection hurt him this much—a grown man who'd suffered heartache a time or two in his day—how much more damaging would it be for his impressionable boys?

32

*T*hanksgiving came and went, and before she knew it, twinkling lights and carols surrounded her . . . on the streets and the subway, at the office, in every shop and store, and even in the library. Not to be outdone, the U.S. Weather Bureau predicted a white Christmas for New York and the vicinity. Honor didn't think she'd ever identified more with Ebenezer Scrooge.

Uncharacteristic blizzard conditions pummeled the mid-Atlantic states, and she was tempted to call and see how Matt and the boys were faring. Instead, she phoned Mercy, under the guise of checking on the new mother and eight-pound, seven-ounce, Cora Marie, born at two minutes to twelve, Thanksgiving night.

"I've never seen snow like this," Mercy admitted. "They're dumping it in the harbor because there's no place else to put it." Baltimoreans had taken to skiing to get around, she said, and the only altercation of any measure happened when two elderly women grabbed hold of the last-standing snow shovel.

"Goodness . . . I hope you stocked up on formula and diapers."

"Don't need formula, but the diaper situation is getting dicey. Austin might just have to break out his snowshoes.

Either that, or *I* might be forced to break out the duct tape, to hold up those size threes I got at my baby shower."

The women talked recipes and Christmas trees, home décor and the Finley's decision to buy an Ocean City condo. "You should come down this summer," Mercy said. "We can laze on the beach and make fun of guys in Speedos."

"I might just do that," Honor said, laughing.

"So are you *ever* going to ask about Matt and the boys?"

"Well, sure." She couldn't very well admit they'd been 90 percent of the reason for her call, now could she?

"I don't get it, Honor. Things seemed to be going really well. Was it your job or his that came between you two?"

"Neither." It was mostly the truth. "Can't break up a couple that never really got together . . ."

Mercy sighed. "Well it's a shame, is what it is. You're perfect for each other."

"Yeah, well, a girl can dream." She took a big breath and let it out slowly. "So they're all okay? Nobody has come down with that weird strain of flu that's going around, I hope."

"No. They're fine. Physically. Well, at least the boys are fine."

Honor gasped. "What's wrong with Matt? Don't tell me he went on a mission and hurt himself, or—"

"The only thing wrong with that man is, his heart is breaking."

Well now, Honor thought, *way to shut a girl's big mouth good and tight.*

"Austin said he got like this after Faith died. Sort of."

Sort of?

"He had the boys to take care of and the house to run. I guess there wasn't time for a whole lot of wallowing."

Wallowing? Matt was the last man on earth she could picture *wallowing*.

"You should have seen him on Thanksgiving." Mercy groaned. "I'll bet he didn't say a dozen words."

Honor sighed.

"You sure know how to mess a guy up, girl. Until you came along, Matt Phillips was just about the most together man I'd ever met."

Honor heard the call-waiting signal. *Saved by the beep,* she thought. "Hey Mercy, can I get back to you? That's Elton on the other line."

"Tell him he needs to get over here and meet Austin's baby girl. If the *snow* ever melts, that is."

She pressed the Talk button to switch from Mercy's line to Elton's, and she barely recognized his voice when he said, "Honor, I need you. It's Bethany."

"Your granddaughter?"

"She was skiing with friends in West Virginia. Blue Ridge something or other. And got off the trail somehow. Nobody has seen her in hours."

Hours. Depending on where she was in those mountains, it could take Honor a dozen hours to get to her in this weather. "But Elton, I just talked to Mercy, and she said the whole city is shut down. Even if I could get out of New York right now, I'd never be able to—"

"I have this friend who owns a private jet. He owes me, big time. I could call him. Ask him to come get you."

Fear and worry had muddled his mind. If Elton had been thinking straight, he'd know that even if his friend could fly from Baltimore to New York, he wouldn't have a safe place to land. She said all that as gently as possible, and then reminded him that Maryland's SAR teams were some of the best in the world.

"I know that," he growled. "But I want *you* on the team."

"Then . . . what about a helicopter?"

It didn't surprise her to hear that Elton had a friend with one of those, too. He told her to get packed; he'd call within the half hour to let her know when and where the copter would pick her up.

The instant he hung up, Honor sat right down to write up a list.

1. Call Buzz.

She'd beg him to take Rerun home with him for a few days, and she had every confidence that he'd say yes. For one thing, he and his wife loved dogs, and it hadn't been long since they'd put their Lab down. For another, he knew that Rowdy had successfully worked several snow missions and that while he hadn't been overly fond of airplanes and helicopters, he'd cooperated. "That dog would ride a rocket to the moon if you asked him to," he'd once joked. In her heart, Honor knew it was true, and while she loved the golden's dedication to her and the work, getting him to that level meant sacrificing one-on-one time with Rowdy. In time, Rerun might become a rescue dog capable of earning medals and awards, but for now, he'd be safer and happier in Buzz's warm, dry family room.

2. Call Austin and Mercy.

This call would be the toughest because she'd have to get their promise that they'd adopt Rerun if anything happened to her.

3. Pack.

Honor grabbed her biggest duffle and started filling it with cold weather gear. She'd never gone snowboarding in her life, but oh, did those guys know how to dress for ice, snow, and wind. The stuff was waterproof, lightweight, and durable, with lots of pockets—ideal for quick and easy access to flashlights and batteries, radios, energy bars and bottled water, and spare pairs of gloves—and a good way to lighten the load of the pack. Plus, because zippers tended to let cold air in, and Velcro loops often got clogged with ice and snow, these manufacturers made use of both, perfect for a person headed into cold and snow.

The five-layer clothing system—under, wicking, clothing, insulation, shell—never failed her in the past, and Honor saw no reason to deviate from it. She'd pack a separate bag with everything she'd need to start the search and stow duplicates in her pack, in the unlikely event she got wet. Socks and boots, a warm hat, a hooded jacket and gloves went into both packs. An oilcloth tarp with big, rustproof grommets and 100 feet of marine rope, matches, stowed in a Ziploc bag, and a fully charged cell battery went into the pockets of her jacket and pants.

4. Leave a key in the flowerpot on the front porch so that Buzz could get in to fetch Rerun.

5. Unplug the toaster and coffeemaker, set the timers that controlled the lights, close the blinds, and lock up.

6. Pack *White Fang* poem and Bible.

One more entry and her list would be complete. Honor's pen hovered over the number 7; she couldn't make herself tap out the dot behind the digit, because that item was her reminder to call Matt. Maybe hearing about the mission from her, directly, would help make up for any hurt feelings still left from her failure to keep her Thanksgiving promise.

Like you need a reminder for that one, she thought as the phone rang.

"You ready?"

"You bet."

"How soon can you get to the Queens Midtown Tunnel?"

"I don't know . . . twenty minutes or so if I don't hit construction traffic. Why?"

"Because there's a helipad there." He gave her the address. "My pal's name is J.R. Kane, and he'll be flying one of two LongRangers: the Weasel or Eagle Eye."

"When will you be there?"

"Just as soon as I can talk my son-in-law into gassin' up *his* baby. J.R.'s on his way. You'll have plenty of time to pick his brain on the way to Spruce Knob." Then he rattled off J.R.'s cell number and hung up.

So she was headed to the Monongahela National Forest, where hikers and hunters and cyclists routinely wander off the trails and quickly find themselves disoriented. Bad enough in the summertime. But in the Allegheny Front, where the average snowfall is 180 inches? While she was picking J.R.'s brain, she'd see if he knew how Elton's granddaughter got out there in the first place, though the better question was *why* she'd gone at this time of year.

"C'mon, Rerun," she said, opening the back door. "Let's take a final run around your grassy knoll." It would be an hour or so before Buzz could get there; no point stressing the dog any more than necessary. While Rerun did his business, Honor packed up a big shopping bag. His favorite toys, collar and leash, food and dog treats, and the pillow he liked to cuddle with at night. She stacked everything near the front door, where she'd told Buzz he could find the dog's things, then sat at the kitchen table to scratch out a quick note: he doesn't mind thunder or lightning, but house flies and bees wig him out, and just for fun, she added that strangers don't bother Rerun . . . unless they were wearing Pittsburgh Steelers emblems.

She made a list of phone numbers, too: Elton's. Hers. J.R.'s, Matt's, though she didn't know why. Cross-legged on the floor, Honor gave Rerun a quick massage and a good long hug. "No telling when we'll get to do this again." She held his face in her hands and looked deep into his soulful brown eyes. "I'm counting on you to be a good boy for Buzz, you hear?"

Then she kissed the bridge of his nose, grabbed her duffle, and headed for the Midtown Tunnel.

33

*E*verything about J.R. Kane broke stereotype.

Instead of the grizzled, pot-bellied guy she'd expected, a tall slender man in his mid- to late 50s greeted her. Rather than a traditional one-piece flight suit, he wore a starched white shirt and snug blue jeans, and on his feet, pointy-toed cowboy boots.

So much for her birds of a feather theory.

"You made good time," he said, hefting her bags into the back.

"When Elton gives an order, people listen."

"How long have you known that old reprobate?"

"Long enough." She climbed into the cockpit and buckled up, then adjusted her headset.

"I see you've done this before," he said, flipping switches and planting his feet on the torque pedals as the rotor geared up.

"Doesn't mean I'm not scared out of my shoes."

"Relax, darlin'. I've been buzzin' the skies in one of these babies since before you were born, so you just sit back and enjoy the ride."

Easier said than done, she thought, considering where they were going. And why.

"Elton didn't tell me you were from Texas."

"Texas!" he thundered. "Whatever makes you think I'm from the Lone Star State?"

"Oh, I dunno . . . maybe it's those boots and jeans and your cowboy drawl?"

J.R.'s laugh filled the space. "I'll have you know I was born and raised in Towson, Maryland. Picked up this twang when I went to college in Mississippi. Drives my wife plum loco, and I don't mind admitting I find that a tad curious, seeing as how this is what I sounded like when she met me, more'n twenty years ago."

Nodding, Honor held on tight as he pitched the craft upward to clear a building. "So did Elton happen to mention how his granddaughter ended up stranded on a snowy mountaintop, all by herself?"

He thumped the cyclic control, and Honor cringed. It wouldn't take much to move the stick forward or back, sending them into a roll.

"I'll tell you what, if that fool young'un was mine, she'd have a hard time sitting, 'cause every pair of trousers she owns would have my size-ten boot print on 'em. Never met a child who could get into more trouble than that one."

He fiddled with a switch above his head, then adjusted his mike. "What kind of fool goes hiking when there are blizzard warnings? All these rescuers, you included, risking your life now to save that little brat?" He harrumphed. "I know it sounds cold and harsh, but given my druthers, I'd druther stop the contaminated DNA right there."

"I've heard it isn't healthy to hold things in, J.R. You ought to learn to speak your mind. The experts say venting is good for a man."

And so it went for the next half hour as he hurtled through the darkening sky like a bullet. He put the LongRanger down at the edge of Briery Gap Road, where a dozen ambulances, fire trucks, and squad cars had lined up near Forest Road 104. "They don't maintain the 104 or the 112 in the wintertime," J.R. said, handing her the smaller bag, "which is only gonna make the going tougher for the lot of you." Slinging the big pack over one shoulder, he walked beside her toward the convergence of county and SAR personnel and stood with her as a woman with a reedy voice called out the coordinates. "Lat three eight point seven ought-ought eight degrees north," she droned as pencils scraped across index cards. "Long seven nine point five three two-two degrees west."

Everybody took care to note where they'd tucked those cards, because in the unlikely event *they* got lost, the numbers could very well make the difference between life and death.

After accepting their assigned quadrants and muttering a few good lucks and Godspeeds, the searchers got down to business. J.R. grabbed her elbow as she tightened the cinch of her pack. "Don't you do anything dumb out there, you hear? You're more valuable than a little ninny who'd go looking for high adventure without a thought to the outcome."

"Thanks, J.R.," she said.

He waved her thanks away. "If you see that old buzzard, you tell him for me that I'm praying for the girl." And with no warning whatever, he wrapped Honor in a hug. "I'm praying for you, too," he said, giving her a little shake.

"I'll be fine. I always am."

"'Course you will." And with that he turned on his tall slanted heel and headed back to his Bell 212. Honor started walking before it lifted off with a swirl of grit and snow and crisp leaves. She wasn't cold, because she'd dressed for this weather, so it was more than a little unsettling when a chill snaked down her spine. Having nothing to compare it to, what choice did she have but to shrug it off?

She did a quick head count of all the people who said they'd pray for her—Elton and his wife, J.R., Mercy and Austin, and a handful of family members who'd gathered at the base of Spruce Knob to wait for the searchers to come back and deliver their loved ones or, at the very least, hope that they'd soon be reunited.

"Of course you'll be fine," she muttered, gaze scanning the landscape for the one thing that didn't belong . . . the thing that might lead them to Elton's granddaughter. She had to be fine. Who'd make sure Rerun knew how to ride in a Piper Cub or a Bell 212 if she wasn't?

The snow under her boots drowned out the quiet shudder of fear that prefaced her next thought:

It's nice to know he'll have a good home, just in case . . .

⁂

If the boys hadn't been so keen to go skiing, Matt might just have skipped the trip. *No* might *about it,* he thought, because his heart just wasn't in it this year.

They'd rented a ski-in/ski-out unit, as always. The change up this year was that they had two bedrooms. One for the boys, one for Harriet, and the pullout sofa for Matt and Cash. The place had the same gorgeous views of Wisp's lifts and trails and a slightly bigger kitchen that came equipped with everything but food and drinks. He wasn't in the mood to cook, either, but because that, too, had been part of their every-other-Christmas tradition: ski all day, then hunker down for microwave pizza or grilled cheese and tomato soup. *Easier to go with the flow,* he thought, *than explain why you're so out of it.*

Tomorrow, day three of their five-day trip, the boys would go tubing while Harriet played bridge with three other nannies and sitters she'd met in the lobby. If he had his way, Matt wouldn't leave the room except to walk the dog. He'd brought along a novel and intended to get halfway through it before the troops returned this evening, or die trying.

Well he didn't die, exactly, but he did conk out at about 10:00 and didn't wake up until Cash nudged his elbow to let him know it was time for another spin around the potty park. As he stepped into his boots, the TV crawler said Wisp would get a foot of fresh snow by morning. The boys would be thrilled. Matt? He just thanked God they wouldn't get slammed by the blizzard that was bearing down south and west of them. The resort was certainly equipped to handle the pounding, but roads in and out would shut down for days. And he'd already spent *five* days in a two-room suite with eleven-year-old twins, an elderly widow, and a skittish dog. Any longer and his patience with family bonding would blow apart at the seams.

He slid into his jacket, but didn't zip it up. Didn't comb his hair, either, and it made him grin a little when a couple of teens going the opposite direction gave him a wide berth. If he really gave a hoot what they thought, he might have explained that he was on vacation. Why clean up to take a slog with the dog and go right back to sprawling on the sofa? At least he'd brushed his teeth, so when two ski bunnies skittered around him, he didn't feel like a total loser doing his Jack Nicholson impression.

Back at the condo, he'd barely hung up the dog's leash when his cell phone chirped. If it hadn't been Liam's name in the caller ID block, Matt would have let the call go straight to voice mail. "What's up?" he said on the second chirp.

"Why aren't you out on the slopes? You didn't break a leg or something, did you?"

Oh, he'd heard *that* tone enough times to know what it meant. Pinching his nostrils shut, he said, "This is Matt's cell phone. If you're calling to dole out a rush-rush writing assignment, you can just take a hike." He let go of his nose to add "*Be-e-ep.*" And then, he waited.

"Are you finished?"

"Liam, *du-u-ude,* lighten up. Life is short, and so's this trip, so—"

"I just got a frantic call from Elton Kent."

"Honor's old boss? What's he want with you?"

"Didn't want me. He was looking for you."

"Me? What for?"

"Seems his granddaughter went to some far-fetched place in West Virginia. Knobby Spruce or some such and got herself lost."

"Spruce Knob?"

"Yeah. That's it. Anyway, so the kid goes up there day before yesterday . . . get this . . . *hiking* with her sorority sisters, and—"

"Hiking? On the Allegheny Front? Wait. Don't tell me. She's blond."

"Man. You're cold. Did you hear me say the kid went missing?"

"Oh. Yeah. Sorry. But sheesh. What did she expect? It's winter. In the mountains. Where the average snowfall is, like, fifteen feet a season."

"Don't tell me. You know this because you're a skier."

"Well, yeah. Why else . . . But wait a minute, here. What does Elton's missing granddaughter have to do with me?"

"He sent Honor out to find her."

Matt's heart thudded against his ribs, and his legs felt rubbery. He sat on the sofa arm and ran his free hand through his hair. "Is she all right? Did she get hurt bringing the kid home? What, Liam? Spit it out, man!"

"The girl is home, safe and sound. GPS in her cell phone led 'em right to her, all curled up in a ball, crying like a baby."

"Okay. That's good. I guess. She's okay, I take it? No frostbite? Broken bones? Bruises on her backside where her parents kicked her bee-hind?"

"She's fine, but Honor's missing. *Been* missing for two days."

Matt was on his feet, pacing when he said, "No way. She's the most careful, cautious . . . She *teaches* SAR for the love of Pete."

"I'm just telling you like it is. Like Elton asked me to do."

"You know, for a newspaper man, you talk like a real dope sometimes."

"Hey. Don't shoot the messenger. So here's the deal. Elton says you're as good, maybe better, at this SAR stuff as Honor is, and that if anybody can find her, it's you."

At most, he was a two-hour drive from Spruce Knob. Harriet could stay with the boys. And he'd come equipped to ski, so warm clothes weren't an issue. But he'd need ropes and climbing gear. A tarp and first-aid kit. A compass. Maps. A radio. Flashlight and batteries. Plenty of batteries . . .

"I'll make some calls," Liam said, "make sure you have all that and then some in the next hour. And I'll call in a favor. Get you transported over there by helicopter."

Until Liam spoke, Matt hadn't realized he'd recited his list aloud.

"You sure this is wise, Matt?"

"Wise? What do you mean?"

"Well, y'know how they say doctors shouldn't treat family and friends—because they're too close to make impartial decisions."

"I'll be fine. And so will she."

She *had* to be.

34

How infuriating that mere inches from her stiff and trembling fingertips, she had matches. A heavy tarp. Water and energy bars. A radio to call for help. And warm dry socks. It was all she could do to remember to wiggle her fingers and toes, flex her calf and thigh muscles to keep the blood flowing. Honor had been with SAR long enough to know she'd broken her left arm when she lost her footing up there and got hung up between two boulders. She'd dislocated the shoulder and cracked a couple of ribs, too, and quite possibly her left collarbone. The only benefit she could see to being this cold was that it helped numb the pain, a little bit, anyway.

She'd been hanging like yesterday's wash for nearly two days now. She could see her cell phone down there, twenty, thirty yards deeper into the fissure. At first, she'd thanked God, because surely it was sending a signal to some nearby mountaintop tower. But if that was the case, help would have arrived by now. At the very least, a search plane would have coasted overhead, one guy piloting while another peered through high-powered binoculars, looking for her telltale red vest.

She'd done her best to keep the snow from piling up on it, but it was falling too hard and fast. The only thing she'd seen overhead in the past day had been a bald eagle. A red-tailed hawk. A peregrine falcon. She'd seen a black bear up there, too, and he'd sniffed the air, trying to figure out where the scent of *human* was coming from. But his poor eyesight and short arms worked to her benefit, and he padded away to find an easier-to-reach meal.

Right now, Honor just wanted to go to sleep. Just close her eyes and slide into slumber and let the Grim Reaper have his way with her. But that same *something* inside her that made her fight every time her drunken uncle Mike crept into her room? That something kept jerking her awake, reminding her how Mike had done just about every vile thing a man could do to a girl . . . everything except *that,* because her will had been *just enough* stronger than his drive to violate her.

In the battle between sleep and fear, the score was Sleep 3, Fear 5. She couldn't just quit. Because what if she found herself staring into her uncle's crazed, glittering gray eyes again? What if her punishment for not going to church, or saying her prayers was . . . sharing the same dark corner of hell with Mike, the way her parents had made her share the corner of her room with him after he'd finished his National Guard training at Camp Legeune? Hell wasn't out of the question, because she hadn't always lived a stellar life, and who knew that better than God!

And what about poor Rerun? Sure, he'd be content, living with Mercy and Austin and—and little . . . little . . . *Lord,* what had they named their baby girl!—but he'd wonder where she'd gone, and even though the Finleys fed him and kept a roof over his head, it wouldn't be the same. He'd always feel as though she'd abandoned him, the way her father had when she stupidly *stupidly* told him what his brother had been doing . . .

"Oh, Honor, what an absolute *mess* you are," she slurred. "You had a chance at happiness, *two* chances if you count John, and you blew 'em both. Didn't have the guts to put your foot down and keep John from going to Ground Zero. Didn't have the spine to admit that Matt was the best thing, the very, very best thing . . ."

Why, you sound like just like your drunken Uncle Mike, Honor Mackenzie. And isn't that just a big fat hoot! Because thanks to Mike, she'd never so much as swallowed a drop of alcohol. Now really, that was funny enough to inspire a good, long cackle . . .

. . . if she could summon the strength . . .

. . . *if she had the room . . .*

". . . if I had the *space* to take a breath!"

She looked down. Saw the mirror-like curve of her flashlight's lamp, peeking from the left-side pocket of her snow pants. Could she reach it? And if she could, would she have enough strength in that hand to grab it?

"Well, dummy, you've gotta at least *try.*"

The pain was excruciating, but it was proof she hadn't died.

Yet.

If she could make her weak, numb fingers grip it, just long enough and just tight enough to transfer it to her *right* hand, then maybe, just maybe she could get it working. And that way, if a plane coasted overhead or even J. R.'s helicopter . . .

A little bit of hope glimmered in her, and she didn't know whether to believe in it, or see it as proof she'd made it to *heaven*, but didn't have enough sense to admit it.

Yet.

"Wouldn't be the first time you didn't have the sense to admit something good."

She should have called Matt that Tuesday before Thanksgiving.

Should have gone back to Baltimore.

And told him how she felt.

Because now . . . now?

"Good thing you memorized that poem. Because now you'll have something pleasant to focus on."

Honor closed her eyes, and let the warmth wash over her as the words he wrote echoed in her head: *Born in silence and weaned on ice, his heart beat, beat, beat with strength. His voice keened, long and low, deep into the night. Up it rose, like warm steam that rode upon the air, and floated in the streams, its echo reaching, seeking, touching every corner of the earth; a call, a plea, a prayer that he might find the one who would love him, just love him . . . when the time was right. When life grew bitter and cruel, though he taught himself to mirror the meanness, his strong and honorable heart wasn't in it. After the battles, he stood proud in his high place, looking, listening, waiting for the one who would love him, just love him . . . when the time was right. Then, at long last, he had found the one who loved him, just loved him . . . for now, the time was right. This was the one for whom he'd fight, to the death if need be, for he was White Fang, who was loved fiercely because he loved fiercely. The spirit of this wolf-dog lived in Rowdy, and lives in Rerun, and in the heart of their mistress, who is loved fiercely because she loves fiercely.*

"I love you, too, Matt," she whispered. "Sorry I didn't say it sooner . . ."

"G'bye . . ."

35

*G*ood grief, Dan," Matt said, shaking the radio, "how'd this happen?"

"My fingers are numb. It slipped out of my hand. Sorry, Matt. Maybe we can fix it?"

It was getting dark, and that storm was close. If they didn't get out of here, right now, all three of them would end up like Honor. Much as it pained him to do it, he had to call off the search. He had two young boys at home. Dan had a daughter and Bill a son, and both men had wives.

"Never mind," he said. "Let's just—"

"What. Is. *That?*"

He looked in the direction Bill had pointed and squinted. And still unable to believe what he saw, Matt knuckled his eyes and looked again.

"Is that . . . is that what I think it is?" Dan said.

All three men stood, gap-jawed and leaning into the wind, staring at the same spot.

Matt held his breath. *Three short, three long, three short.*

"I don't believe my eyes," Bill said. "It's Morse code, all right."

Dan shook his head. "Think she's got a working radio?"

Matt nodded. "But it's either out of reach or inoperable."

"Well, let's get a move on." Dan started moving forward.

"No, wait," Bill said. "From the looks of that light, she's a good two, three miles out there."

"He's right," Matt agreed. "Snow this deep . . . it could take half an hour to go that distance. Hand me that radio, Dan. They know approximately where we are. If we can get the thing working long enough to call the base . . ."

". . . they could have a medevac unit here in no time." He dug in his pack and withdrew the cracked device. "It doesn't look all that bad," he said, popping off the black plastic backer. "We can jury-rig her, I'll bet." Matt grabbed his flashlight. "Give me a beam, Bill."

"You want I should signal back to her, let her know help is on the way?"

"Not yet," Matt said. "Might make her think it's okay to quit."

"But we know right where she is."

"We do *now*. But the way the wind is blowing the snow around? That whole landscape is gonna shift and change a hundred times before we get to her." He shook his head. "Let's just get this baby working and worry about telling her the cavalry's on the way once the cavalry's actually on the way."

❧

Her voice was so rough and raspy that she could barely whisper "Matt!" But after a sip of water, Honor managed to croak out, "I never thought I'd say this, but when I first saw you, I thought I'd died and gone to heaven."

Relief surged through him as he gently wrapped her in a space blanket. "Shh," he said. "Lie still."

She huddled deep into the silvery cloak. "H-how did you find me?"

"We had your last coordinates as a starting point. And then we saw your light. Now seriously, pipe down. You're a mess."

Dan held up the radio. "He's right. Not that you're not a mess. Well, you are, but that's not . . ." He waved a hand in front of his face. "Help really is on the way."

She was trembling from head to toe and almost as white as the snow, yet she managed to say "You sent a message . . . with *that?*"

She was having trouble focusing. Matt could tell because her eyes were rolling in their sockets.

"It looks worse than the one I dropped down . . ." Pausing, she licked her lips. ". . . down into . . ."

"Matt jury-rigged it." Dan held it closer, so she could see the bootlaces that held the back in place. "You think this looks bad, you should see how it looks on the *inside.*"

She started to say something, but Matt cut her off. "Honor. I'm not kidding. Hush. You're in shock. You know what that means as well as I do."

Nodding, she said, "Okay . . . *MacGyver.*"

She was smiling when a seizure took hold of her . . . and then she went completely still.

❧

During her ten-day stay at Johns Hopkins, Honor was in surgery four times. The first operation stopped internal bleeding and reinflated the lung punctured by one of three broken ribs. Next, the docs needed to set the compound fracture of her femur. Two steel pins replaced her ulna and radius. And her fourth and final trip to the OR repaired a shattered nasal bone.

Through it all, Matt didn't hear a word of complaint . . . but a big box of chocolates coaxed the truth from a savvy old nurse. "She's as compliant and cooperative as can be when she's awake," Esther told him while Honor was down getting X-rays.

"Maybe it's the drugs?"

"Not a chance. She's hooked up to a fentanyl pump, but she isn't using it."

"But they carved her up like a Thanksgiving turkey. How's she handling the pain?"

"Y'got me by the feet. I couldn't do it. Mmm-mmm-mmm, no way."

Matt shook his head. The longer he knew Honor, the more he saw her as a puzzle, with pieces forced into places where they didn't belong, and pieces missing.

"But when she's *asleep*," Esther continued, "oh, the scary-awful dreams that poor girl has!"

Esther told him about Uncle Mike, the drunken inventor, and Daddy, who claimed if he stayed, he'd end up in prison for murdering his pedophile brother. "Then there's Mommy, who found all sorts of creative ways to pay the rent . . . and died of AIDs two years after Daddy disappeared. And the whole mud-dled mess is entirely Honor's fault, don't you know." Esther popped a vanilla butter cream into her mouth, then put the lid back on the box and tucked it under one arm. "I've asked her about the dreams," she said from the doorway, "but she acts like I've confused it all with a grade-B movie. It's a crime, I tell you, what she's been through."

She'd been gone all of two minutes when an aide rolled Honor's wheelchair into the room. "Good to see you," she said, smiling.

"Good to see you, too. You look sleepy. Want me to come back in a couple of hours? Give you a chance to take a nap?"

"Do you think it's too soon for you to bring the twins in to see me?" She shrugged her good shoulder. "On second thought, I guess I'm pretty scary looking, with all these bandages and casts and tubes running every which way . . ."

Matt didn't know how he felt about bringing the boys around, even after all the wires and tubes and casts were long gone. "It won't be long now before they move you to a rehab facility, so you can get your mobility and strength back." Honor had a lot of healing to do, inside *and* out.

"I can promise you this: I'm going to work hard, harder than I've ever worked at anything, because oh, how I want to go home."

Home to Queens? Or to her little house in Baltimore? "Understood." He'd had a lot of time to think and pray on things since that night in Queens, when she'd cooked him supper. "So, have you talked to Buzz lately?"

"This morning." She brightened a little. "He says Rerun is doing great."

"Bet he misses you like crazy, though."

"I miss him, too." She shook her head. "But if I ever hope to be strong enough to get him back, to get my *life* back, I have to concentrate on getting better."

"Well, *that's* the sanest thing I've heard you say since you got here."

She frowned. "Is that even a word? Sanest, I mean."

"Hey. Who's the Pulitzer winner here?" he teased. Then he stooped to drop a kiss on her forehead. "I'm outta here. Get some sleep, will you?"

"I'll try."

"Someone very smart once told me 'Do or do not; there *is* no 'try.'"

"You said it to me first."

"Did I?"

"You did."

"I almost forgot to tell you. Remember that girl who went missing months ago? Macy somebody?"

"Yes. How could I forget? Broke my heart when they called off the search."

"Well, then you'll be happy to know she's home."

"Alive?"

"Yep. And getting ready to start high school."

"Where *was* she?"

"Seems despite the perfect picture her folks painted, she had a few, shall we say, problems. I have a feeling Mom won't entrust medication dispensing to Macy anymore."

Honor got a far-off look in her eyes. "So she ran away . . ."

"To a shelter in the city, where she gave the administrators a phony name and convinced them she'd been abused and abandoned."

Eyes narrowed now, Honor frowned. "What a horrible thing to do." She heaved a frustrated sigh. "What made her go home, finally?"

"She missed her mother."

"Hmpf. As I recall, she disappeared on the very night her teacher told her she got the lead in the school's production of *Sound of Music*. Looks like Macy's perfect for Tinseltown."

"Well, she's home, anyway. Safe and sound. Which is where I'd better go before the boys think I've abandoned them."

He'd said it without even thinking, and when Matt saw her flinch in response, he groaned inwardly.

"Tell Steve and Warner I said hi."

"You bet." He kissed her forehead again, this time as a silent apology for the slip of the tongue. "Get some rest," he said again, backpedaling from the room.

He wanted to do the right thing, for Honor *and* his boys. For himself, too, if the truth be told. That meant he had lots to think about, lots more to pray about.

Because his decision would impact four lives in a very big way.

EPILOGUE

Hard to believe it had been two years. Some days, it seemed like twice that. And others, it felt like yesterday.

Honor hadn't explained why, when Buzz all but handed her a chance to come back to Baltimore—same title, same pay—she'd chosen to stay in Queens. It didn't make a lick of sense to him, because she didn't know a soul up there and couldn't participate in nearly as many of the SAR missions she loved so much.

It hadn't been easy, letting her go, especially after spending countless hours in the rehab center, cheering her on as she struggled through painful exercises, holding her up as she graduated from the wheelchair to crutches, from a cane to standing on her own, holding her close when she got word that Buzz died of a heart attack.

His conscience was clear because he'd kept every promise made to her. How much easier life would be, he thought, going through life the way Honor did: if you never made a promise, nobody could hold your feet to the fire when you broke it. No, not easier, because when all was said and done, what did she have to show for her less complicated life?

It had been a good decision, keeping her from his sons. If losing her hurt him this much, how much more would they have suffered, after putting their trust in her hands, only to watch her walk away. That box of chocolates, paid to Esther in exchange for information about her patient would have been a steal at a thousand times the price because the awareness it bought had all but erased his anger and gave him hope.

They'd stay in touch. He'd see to it. Maybe in a month, or six months or a year, they'd figure things out. Yeah, she was a mess, but so was he. If he hadn't been such a proud and idiotic fool, Matt would have *told* her how he felt, instead of writing it down and hiding it in the pages of a book.

That, at least, would have given them *both* a shot at love . . . and honor redeemed.

Discussion Questions

1. What do you see as Honor's strongest character trait (and her weakest)? Why?

2. In what ways do you identify with these traits?

3. What would you say is Matt's most endearing personality quirk (and what makes it endearing, as opposed to annoying)?

4. Name two people in your circle of family and friends who most remind you of Honor and Matt. Why do these "real, live" people seem so similar to the characters in *Honor Redeemed*?

5. If you've been the victim of a rumor (vicious or otherwise), how did you cope with the fallout? What advice would you give someone whose life has been affected by gossip or innuendo?

6. How do you react when others gossip in your presence?

7. Have you ever participated in spreading a rumor? If so, how did it make you feel, afterward?

8. Can you refer to Bible verses or life principles that explain why gossip and rumors are harmful . . . and wrong?

9. Have you (or a loved one) survived a life-threatening situation? If so, what kept hope alive until the situation was resolved? (If not, how do suppose you'd behave in life-or-death circumstances?)

10. Like Matt, we've all lost treasured loved ones. What's your opinion of how he coped with the loss of his wife, Faith?

11. What would you say is the biggest difference between "ordinary people" and those who voluntarily put themselves at risk to save others?

12. When was the last time you thanked a first responder or soldier for his/her service to the country?

13. How do you feel about Austin and Mercy finally getting together?

We hope you enjoyed Loree Lough's *Honor Redeemed*, the second book in her First Responders series. Here's a sample of her third book of the series, *A Man of Honor*, which will be out in Fall 2012.

A Man of Honor

Loree Lough

1

05:30
May
Gunpowder State Park, near Baltimore, Maryland

A light rain painted the blacktopped path with a silvery glow, and overhead, newly unfurled leaves fluttered on the soft spring breeze. The occasional *whoop* of police sirens drowned out the croak of frogs and cricket chirps, and the steady flash of emergency vehicle strobes sliced through the early-morning darkness.

Dusty pulled up the hood of his sweatshirt and gave the thumbs-up sign as he passed two cops, interviewing a runner in a skin-tight running suit. "He's the best-behaved dog I've ever owned," the guy was saying, "but all of a sudden, he went completely off his nut, right about there." Pointing, he indicated a break in the tree line, twenty or so yards ahead.

Slowing his pace, Dusty took note of the golden's stance—ears pricked forward and tail straight out as it stared at the spot. "It's probably nothing," the owner said. "Dead squirrel or rabbit, maybe, but with that young girl still missing . . . couldn't have lived with myself if I didn't make that call."

The tallest cop tucked a tablet into his shirt pocket. "We appreciate the help. If we need anything more," he said, patting the pocket, "we know how to get in touch."

In other words, go home, get out of our way, and let us do our jobs. Marathon Man took the hint and led his dog away as Dusty joined the circle of search and rescue workers. Jones, this mission's operation leader, quickly brought them up to speed: the high school girl who'd gone missing on the night of her prom had last been seen miles from the area, but when the golden started acting spooky, it made sense to start another search, here.

"It's been five days," the Operations Leader said, "so prepare yourself for the worst."

Meaning it wasn't likely they'd find her alive. They all knew the drill, but Jones went over it anyway. "Try not to make too big a mess, stomping through the underbrush."

Because the cops will need every scrap of evidence we find, Dusty told himself, *to catch the animal who did this.*

Now the OL reminded them to double-check their field packs, to ensure they contained standard first aid: compass, knife, matches and rope, snakebite kit, sterile dressing and bandages, space blanket, and metal mirror. Dusty thanked God that he'd never needed that last item to find out whether or not a victim is breathing.

They slid into surgical gloves and field-tested their radios, then counted off, starting with Honor Mackenzie, a seasoned dog handler, and ending with Dusty, who said, "Eleven." Later, he'd ask why she'd brought Rerun along this time, instead of

Rowdy. He said a little prayer that nothing had happened to the amazing golden retriever that had earned the respect and admiration of anyone who'd ever worked with him.

"You volunteers," Jones said, interrupting his thoughts, "pair up with somebody who's wearing a pack."

Technically, they were all volunteers, but SAR personnel were required to earn wilderness certifications, while the rest, friends and family of the girl, mostly, had probably never undertaken anything like this before.

"And you with packs, make sure your partners are wearing gloves, too."

Nodding and mumbling, they marched forward.

"Mind if I follow you?" said a quiet voice near his elbow.

If you think you can, he thought, grinning as he waved her on. To her credit, she stayed with him, every slow and methodical step of the way. He said a silent prayer of thanks that she wasn't the chatty type, though cute as she was, putting up with the noise wouldn't have taken much effort. If she passed muster—and wasn't married or engaged or whatever—maybe she'd let him buy her a cup of coffee afterward, to find out what else they had in common. Dusty started to ask about her connection to the missing girl when the toe of his left boot brushed against something. Instantly, he froze in place and, squatting, gently combed his fingertips through the grass. What he'd bumped, he realized, was a sparkly shoe. He automatically scanned the area, and six inches farther left, Dusty saw its mate. Then, a few yards ahead of that, the girl who'd worn the sparkly high heels to her prom.

Standing, he radioed his position as his cute little shadow sidled up beside him. "Lord, Lord, Lord," she chanted. "It can't be."

"Can't be what?"

"Melissa." She ran a trembling hand through her hair. "She's
. . ." Tilting her face to the heavens, she exhaled a groaning
sigh.

He looked at her, *really* looked at her for the first time. "You
know her?"

"She's one of my students."

He heard her gulp and swallow. Hard. And then Jones and
a couple of the others jogged up. The OL stopped short, jerking his head back and muttering under his breath.

Another joined him, wrinkling his nose and blinking rap-
idly as his eyes started to water.

Dusty drew their attention to the teacher. "This young lady,"
he said, "tells me that she knows the, ah . . ." The accurate term
was *victim,* but he didn't feel right, using it with the girl's distraught teacher standing right there, doing her best to look at
anything other than the body. "She's a teacher. The girl is one
of her students."

"*Was* you mean," said a voice Dusty didn't recognize. He
turned, intent on asking the guy if he knew the meaning of the
word *tact,* when Jones started barking into his radio. Minutes
later, the area was crawling with cops. SAR personnel and the
rest of the volunteers recited name, rank, and contact info,
then disbanded.

Half an hour later, Dusty ran into his shadow again on the
path. She'd peeled off her gloves and stood clutching them in
one hand while the fingers of the other seemed to have been
permanently tangled in her dark wavy bangs. She'd earned a
few points back there, for keeping up with him, for not falling
apart when she got an eyeful of the grisly sight. Dusty thought
it only fair to give her a few more because she was holding it
together now, too, despite the onslaught of rapid-fire cop questions: to the best of her knowledge, what was the girl's full
name and age? Which school had hosted the prom? Had she

been the date of some boy who attended classes there, or was she a student, herself?

"Do you know how we might get in touch with her parents?"

For the first time since the interrogation began, her voice wavered slightly. "Her mother is a widow. It hasn't even been a year since Melissa's father . . ." She bit her lower lip and squared her shoulders. "As far as I know, her mom doesn't have family in town. I can sit with her, if you like, when you . . . when . . ."

When you tell her that her little girl was slaughtered. Dusty ground his molars together. If he ever got his hands on the animal who—

". . . when you break the bad news," she finished.

Dusty's cell phone rang. Turning, he took a few steps away to answer it. It was Blake Carlisle, his assistant pastor at the halfway house, checking to see if Dusty would be back before dark, or if he should arrange to stay overnight.

Dusty glanced over his shoulder, thinking to get a read on the pretty little teacher; if it looked like she could use some moral support, he'd volunteer to go with her to the police station. But she was gone. "Hold on a second, Blake," he said, then took the phone from his ear. "Where'd she go?" he asked the nearest cop.

"Home. Somethin' about a cat or some such," he said, then turned back to his partner.

He could've kicked himself for not asking her name earlier. Oh, he could get the information, but it would be like pulling teeth without benefit of anesthetic, trying to pry the information from the cops.

His grandpa's favorite adage pinged in his head: "He who hesitates is lost."

He pressed the phone to his head again. "Back," he said.

"So did you guys find the missing girl?"

Dusty heard concern in Blake's voice. "Yeah, 'fraid so."

"Dead?"

"Uh-huh."

"Exposure?"

The image of her battered body flashed in his mind. "'Fraid not."

"Lord. Any idea who did it?"

"Not a hint. At least, not yet."

"I'll pray for her."

"Good idea."

"For her family, too, and that the cops find something that leads to her killer."

Butcher was more like it, but Dusty didn't say it. "Say one for the girl's teacher, too. She was practically in my lap when I found the body."

"You got it."

And while you're at it, say one for me. Because he wanted to call her, see how she had weathered the ordeal, but to do that, he'd have to find her first. Gut instinct told him it would happen. Soon. When it did, he hoped she'd let him buy her that cup of coffee because he really *did* want to find out what else they had in common.

Want to learn more about author
Loree Lough and check out other great
fiction from Abingdon Press?

Sign up for our fiction newsletter at
www.AbingdonPress.com/fiction
to read interviews with your favorite authors, find tips
for starting a reading group, and stay posted on what
new titles are on the horizon. It's a place to connect
with other fiction readers or post a
comment about this book.

Be sure to visit Loree online!

www.theloughdown.blogspot.com
www.loreelough.com